Ryan looked away from me to s that look. It was the way a game poacher, or a policeman at the tread he hears a tiger on the jungle path. I ... through the night.

"What – "

He held up a hand for silence.

I had heard nothing and looked in vain down the street, trying to follow his gaze.

In the distance, two men emerged into the lit circle beneath a streetlight. They were indistinct, but I had an impression of broad-shouldered types in long coats, moving rapidly towards us, side by side. They were too far away to make out their faces or anything about them, but their gait conveyed something of relentless determination. It was as though they went on rails rather than striding.

"Run, Stubbs!" Ryan ordered.

I have never been one to run from a fight, but this was a categorical order, and there was something about those marching figures... I do not know what I would have done if I had been on my own, but my legs seemed to move of their own accord as soon as he spoke.

I thought I saw something in Ryan's arms. He had not held anything a minute before—I would have sworn it—but he seemed to be opening a long leather case, of the sort that might hold a rifle.

But it was only an impression, and I was already going.

"And for God's sake," Ryan shouted, "don't look back!"

ISBN 978-1-948929-88-2

For information address Crossroad Press at 141 Brayden Dr., Hertford, NC 27944
A Macabre Ink Production - Macabre Ink is an imprint of Crossroad Press.
www.crossroadpress.com

First Edition

MASTER OF CHAOS

Book 4 of The Harry Stubbs Adventures

by DAVID HAMBLING

Macabre Ink

For *PRE*

Professor Sigmund Freud and his school have, in recent years, discovered a part of this body of Truth, which has been taught for many centuries in the Sanctuaries of Initiation. But failure to grasp the fullness of Truth… has led him and his followers into error.

—Aleister Crowley, "Magick in Theory and Practice"

Both the Modernist artist and the schizophrenic are characterised by a pronounced thrust to deconstruct the world and to subjectively reconstruct human experience without reference to objective reality. Layers of reality exist side by side, frequently fusing into each other, and … a profound sense of alienation from the empirical world runs rampant.

—Brigitte Berger, "Schizophrenia: Chicken or egg?"

London, 1925

Prelude

Sitting comfortably, as I hope you are, with a drink at your elbow and thoroughly at your ease, you are secure in your world.

You have no reason to fear that the floor will give way beneath you, precipitating you into a fathomless pit. You are not afraid of being sucked up into the sky, or that the building will collapse around you like a house of cards. Your world is solid, reliable, predictable.

I was once equally secure. Then the floor gave beneath me, and if I have climbed back out of the abyss, I will never sit quite as comfortably again.

Madness is something we can all laugh at. In less enlightened times, people would go to see the lunatics in Bedlam for entertainment, as if they were animals at a zoo. You might sympathise with the poor chap with his broken leg in a cast, but someone with a broken mind is ridiculed for his injury.

There was a time when I wanted to tell the world about my adventures, the discoveries that I had made, and the secrets that lie beneath our everyday existence. I burned to tell the truth, to let everyone know about the occult powers and alien beings that moved among them.

That impulse has left me.

Like the other documents I have deposited with Latham and Rowe, these pages are sealed, with strict instructions that they are not to be opened until after my death. I am determined that nobody will read them while I am still living—not merely from personal embarrassment, but because of the damage that will be done to my reputation as a man of sound mind and good judgement.

There is no earthly reason for you to believe any of what I say. I can hardly enclose the tooth of a dragon I have slain with this manuscript as a token of my good faith. So, I only have one reason to expect your credence.

Many who fought in the Great War never spoke a word about their experiences when they came home. They knew that they could never be understood, that their words would make no sense to those who had not experienced the terrible conflict for themselves. I leave these words for a future generation because this is a war which is not over.

You may recognise certain patterns in these pages which echo events of your own time. This alone might cause you to be receptive. In that unfortunate instance, you will want to know what has been unleashed on the world, and I might be able to provide some slight insight. It is little enough, but to those who collate such intelligence, it might contain some vital clue to the survival of the human race.

There—I am sounding properly mad now. If you have stomach enough for a deal of death, destruction, and madness beyond the ordinary, and if you are not afraid to approach madness yourself, then read on. I will give you a full account of my dealings with that being that I call the Master of Chaos.

Chapter One: Meal Duty

The trolley announced its progress down the corridor between the rooms of the segregation wing with rhythmic squeaks from one wheel. The trolley was a massive thing, and at another time it would bear two full tea urns or a hundredweight of laundry. Today, it rolled easily, its only cargo a half-dozen tin trays, each bearing two dishes under domed metal covers, and a water jug. There were six portions of fish pie, each with runner beans from the garden, and six bowls of stewed plums with custard for the segregated patients.

The fare was not perhaps the sort of thing they serve at the Savoy Hotel, but it was decent enough grub. My own lunch had been comprised of the same food from the same kitchen, and I could vouch for it. Bringing the trolley to a gentle halt, so as not to spill the water jug, I cleared my throat and knocked on the first door.

"Good afternoon, Mr Collier," I said. "Time for lunch." Having knocked, I peeked through the spy hole.

Collier was a slight individual, made smaller by his way of hunching over and wrapping his arms around himself. His dark hair hung limply around his face. He was rocking back and forth on his bed, which was the only furniture in the room. He stopped when I opened the door.

Collier was one of the melancholic sort. They were the commonest type in the place, men who had been beaten down by circumstance and, due to some flaw in their mental constitution, had been unable to get up again. It was not always easy to tell them from the dipsos—the dried-out alcoholics, or "suffering from Korsakoff's Syndrome," as we were supposed to call them—or from the shell-shock cases. In fact, those categories were not mutually exclusive. There were unfortunates who could be classed as all three.

They were listless, spiritless beings. Everyone there, except for those few in the grip of mania, was subdued, muted. Something in the air drained their energy. It aged them: it was a world of shabby, stoop-shouldered men, who were prematurely bald or greying. They all resembled each other, but none of them saw it. Ten times a day, someone would stop me and explain that he was not like the others, that he did not belong in there, and that the doctors or the superintendent or some imaginary authority could vouch for him. All he needed was a chance to explain his case. I always nodded and agreed.

"Time for lunch?"

Collier seemed to come back from a great distance.

I allowed him a minute to understand the significance of the tray I held out.

"No, I'm not hungry."

The room smelled of carbolic, as did the rest of the asylum, with a whiff of something less pleasant. There was a grate over a drain in one corner for the occupant to relieve himself. The overall effect was not appetising. "You don't have to eat every meal," I said. "But if you choose not to eat, I am required to record that fact in the register."

He knew well enough what that meant. There were plenty there who tried to starve themselves. Sometimes it was to mortify their flesh, or because they thought they were being poisoned, or for more inscrutable reasons. And there were hunger strikes. Any missing of meals was recorded, and if it continued to a certain point, a warning was issued.

If a patient failed to heed the warning, a regime of force-feeding would be instituted. This was a highly unpleasant procedure, falling not very far short of torture. Based upon the other attendants' accounts of their experiences, it was not a process that I ever wanted to be involved with.

"I had breakfast," he said heavily. "I'll eat dinner. But nothing now."

The evening meal would be cold, probably just bread and meat paste, and nothing nearly as appetising as what was on my cart. "It's a pretty decent fish pie," I said, by way of encouragement.

Collier looked at me as though I was having a joke at his expense.

He shook his head.

"Would you at least like some water?" I said.

"Yes, please."

Politeness was a habit with many of the inmates, however withdrawn they were. Sometimes, it was the last thing to go. I poured a tin cup of water, and Collier drained it quickly, suddenly discovering that he was thirsty. It got warm in those rooms, which had no windows to open or fresh air to breathe.

He accepted the offer of a refill.

"Last chance for fish pie," I said, but Collier shook his head.

It seemed impolite to refuse a meal that had been brought round specially. Collier could have at least taken the tray, moved some of the fish pie around with a spoon, and scraped the custard off the stewed plums, which were a little on the sharp side. One would have thought he would want to show a little appreciation for those who were, in effect, his jailers, and that he would go to lengths not to offend them.

If I had learned anything, though, it was that the inmates in the place were unfathomable, and their ways were not the ways of men on the outside. They had their own manners of thinking.

The story that I had heard was that Collier's two children had died of measles. He had gone into a decline and had given up his work—or been fired from it. His wife left him, and in the end, he had tried to hang himself. The attempt had failed, and he wound up in the asylum. The idea of self-destruction came back to him at intervals, though, which was why he was in segregation, where the tiled cells limited the methods by which a man could harm himself.

The occupant of the next room was a well-spoken man called Ross. If you did not know he was mad, you might think he was permanently hungover. He was not one of the ex-drunks, though, whose damaged brains processed even the simplest question at quarter speed and sometimes produced no answer at all. Ross was a victim of night terrors, which deprived him—and everyone else nearby—of sleep.

Ross would scream at volume and for a protracted period almost every night, usually several times. He still seemed to be asleep when he did it, and the others would shake him and slap him until he came around and stopped screaming. He wore a haunted look.

I was not clear why Ross was in segregation, whether he was actually considered to be in imminent danger of harming himself or others, or whether the move was an administrative measure to move him out of the ward for a while, so he did not wear on the nerves of others. I could well believe that some of his roommates would be highly disturbed by his terrors. It was never the most peaceful place to spend the night, but the volume and intensity of Ross's night terrors were unique.

I had never heard what his story was. Men who had been in such disasters as train crashes or shipwrecks sometimes had night terrors like that—and of course, some of the shell-shock cases from the war.

"Ah," Ross said, looking up as I opened the door. "Stubbs. I thought it must be you. Very quiet, not clattering around like the others."

He was tall and on the lean side, hollow-cheeked, his features marked with the lines that come with prolonged mental anguish. He was standing in the middle of the cell. Ross was given to pacing around in circles, seemingly following the pattern of some dance in his head. He was always pleasant, barely on the right side of ingratiating, and knew all of our names.

"Fish pie today. It's Friday," I said, handing him the tray.

"Very welcome, I'm sure." He lifted the cover and inhaled the aroma. "So, it's Friday then. Easy to lose track in here. It'll be the weekend for you soon, then."

"We have to work shifts on weekends too," I reminded him. The job played havoc with any sort of social life you might want to lead, eating into evenings and weekends and holidays alike. They needed more staff.

"No rest for the wicked, eh?"

"Enjoy your lunch, Mr Ross," I said, passing him a cup of water.

"I say, you haven't got a cigarette, have you? I'm dying for one."

The inmates were permitted to smoke, though only under supervision, and of course they were never allowed matches or lighters in their possession. Cigarettes—invariably Woodbines, as they were the cheapest—were a kind of currency. As it happens, I did not smoke. When I was a lad in the Army, I found I could swap my cigarette ration for others' chocolate, so I never developed the habit.

"You can have one as soon as you get out of here and back to your block," I said. Asking favours was one of those signs that they were trying to get around you and strike up a friendship. Giving him a cigarette when he asked might mean being tricked into giving him something he could kill himself with later. Even when the rules seemed harsh, they were there for a reason.

Ross bowed, indicating that he understood, and I departed.

Hooper, in the next cell, was unpredictable, swinging between wild activity and sullen inertia. When he was in an excitable state, he could be dangerous. He was cooling off for a few days in segregation after a scrap with another inmate over, of all things, a cleaning cloth. The men spent some time on inefficient cleaning fatigues, some working at half-speed and others sweeping dirt back where it had come from. Three of them could do the job of one ordinary man, but they prized the opportunity to do work.

Hooper seemed calm enough. In any case, the gross disparity in our sizes—I was twice as big as he was, and he had no muscles to speak of—meant that any trouble would be short-lived. Hooper had a round moon face and curly hair, and seemed pleased to see me, lifting the lid from the tray as soon as I passed it over.

"Friday—fish pie," I said.

"Fish pie, Friday," he replied at once, like a sentry giving the countersign. "Friday, fry-day. Why isn't the fish fried, eh, on Friday?" He looked up at me with big eyes.

"Maybe they fried it before they put it in the pie."

"Pie, pie, pi, pi," he said. "Twenty-two over seven is an irrational number—you can't work it out however long you try, and I did try. My, my how I tried. That was irrational! Who said anything is easy as pie? I say, do you know why pies are circular?"

"I've no idea," I said.

"It's so there's more to go round!" he said, laughing merrily. "It all goes around and around, you know. It's all irrational." Hooper was a pleasant sort when he was in this mood, and seemed entirely harmless, for all that he did not make much sense.

"Well, you enjoy your lunch, now," I said.

"They came for him next door," he said, suddenly serious, jerking his head to indicate the room on the other side. "Just now."

I had not heard or seen anything, which I surely would have

done if something had happened. Gillespy, in the next room, was not scheduled to be moved. The chalkboard at the end of the corridor showed who was in each cell, and it had not been amended. I suspected that this move was part of Hooper's fantasy world.

Many of the patients lived at least partly in worlds of their own. Some of them talked to themselves, or responded to voices only they could hear. One of them dragged a piece of string behind him, apparently in the belief that he had a dog. Another would pull on an old pair of cleaning gloves and stamp down the corridor emitting engine noises and making hand signals before he turned. It was comical, but there was also something pathetic in how these men clung to rituals from their previous lives, as though they could bring the past back by re-enacting it in symbolic form.

Hooper, of course, was adamant that his neighbour had been moved. "Oh, but they did take him," he said. "No fried Good Friday fish pie for him. The fish won't feed him. He'll be feeding the fishes. It all goes around!"

"Who came for him?" I asked. Of course, it was a foolish question, but trying to gather information had become second nature.

Hooper rolled his eyes. "Oh them, them, the ones that come round for you. Soft-footed, slow-thighed, steely-eyed, blank, and pitiless. They come round and round." He made an odd circular gesture with one hand and muttered something that sounded like "Robber-row, robber-row, robber-row."

"What's that?"

"Protection," he said. "I'm still here, but he's gone." After a moment of what seemed like sober reflection for the man who had supposedly gone, Hooper tossed his head, took up his wooden spoon, and started eating with every sign of enjoyment.

I left him to it.

"Oi, Harry!" Miller hailed me from down the corridor as I turned the key in Hooper's door. Miller was an attendant, a burly man with a bald head and something of the bulldog about him.

As soon as he was in range, Miller threw a sloppy punch at my jaw, which I blocked easily. Miller was a good man in a grapple, and skilled in the art of subduing patients with the minimum of fuss by using his weight and strength. His boxing, however, continued to be woeful. I blocked a left, and a right, and another left. The blows were getting wilder, and the next right completely sailed past my head. I let it go and counterpunched, striking him below the sternum.

Miller let out an "Ooff" and stepped back, wincing and grinning broadly. One of his front teeth was missing. "Every time!" he said. "You get me every time, and I can't even touch you."

Horseplay was part and parcel of Miller's character. Although a good ten years older than I was, he was a boy at heart. Miller never tired of arm wrestling, or trying to lift someone off the ground, or seeing who could balance a penny on their nose longest. He still could not resist the temptation to trade punches with me, long after the novelty of having a "famous boxer" on the staff had paled with the others. Along with an Irishman called Donnelly, and a Cornishman called Vanstone, Miller and I formed a close circle within the group of attendants.

"You need to practice with a bag," I told him, "so at least you can hit a man standing right in front of you."

"Here, Harry," he said, suddenly abashed and looking down at the trolley. "You haven't got one tray over, have you?"

"As a matter of fact, I do," I said. "Collier wasn't interested."

"That's what I hoped! It's just, well, Harry, I dropped one going round the sick ward, and I thought maybe..."

Miller was as tough as they come. I'd seen him singlehandedly pin down a maniac who had torn off a straightjacket and thrown another attendant clear across the room. A long white scar ran down his arm from wrist to elbow, left by an inmate with a jagged piece of metal. They said Miller disarmed the man, with his blood pouring all over the place, and kept him subdued until help arrived. At the slightest provocation, he would show you the indented scars on his calf that had been left by an inmate who'd clamped on with his jaws like a terrier and hung on for ten minutes, while Miller waited for others to remove him.

For all his physical courage, Miller was scared to go back to the kitchen and tell the cooks he had dropped the tray. He was as frightened as a schoolboy who had broken a window. I handed him my spare tray. "You weren't trying to balance it on one finger again, were you?" I asked. "Hold that tray with both hands, now."

"You're a pal, Harry!" Miller said.

Miller was essentially good-natured. He was no intellectual, but anyone who could cope through the rough-and-tumble and keep smiling, as Miller did, was a treasure. He might have been more prone to accidents than most, but if it was a member of my family in the wards, I would far prefer to have an overgrown boy like Miller looking after him instead of the surly types who would let a patient go without lunch if they were a tray short.

"You haven't heard anything about them moving Gillespy, have you?"

Miller looked at me dumbly for a second. "He's in room four. What would they move him for?"

"I dunno," I said.

Miller seemed to doubt himself. He put the tray down, went over, opened the spyhole to room four, and stood back.

"Is he there?" I asked.

"Oh dear" was all he could say, but his tone was eloquent. "Oh dear. Better open it up, Harry."

The spyhole gave a limited view of the room, but I could see a man propped up against the far wall. I did not like the way he was arranged. It was not a natural position for a living human being.

I unlocked the door with a sinking feeling in the pit of my stomach. The men in this place did strange things. They adopted peculiar postures and could freeze into statues for hours on end, but Gillespy was not one of that type.

His eyes were open, but he did not seem to be breathing, and there was no pulse in his neck. His flesh was warm, but perceptibly cooling.

"Oh dear, oh dear," said Miller, squatting down next to me. "How did he do it?"

The inmates in the segregation ward were searched thoroughly, but there was no indication that Gillespy had cut himself, and there was no suspension point for a hanging even if he had the rope for it. Some of the wilder ones threw themselves at the walls, but I could not see any sign of contusions.

"How did he do it?" Miller repeated. He took Gillespy's chin and moved it left and right, up and down, looking for any signs of choking or strangulation. "He must have done something to himself."

"Poison?" I said.

"He hasn't had his lunch yet," said Miller, as if that was evidence. "Dear, oh dear."

"I'll go and tell Dr Beltov," I said, standing.

Miller seemed unwilling to leave. "He must have done something," he repeated.

There was nothing else in the room except the bed, which was fixed in place and gave no clues. The bedding was in place. The tiled walls stretched up blankly to the ceiling, and the floor was bare.

Miller was still frowning at the body, as though it would all come clear if he looked hard enough. I made a conscious effort to scan everything for details. The heels of Gillespy's shoes were scuffed, which was not so very unusual. There were no signs of fresh injuries on him, but he was pushed up against the wall in a distinctly unnatural posture. His neck seemed partly discoloured, but that was probably from the angle at which he was lying.

"I'll tell Dr Beltov," I said.

"Weird," said Miller. "I never saw one like this before, did you? How do you think he did it, Harry?"

Chapter Two: Hunting the Tiger

It was a fine autumn evening, rather warm and humid if anything. The summer seemed to be dragging on, and it was becoming interminable. It had not rained for weeks, and everything was looking brown and parched. It took something to get Londoners to complain about the lack of rain, and that Indian summer was doing just that. The dusty, smoky air burned your throat, and it wanted a good cloudburst to settle it, but the sky, though often hazy, refused to yield a single drop of rain.

I was therefore in something of a desiccated condition when I visited the Conquering Hero, and very much more refreshed on my way home. It was dark, despite the street lighting, and I did not see the man who hailed me.

"Stubbs!"

I stopped and looked about before seeing him sitting on the bench. It was only the glowing cigarette that drew my eyes to him—otherwise, he might have been a part of the bench itself. He was wearing a hat, and his face was partly shadowed. There were many butts scattered about his feet. They could not all have been his, but somehow I felt that he'd been waiting for me a not-inconsiderable amount of time. I stepped closer.

"Got a minute?" he asked.

He was well-dressed, in a city suit with shoes that had been recently polished. Neither his hoarse voice nor what I could see of his face rang any bells. "Do I know you?"

"Ryan," he said. "From head office."

"I think there may be some confusion," I said.

"Only on your part." Ryan put the cigarette between his lips and passed me a business card. Holding it up to the light, I saw it was identical to the ones I had for Lantern Insurance, the fictitious company I worked for as the only employee. It had the same typeface and the same stock image of an old-fashioned lantern shedding beams of light. Only the name was different: J Ryan, and the title: Regional Manager.

At first, I thought there had been some peculiar mix-up, that there was another Lantern Insurance which happened to use the same symbol, that he had come into possession of one of our cards and mistakenly thought that I worked for the same firm. Then I noticed, in tiny letters underneath the company name, the legend "A Division of TDS."

TDS was the secretive organisation which was my real employer.

The initials TDS might have stood for Theral Development Society, as I had originally been told, but then again, they might be more mutable. My research had also turned up a few others, including a Tribus Dies Syndicate. It was a shadowy organisation to say the least, dedicated to stamping out interference in human affairs by violent means. I was a reluctant participant, kept in line by the threat of blackmail and violence to my family. You were either with them or against them.

"Where is Miss De Vere?" I asked, referring to my superior. She was a doctor of psychology, among other things, and the only contact I'd had with the organisation thus far.

"Our Lady of Holocausts is in Chicago… or New York, Boston, some damn place." Ryan did not care for Miss De Vere. "You can talk to me instead. Take a pew."

It had not seemed polite to loom over him, though I think I was more bothered than he was. I took a place a respectful distance from him. Ryan sat immobile. Normally, someone might adjust their posture when you move close, but Ryan was like a shop-window dummy, turning only his head.

"The famous Harry Stubbs," he said. "The Norwood Titan. The last man standing."

"Not that famous," I said.

"Not that famous," he agreed. "But with a reputation in certain circles." Ryan was weary and irritable. He did not want to be there any more than I did. Also, there was something peculiar about his eyes—one of them might have been glass, but I could not tell which one.

"I've been waiting for instructions," I said.

My orders had been scant indeed—barely a couple of lines typed on a slip of paper instructed me to get a job as an attendant, with the reference from Miss De Vere. I had sent my weekly summary report to a Post Office box, but there had been no further indication of what I was to do. And when I summoned the nerve to call Miss De Vere's answering service, I found it had been cut off.

"I'm maintaining a complete record of my observations on a day-by-day basis. It's difficult without knowing what to look for. There was a death today, but I'm in the dark as to precisely what I'm supposed to be doing."

"God," he said slowly, with an exhalation of smoke, as though appalled by my breach of good taste. "You really are like they said."

Aware of how much I had drunk, I reined in an impulse to answer back with anything like the irritation I felt. "You wanted a word with me," I said. "Mr Ryan, you are the senior manager from head office, and you have my full attention. The floor is yours." I made a sweeping gesture.

"It's dangerous enough, my being here now," he said. "We haven't kept you in suspense for the fun of it." He looked up and down the street with the searching gaze of a hunter. You could see down the row of streetlights in each direction, and there was nobody under any of them.

"I'm sure you haven't," I said. "I'm sorry if I seemed insubordinate."

"No matter." He looked at me and tapped his own ear in the place where part of mine was missing. "That ear—lose it in the War?"

"Our war," I said.

"Piece of advice. Don't let Them fix it for you." I did not need to ask who he meant by 'Them.' He cleared his throat then went on in a different tone. This was the briefing. "Before I got into this game, I used to shoot tigers." He might have meant to be matter-of-fact, but his manly pride was obvious. "It's quite an exciting pastime. Useful too. A man-eater can kill dozens of natives, or more. Tigers are quite a pest. They kill more than they need for food—hunting is as much a sport for them as it is for us. That's my conclusion, anyway. They have a fiendish intelligence, tigers."

He leaned back and briefly seemed to contemplate the darkness above us for a moment before continuing. Under other circumstances, that glance into the sky might have seemed eccentric, but there was something ominous about it, as though he was on the lookout for aircraft. "Lions are dumb brutes. Stupid as sheep. Shooting lions is a game for bravos who want a pelt for the fireplace to impress their neighbours. Leopards are more like it. Tigers though, are a sport for men. Point being that a tiger isn't wandering around with a target on its back, waiting for you to plug it. The things are damn near invisible when they want to be. When you're hunting a tiger, the last thing you are going to see is the tiger."

I recalled the paradoxes that my Chinese friend, Mr Yang, had so enjoyed—this sounded like one of them. *You don't see a tiger when you're hunting tigers.*

"You won't just blunder into a tiger on the trail, not unless you're very lucky, or very unlucky. A tiger can maim you with one swipe." He looked involuntarily down at his legs then looked up again. "It's not like shooting a pheasant. As soon as the tiger knows you are hunting him, he starts hunting you. You have to track a tiger by the signs he leaves. The claw marks in trees and the spoor that mark its territory. Spoor—that's shit, if you didn't know."

"I'm familiar with the term," I said.

"You can learn a lot from tiger shit," he said, relishing the word. "See what it's been eating and when. Footprints, sometimes, in the soft mud by a water hole. But mainly, you track a tiger by its kills. That's what tells you where it is. The spread and timing tell you about its range and the times of the day it's active."

I felt that I should be taking notes, but also that it was all a preamble. Ryan checked up and down the street again.

"You can tell from a kill the animal that did it. An experienced man-eater will break the neck at once, but young animals leave a bloody mess. Timid animals might only eat the liver, then go off when they're startled and not come back. Bolder animals get all the meat off the carcass. The claw marks, the teeth marks, they are like the fingerprints of the criminal. Except, unlike fingerprints, the kills tell you something about the personality that left them. Anyway, you appreciate what I'm saying?"

"The general principle is clear enough," I said.

"Well, it's the same here. Except in this case, our 'tiger' is leaving a psychic trail. The patterns of trauma in his wake show where it has been, maybe where it is going. The people in that hospital—some of them—if you could read their brains aright, would be like a map of his area of operations. His hunting grounds."

I almost spoke up to mention Renfield, the madman in Bram Stoker's great Gothic work, *Dracula*. Renfield had been driven mad by an encounter with the vampire. His madness, which centres around an obsession with eating flies and other insects for their blood, is a lunatic echo of the evil Count's own modus operandi. Ryan, though, was not the sort to be impressed by analogies with popular novels.

"You say 'he,' but what is he? Surely not anything like an actual tiger?"

Ryan flicked ash from his cigarette like a cat twitching its tail. Miss De Vere was sensitive about information being given out. She was prone to extreme measures to prevent knowledge from being spread. It would not be an exaggeration to describe it as a scorched-earth policy. Ryan would surely have to tell me something, but not necessarily as much as I would have liked to know.

"We can't say for sure. Most likely, it will look human, at least superficially. They tend to. Some extension or projection of it, anyway. All we can say for definite is that it's an intruder here. And it's dangerous to sanity."

My previous experience with the uncanny, with things that do not originate in our world, suggested that susceptible brains could be damaged by encountering them, as an eye is damaged by staring at the sun.

"Even more so than most of them," he said, as if following my line of thought. "Not just the incidental shock of something that human beings are not built to cope with. This is deliberate psychic damage."

"I don't understand," I said.

"You don't have to," he said bluntly. "But remember it breathes madness. Get too close and you'll go mad, too. As Gillespy did."

It took me a second to make the connection, hearing the name out of context like that. "Gillespy—the one in the asylum?"

"He is—or was—one of us." Ryan said "us" in a way that included me. Ryan was, like me, a reluctant recruit, without any great enthusiasm for the job. He did not have Miss De Vere's missionary zeal. He was a tiger hunter, not a crusader. "One of my beaters, you might say. Your predecessor. He was on the trail of an umbrella-maker who had gone mad while pursuing occult interests—and he suddenly cracked up."

"He just died," I said.

"What?"

"Gillespy died, of heart failure, supposedly. But, I dunno…"

Ryan looked out into the night. For once, he was not looking at or for anything. After a moment he sighed.

"That's rough," he said at last. "Gillespy was a decent sort. Heart failure must have been quick. Best any of us can hope for. Do they still bury lunatics in unmarked graves? Even better. Let him rest in peace."

"Do you think… he was killed?"

Ryan looked at me sidelong then scanned up and down the street. He ignored a single car speeding noisily past us. "Undoubtedly."

"But how?"

Ryan smiled with half of his mouth. "If you ever get an answer to that question, be sure to include it in your report," he said. "Poor old Gillespy. Still, his shuffling off is convenient. They had intimated they would prefer him that way. Dead men tell no tales, et cetera."

Them, They.

"Lucky I didn't have to ask you to volunteer for that particular fatigue," he said.

Ryan was the tough sort who would shoot a wounded comrade rather than see him slowly bleed to death in no-man's land. He would expect the same treatment himself, if it came to it. I could understand that view, but it takes a hard, hard man to pull the trigger on one of his own. The army is dead set against it, but hunters are not soldiers.

"As to the question of what we're tracking," Ryan resumed, "we have to thank your friend, Miss Horniman, for summoning it."

Miss Horniman was an individual whom I had encountered in my previous case. A scion of the Horniman Tea family, she had been instrumental in helping identify a certain object in the Horniman

Museum, though I had not acquainted her with the full facts of the case. In her youth, Miss Horniman had been a member of the Golden Dawn, an esoteric society dedicated to magical research.

In the course of the Horniman case, I had alerted TDS to the fact, some decades earlier, that her group might have been more dangerous than they thought. Most supposed psychics were tricksters, or deluded themselves. A few were not. Evidently, an investigation had been launched.

"There was a group of women within the Golden Dawn, who called themselves the Sphere. Well-meaning do-gooders trying to use their powers for world peace." From his tone, Ryan might have been talking about the Calcutta Ladies' Society for the Prevention of Cruelty to Bengal Tigers. "Seems they made psychic contact with an entity in the late nineties. It disappeared, supposedly for another plane of existence. But maybe it has just taken that long to get here in person after they opened the door."

I tended to take astral planes and psychic beings with a generous pinch of salt. Most of the people who went in for that sort of thing just had overly active imaginations. As my friend and former business partner Skinner remarked, it is funny how many people who believe in psychic powers think they're gifted, or sensitive to vibrations, or are the reincarnation of someone important. I read once about a party where two grand ladies ended up refusing to speak to each other because they both claimed to be Cleopatra in a previous life… They and a hundred others.

But, occasionally, there is a genuine talent, a real phenomenon. Which is something I would not believe had I not had ample first-hand experience.

"What was this entity?"

"No real name. They called it the Egyptian Astral," he said. "Don't read too much into that. They summoned it using Egyptian symbols. Popular back then. Miss Horniman eventually twigged that it wasn't exactly benign, that it was something alien and malevolent. They carried out a banishing ritual, but there's an old saying about not calling forth that which you cannot put down. And now it's here, feeding off humans, or…"

The pause stretched out. I knew he would finish if I gave him time.

"Or maybe it's just playing with us," he said.

I wanted to press him on what I should be looking for or taking note of. Would this entity be something that had landed from outer space, like a falling star? Would it be a miasmal, malevolent presence, or a concrete being, and if the latter, what form might it take? I had seen alien beings before and knew they took a variety of forms.

Ryan's head snapped round suddenly, and he looked away from me to stare down the street. I knew that movement. It was the way a gamekeeper turns when he hears a poacher, or a policeman at the tread of a burglar, or a hunter when he hears a tiger on the jungle path. Ryan's eyes bored through the night.

"What – "

He held up a hand for silence.

I had heard nothing and looked in vain down the street, trying to follow his gaze.

In the distance, I could see two men emerging into the lit circle beneath a streetlight. They were indistinct, but I had an impression of broad-shouldered types in long coats, moving rapidly towards us, side by side. They were too far away to make out their faces or anything about them, but their gait conveyed something of relentless determination. It was as though they went on rails rather than striding.

"Run, Stubbs!" Ryan ordered.

I have never been one to run from a fight, but this was a categorical order, and there was something about those marching figures... I do not know what I would have done if I had been on my own, but my legs seemed to move of their own accord as soon as he spoke.

I thought I saw something in Ryan's arms. He had not held anything a minute before—I would have sworn it—but he seemed to be opening a long leather case, of the sort that might hold a rifle. But it was only an impression, and I was already going.

"And for God's sake," Ryan shouted, "don't look back!"

I took off like a rabbit into the shadow between lights, hoping there were no slippery leaves underfoot.

A dull boom, more like muffled thunder than a gunshot, swept over me. It was oddly drawn out. My back prickled as I ran. As

I rounded the corner, there was a tremendous shriek. My first thought was that it was a human cry, but the sound rose to the pitch of grinding metal, the noise a locomotive makes when the wheels stick and slide along the steel rails.

By an effort of will, I did not turn my head but ran on, as fast as I could, past street after street until I made it to the safety of home. I fumbled and dropped my latchkey on the doorstep. There was a pounding in my ears, but I registered that it was only my heart, not pursuing footsteps. I was almost calm by the time I entered then closed the door, but I took care to bolt it behind me.

That night, I was troubled by a recurrent dream in which I was pursued down dark streets by pairs of men running on silent feet. Every time I thought I had lost them, they appeared again out of the shadows, closer than before. Their faces were bland, there was something wrong with their hands, and I knew it would be death if they caught me. I managed to stay ahead somehow—I've always been faster than most men of my size—and some time before dawn, they stopped pursuing me, and I slipped away into the quiet byways of quaint domestic dreams.

Chapter Three: Inside the Asylum

Dr Beltov was the senior physician and greatly respected, if not liked, by one and all. He had studied in Vienna and Paris and Berlin, where his mind had taken on a fine edge by honing against the finest thinkers in Europe. I don't know how many languages he spoke—and I'm sure it was quite a few—but his English was as correct as a BBC announcer.

Beltov was rather direct, without the polished manners of the other doctors. Unlike the others, who came and went as though they passed through a revolving door, Beltov was not planning to move on to his own practice, where he could help fashionable ladies with their neuroses. He did not have the right look; he favoured jackets a few shades too bright and in unlikely colours, paired with equally unexpected shirts and ties.

Also unlike the others, Beltov had a passion—you might almost call it a mania—for the precise recording of clinical data. He had no time for vagueness or intuition, but insisted that every piece of information must be recorded accurately, as if he was a detective collecting pieces of evidence to catch a murderer. You had to respect his thoroughness, though I could see why the other doctors found him to be such a trial. Nothing got past him that wasn't stamped, certified, and guaranteed.

"He's a stickler," was Miller's verdict, which he unfailingly attached to every anecdote about Beltov's insistence on forms be filled in and details noted, all the way down—and I do not exaggerate—to recording bowel movements.

People thought Beltov was a humourless medical machine, but I do not believe this was true. As a case in point, while the other doctors had two or sometimes three framed certificates on display,

Dr Beltov had at least a dozen covering the wall beside his desk, some of them rather extravagant. He caught me scrutinising one once. I'd been trying to decipher the gothic curlicues, but even the language was impossible to tell.

"This one records my achievement in swimming twenty-five metres in primary school," Beltov told me, with an entirely straight face. "My research indicates that the content of the certificates on the wall is not relevant for their effect, just the total number." I'd assumed this was his sense of humour.

Beltov was a man of contradictions. Insisting that patients needed to be treated rather than merely stored, "like cabbages in a barn," as he said, he was the one responsible for the therapeutic regime. He instructed all sorts of therapies be carried out, some of them most inconvenient for all concerned and with little obvious utility, with their failures duly recorded in great detail. But he was the most sceptical of any of the doctors when it came to individual treatments. He openly doubted their efficacy, and always demanded more data when one appeared to have succeeded.

"Five centuries of chaining up patients in the dark, and of whipping and abusing them, has proved that it is possible to worsen their condition with suitable treatment," said Beltov. "All we need is an equally reliable means of improving their condition. This will probably take longer."

When I came to Dr Beltov with news of Gillespy's death, the first thing he did was to note the time on the clock on his mantelpiece. The splendid clock was Beltov's pride, unique in its having a case made of glass, with all of the moving brass innards visible. Having checked the clock, he double-checked the time again against his pocket watch. The glass clock, though impressive, was not an especially reliable timepiece, and it required constant adjustment.

He rattled off a string of questions about how and when we had found Gillespy, and I answered him.

"I will investigate," he said. "You must answer my questions in writing and record everything that happened, as soon as possible. Memory is fragile. No detail must escape."

He left me there with pen and paper, returning twenty minutes later.

"It is a tragedy," Beltov said. He sounded tired. "All men must die, but they should not die so young. The provisional cause is heart failure, brought on by choking, and the coroner will confirm this."

I had heard that men could swallow their own tongues and choke themselves deliberately. Perhaps this was one such case.

"But in the end, we are responsible. Would he have died if he were not in this place? We cannot know." He looked at the clock. "We know so little, and there is so little time. We cannot undo the past, but we must learn what we can. Write!" I had slackened in my note taking to listen to him. "Write everything before it fades."

It was as though Gillespy's death might still be worthwhile if we could gather data from it. Beltov was of course correct about heart failure, being a doctor as well as a psychologist. The exact cause, assuming there to be a triggering factor, remained unknown.

"I will do the autopsy," said Beltov. One of his more gruesome habits was to dissect the brain of every man who died in the hospital, searching for physical signs of pathology. Sometimes, madness could be explained by a tumour or growth pressing on a part of the brain, but nobody knew what caused such tumours. It had been suggested that the tumours were caused by a bacterium and might spread by infection. Nobody knew, but Beltov was painstakingly adding to his notes.

"For all the good it'll do," Donnelly said to me later. Donnelly was a cheerful cynic and a great help to me. "He knows more about the bowel movements of every man in this place than I know about my own. If there was a Nobel Prize for counting shit, your man would be saying hello to the king of Sweden."

I had come to assist him in restraining a patient while Dr Easton took a sample of spinal fluid. Easton was hearty rather than precise, and he did not share Beltov's mania for precision. The rather vampiric procedure he was undertaking involved sticking a long needle in between the vertebrae. The patients were understandably anxious and prone to resist.

"This might sting a little," Easton said lightly as he stabbed in the immense needle, having checked that the man was fully immobilised. "I know it hurts, but it's necessary."

Dr Easton was a ruddy, fair-haired man, as utterly English as Beltov was foreign. He had the build of one who had played rugby for his college ten years previously, but was now more in the habit of enjoying a good dinner. Easton adopted a rather casual style rather than adorning his speech with medical jargon, so everything he said sounded like plain common sense. There were limits to his patience, though—he had a way of standing too close and talking too loudly when he was asserting himself with recalcitrant patients.

"Hope for a negative result," Donnelly said afterwards.

"Hope for a positive one," said Easton. "That way we can treat him."

The test, Donnelley explained, was for syphilis, which caused a sort of dementia that could be cured. The cure, however, was not so pleasant, as it involved deliberately infecting the patient with malaria. Apparently, the malarial fever burned out the venereal disease.

"An ingenious treatment," said Easton, "and with a pretty good success rate. Maybe a bit uncomfortable."

"I'd rather stay mad," Donnelly said, "and stay safe in here with three meals a day and no work to do, instead of going back and telling me missus I had the clap and getting what for."

"That's because you're a feckless Irishman with no sense of responsibility," said Easton, but he said it lightly. Donnelly was a good worker and a reliable colleague, even if the doctors found him too clever by half.

Beltov continually clashed with the other doctors. Dr Hamilton, a Scot who was a specialist in the field of talking cures, generally gave him little trouble. Hamilton had the humility to admit that such treatments had little utility in the asylum setting and was content to learn, though he still put forward theories about archetypes and other theoretical entities, all of which irked Beltov.

"You say this is true because you learned from Spencer, who learned from Kaufmann, who learned from Jung, who learned from the great Freud himself," he fumed. "One day this spiral will grow until we are all students of students of Freud. But what is at the centre of it all? What is the source? How does Freud know?"

"Revealed truth, perhaps, Dr Beltov," said Hamilton.

"That is not science."

Hamilton was content to leave it at that. His world might contain other types of truth than those admitted by Beltov, but in the hospital where Beltov reigned, only scientific cures were acknowledged.

Dr Easton was more of a brawler and engaged Beltov at every opportunity. I once caught the two arguing when I went to empty the ashtrays in the doctors' common room.

"If we can get Ross's war record, I'm pretty sure we can diagnose him with shell shock," said Easton.

"Shell shock is nothing more than a convenient portmanteau into which you can stuff every case that suits you," said Dr Beltov.

"Hardly," said Easton, without rancour. "We have a patient with the worst night terrors I've seen, and numerous other symptoms that tally with shell shock, and if his service history shows he was under fire—"

"I was taking issue with your interpretation of shell shock as physical brain injury," said Beltov.

"Shell shock, as we understand it, is surely caused by the shock of shells," said Easton. "The percussive impact of a shell-burst is damaging, and the brain is a sensitive organ. If—or when—you open up the cranium and see the haematomas, we could prove it, but the external signs are a fair indicator, wouldn't you say?"

"I would not say," said Beltov. "The correlation of shell shock with explosions is questionable… What is it, Stubbs?"

"I'm sorry, Dr Beltov, I didn't mean to eavesdrop on your conversation," I said, and started to move away.

"But I think you have something to say to us," said Beltov. "Say it."

"Not really," I said. "At least not medically. I'm not qualified. But I served in the Royal Regiment of Artillery in the war. Only as a bombardier. But they always taught us that the blast from a shell wasn't effective."

"Not effective?" said Easton, an ironic smile about his lips. "I've seen pictures of a whole landscape of craters, and I don't think they were left by moles!"

I laughed politely. "Not effective against personnel," I said. "That's why we had to have shrapnel shells, you see. It's the shell fragments that do all the damage. The blast itself… The explosion is very loud." Exactly how loud you will never know until you have been under bombardment yourself, which is a memorable experience. I doubted whether Easton had ever been on a battlefield. "It pounds your ears like nothing else, but it doesn't have much real force. Blasts can destroy fortifications, but shrapnel is what causes casualties."

"Thank you, Stubbs," said Easton, still ironic. "Fascinating anecdotal evidence."

"Yes, very interesting," said Beltov, taking out a notebook and a mechanical pencil to scribble something down. "It should not be difficult to discover the actual pressure exerted by a shell."

"Even if the individual shell-burst is not that powerful, perhaps it is the cumulative impact of many of them," said Easton.

I coughed awkwardly. Beltov smiled and nodded for me to go on.

"Begging your pardon, Dr Easton," I said, "but I have some small personal experience of blows to the head, as well as cases of shell shock. I've seen men get hit in the head far more than is good for them, without suffering mental problems. I've also seen shell shock in men not exposed to artillery, who have only been shot at by prolonged machine-gun fire."

"Mr Stubbs has the makings of a clinician," said Dr Beltov. "He presents cases which destroy your hypothesis from both sides! Perhaps this 'shell shock' of yours is nothing at all to do with impact, as I was suggesting."

Easton blew his cheeks out to express that there was no point in arguing with anyone who chose to deny such obvious facts and who has no knowledge of medicine. I bowed to them, embarrassed in case I should be called on to make further comments, and moved away.

"Railway spine, caused by impact, is an established condition in *British* medical literature," said Easton. "I can't help feeling that anyone who looks at the clinical notes will wonder how we can be so obtuse as to not connect cause and effect. Perhaps a provisional diagnosis…"

"Not simply for the sake of respectability," said Beltov. "You want Ross's case to be classified as shell shock because that will make him one of the *blesse de guerre,* a hero of the war. I will not allow this without your presenting concrete evidence. No supposition and inference."

That was typical Beltov. He was always playing devil's advocate and shooting down the diagnoses proposed by the others. "A good clinician claims to know nothing," was one of his sayings.

I worked hard to stay in Beltov's good books. He was the master of the place, and a word from him would see me dismissed. Perhaps I succeeded too well and volunteered too conspicuously. Beltov seemed bemused by my determination to help, I realise now he must have sensed an ulterior motive from the start. Donnelly laughingly called me Beltov's stooge.

The lofty lords of bedlam have their own scientific system of classification for the various forms of madness, and you can listen to them arguing about it for hours. The thing is though, it never makes the blindest bit of difference what the exact technical term is. We attendants have our own system of classification which is a deal more pragmatic and of much more useful application.

There are the sullen mad, who rarely move or speak and give little trouble. Then there are the talkative ones, who want to tell you all about it and are harmless enough. Of course there are a few raving ones, and it's no-holds-barred with them—watch your fingers, because they bite like mastiffs. The most dangerous, though, are the sly mad, the ones who are clever enough to act normal most of the time.

"What does it matter what the Latin name is for it?" I asked Donnelly one day. He had been an attendant for ten years and had been most helpful in showing me the ropes. Miller was a pal, but tended to forget the details when explaining things. "It's not like they can cure any of them."

"Ah, that's a fine metaphysical question," said Donnelly. He was an Irishman who had a fondness for discoursing at length on obscure matters that nobody else had ever considered. He might have looked and sounded like an illiterate navvy, but Donnelly had a surprising fund of knowledge and could reel off poetry by the yard. If you ever wanted to know how many angels can dance on the head of a pin, Donnelly was your man. Not that he would ever give an exact answer, but he liked to chew on the question.

"The way I see it, the doctors are doing the same job as the priests in the old days—casting out demons. And to get power over a demon, the first thing they always asked was its name. 'Dementia praecox' even sounds like the name of a demon, doesn't it, now?"

"Why does the name matter, though?"

"She'll never guess my name is Rumpelstiltskin," said Donnelly. "My name is Legion. His name is Abaddon, and in Greek he is called Apollyon. Belial came last, than whom a spirit more lewd never fell from heaven. The power is in the name." His eyes seemed to twinkle, and as usual with Donnelly, I could not tell if he was having me on, or just enjoying his flight of fancy.

"At least you can trick a demon into telling its name," he went on. "But with this crowd"—he stuck out his lips and flicked them with a finger—"bl-bl-bl-bl-bl. It's nothing but nonsense."

"I suppose putting a name to a physical disease makes a difference," I said.

"For five hundred years, the doctors were bleeding and purging and making up Latin names for conditions without doing a blind bit of good," said Donnelly, echoing one of Beltov's favourite sayings. "The wonder is that the trade lasted long enough for them to work out how to treat anything. This lot have about another four hundred to go."

Dr Beltov was the senior physician, but by no means the top of the chain of command. That honour went to the superintendent, a man who I had seen precisely once. He answered only to the Board of Trustees, a vague and distant body which met infrequently. For all intents and purposes, the superintendent was the supreme power. I gathered that he was only in his office one or two days a week, and he did not generally concern himself with the running of the place. Apparently, he was to be found at the North Surrey Golf Club on most days. But he did insist on interviewing the staff personally, and after I submitted my application to take up the post of attendant, I was summoned to his presence.

The superintendent enjoyed a grand office on the third storey, which was to say the top of the building, with two walls lined with what I took to be medical textbooks. The ceiling was high, and windows took up the entire height. What caught my eye were the double glass doors, which opened onto a large balcony. You could stand on that and look out across the quadrangle, defined by the three sides of the hospital, like a king. The afternoon I met him was as warm and golden as melted toffee, and the doors were open to catch the faintest breath of wind. Paperweights—gorgeous things of polished stone with coloured veins running through them—held down each of the stacks of paper on the superintendent's desk.

The superintendent himself cut a majestic figure with a full head of silver hair, looking much as I imagined a high-court judge or a Roman senator would appear. His eyes were heavy lidded, and he spoke slowly and deliberately, but his gaze was keen, and every word was selected carefully.

"Your references speak very highly of you," he said, holding down two letters on the expanse of walnut before him. He did not say it as though it impressed him. "Dr De Vere and… Mr Rowe."

Estelle De Vere was a qualified psychologist, but she was young, female, glamourous, and American, all of which probably counted against her. She had considerable powers of charming, but she had not charmed him. The other referee was Mr Rowe, of Latham & Rowe, a legal gentleman and my former employer.

"Do you understand what sort of job you're taking on?" he asked. "Boxing credentials mean nothing. There's to be no hitting people here, no punching. We don't want a thug."

I did not know it then, but the attendants were generally older men who were more steady and reliable. Seeing my background, as well as my physique, the superintendent had formed a premature conclusion.

"I understand that perfectly, sir," I said. "No violence at all. Restraint, yes, but only as and when necessary. It should be used, as you might say, with restraint."

"It seems to me that you're a combative fellow," he said, having apparently not heard me. "If somebody strikes you—and they most certainly will—are you going to turn the other cheek? Have you, in fact, ever done so? Because I should like to hear about it."

The sun through the tall, leaded windows marked out a cross-grained pattern on the parquet floor. I looked at it as I answered.

"Without getting technical, sir, I suspect I can take a punch better than any man in the building. Rolling with the punch is not just a figure of speech. It's an important skill for a pugilist." I explained briefly about how even a slight movement can have the effect of thick padding, extending the moment of contact the same way a block of rubber would do. "That is, if I can't block it or dodge it, which is generally what happens with amateurs. As for responding, well, I'd always hold a man rather than hit him," I said, aware that I had been talking rather freely about fighting.

"Is that so?" His eyes were on my hands, which I had raised involuntarily during my reply. They were twice the size of his own.

"You see, sir, the advantage of having an abundance of physical force at my disposal is that I can apply techniques, such as pinning the arms to the sides, which are not available to others. I can restrain where another man would not be able to."

"But surely you soften them up a bit first to make it easier?" he asked, raising an eyebrow.

"Oh no, sir. That would be a beginner's error. Once you go down that road you're buying no end of trouble. When you're in the debt-collecting line, which I was for some time, hitting a man is a terrible mistake."

"Oh? How so?" He sounded genuinely curious to hear my logic.

"If you hit him, he can't very well pay up without looking like he's been beaten. Whereas, if you simply grab him, and explain that he owes—well, he might swear a bit, but you've got him focused on the matter at hand, his schedule of repayment, and not grieving about being attacked. His resentment is channelled on his situation, or his creditor, and not on the agent of collection. That's the psychology of it."

The superintendent smiled to himself. I had enriched his knowledge of the world, be it ever so slightly. "A fair point. A fair point." He turned over sheets of paper, pausing to read a line here and there. Evidently, he was rebalancing his opinion of me, looking at the evidence again with a more open mind. "You've never been in trouble with the law, and your army service is exemplary. But tell me, what do you know about mental illness?"

What I knew about mental illness was effectively nothing. While I had met my fair share of lunatics and odd cases along the way, and had made the most of that in my application, I was in no position to generalise. All I had were odd scraps of learning, and I groped for one, obscure and irrelevant as it might be. "Paracelsus said we should not mistreat the mentally ill," I said. "They are not possessed by evil spirits, but rather are our brothers, who are victims of a malady. That seems about right to me."

Paracelsus was a physician, alchemist, and lord-knows-what-else back in the fifteenth century. He kept cropping up in connection with cases, and consequently, I had read some of his works. My conclusion had been that he was right about most things, though few people understood half of his writings.

The superintendent nodded slowly. "Paracelsus, eh? His stock doesn't stand too high with some people, but I'm very much inclined to agree. Yes, though it took the rest of the world three centuries to catch up with the old alchemist, you've about hit the nail on the head."

The name "Paracelsus" might have been a secret code word, given how rapidly my uttering it seemed to change the superintendent's mood. The rest of the interview seemed like a formality. "Why do you want to work here?"

"I want to put my talents to use where they will do some good," I said. "And, as you may be aware, the employment market is in somewhat of a slump at present."

"That's as honest an answer as I've heard," he said drily. "I get a lot of flannel from men who think that they'll get an easy job here. I don't think you're one of those. I think we can try you for six weeks' probation. Do a decent job, and you'll stay on."

"Thank you very much, sir," I said.

The superintendent leaned back, the main portion of the interview concluded, and steepled his fingers to address me.

"You have to understand, this place is an asylum in the true sense of the word, a place of refuge from the world. Consider that every one of those men is Christ—'I was a stranger, and ye took me in.' It is a sanctuary, literally a sacred place—it is sacred to them, and we are the keepers of a sacred trust to look after them."

He went on more in the same vein. To him, the place was a way station for lost travellers until they could get back on their feet. They were not kept there to keep the world safe from them, but to keep them safe from the world. Out there, they would be victimised and bullied, and they had been outcast from their families. It was our Christian duty to tend them and look after them.

I could only admire the old man's lofty ideals. I did not need to visit the wards below to know that to those incarcerated, and to those holding them, the reality would not be quite so benign. But what mattered was that I get that job, and with a little help from Paracelsus, I was in. It was my first job working undercover.

I phoned Miss De Vere's answering service to give her the news and found the line was dead. With no means of contacting her, and no instructions on what I was supposed to be doing, I was on my own.

Chapter Four: The Book of Job

Much of our time was spent escorting patients around or watching over them and occasionally telling them off or physically restraining them. We sometimes supervised their craft sessions, mainly basket weaving—or "making nests for cuckoos," as Donnelly put it—and their somewhat ineffectual attempts at gardening and cleaning. Thankfully, little time was spent handling what Donnelly called "amateur theatricals" from the inmates. We were waiters and porters and cleaners, ever busy with carbolic soap and scrubbing brushes. The job had many of the less-attractive features of being a lavatory attendant at a railway station.

One day, I was clearing up the remains of an incident with a bucket of sawdust when I felt Grogan's eyes on me. Grogan was effeminate, sometimes flagrantly and brazenly so. Officially, there is no bullying here, but Grogan often sported bruises. Some people took exception to him. I myself was not entirely comfortable under his gaze, which may have had something lascivious about it. That is no excuse to hit a man though, not in my book.

"You look like Hercules cleaning the Augean stables," he said. "Funny seeing a big strong man like you mopping up."

"I'm sure Hercules had his reasons, too," I said.

"Oh, he did," said Grogan. "My friend was a painter, and he told me all about it. Hercules had to do penance."

I squeezed out the mop, wondered if I could call it a day at that, but decided the floor needed another go-over.

"He painted Hercules looking just like you, except only wearing a Nemean lion skin," said Grogan.

"What's a Nemean lion?" I asked. Mythology seemed like a safer topic than his artist friend or the semi-clad Hercules.

"It terrorised the people of Nemea," said Grogan. "Its skin was impervious to swords or arrows."

"If its skin was impervious," I said, squeezing out the mop again, "how did Hercules manage to skin it?"

"With the lion's own claws," said Grogan. "They were the only thing that could cut it."

"A paradox," I said. "The only thing you can kill it with are its own claws, and you can't get them without killing it first. Makes you go round in circles."

"Hercules found a way," said Grogan, tossing back his head. "He had big, brawny hands like you, and he strangled it to death. Like Gillespy was strangled."

Before the conversation could progress further, Dr Beltov and Dr Easton rounded the corner, arguing loudly, and Grogan slipped away. The issue at point was Sunday service, which had been discontinued some time ago, but which seemed likely to be revived.

"You think a vicar can cure patients by a laying-on of hands or casting out demons?" complained Beltov, stopping in front of me as if at a traffic signal. "This service will be a disturbance—not good for mental hygiene."

"Think of it as a new type of therapy," said Easton.

"Pah. One that has failed for two thousand years."

"But surely, even you wouldn't deny the patients the consolations of their religion?" Easton knew he was on the winning side, and he moved to a more conciliatory tone. "Can we ignore the spiritual aspect of their malaise?"

Beltov's expression suggested that he would be more than happy to do so. He was suspected of being an atheist, or at the very least a Bolshevik. Religion might well have been one of those delusions he was trying to cure, but he knew which way the wind blows. "You cannot cut people off from a being who is everywhere," Beltov said. "Let them talk to God if they wish. There is no obstacle."

"Now, now," said Easton. "We can't interfere there. Science has nothing to say about God."

"On the contrary. Science has found God, but he is 'not such a God as men would wish to worship,'" said Beltov. "That was William James, whom you all seem to admire so much."

I knew nothing of William James, but Beltov often invoked him as an unscientific influence who was poisoning psychology. Beltov's heroes were surgeons and chemists, men with facts and figures and nothing supernatural about them.

"I can't speak for William James," said Easton. "But you accept the need for a Sunday service?"

"I accept that my views on the matter have been overruled by the superintendent's order, thanks to your interference," said Beltov. "The decision is out of my hands. The vicar can hold his Sunday service, and they can sing hallelujah. But no communion."

"No communion?" Easton might have been a child who had been denied pudding.

"I have professional experience with religious manias," said Beltov. "'Drink my blood and eat my flesh'? It is not well to encourage cannibalism to men with disturbed ideas. No communion."

"As you wish," said Easton complacently. "I think you'll be pleasantly surprised by the results a sound Anglican vicar can produce on a body of patients."

"We can only hope so," said Beltov.

There was no question that the number of patients was increasing. I had been taken on not to fill a vacancy left by a departing member of staff, but as an addition to swell the ranks. The number of patients had been steadily rising.

I gathered from the others that previously there had been spare capacity and empty beds in the asylum. Recently, they were cramming beds in everywhere—in one of the dormitories, you could see ceiling decorations indicating it had once been a billiards room. In other wards, the beds had been moved closer together to accommodate ever-larger numbers.

Naturally, after what Ryan had told me, I kept my ears open for any indication of what was producing this influx of mentally afflicted patients. Among the attendants, the increase was variously put down to a desire for greater profits by the board, and to a shift in changes in the municipal boundaries of the boroughs of Lambeth and Croydon. Those who had been there longer said that it was because of the war: admissions had dropped to practically nothing from '14 to '18, but after that, they had rebounded sharply, as though people had been putting off going mad until after the war. Since then, the numbers had been steadily on the increase.

Many of the new admissions were cases of shell shock, which had not come about until years after men had returned from the front.

The doctors did not express any very definite views. From what I gleaned from the journals left lying around their common room, there was a multitude of clashing schools of thought. Some thought that it was the manifestation of a degeneracy in Britain, that our mental well-being had been corroded by decadence and the influx of poor racial stock, and that if we looked hard enough, the inmates would all be found to be the result of poor breeding some generations back. They did not blame the Jews in so many words, but that was the import.

Others blamed the influence of modernism, a term which I confess I was driven to look up because it was thrown around so freely without the slightest explanation. Modernism, it seems, is a movement in the arts, which started around the year 1900. It abandons traditional values and techniques, and instead places importance on individual experience and revels in nihilism and absurdity, placing no value on traditional morals or religion. Modernism destroys the moral fibre of those exposed to it.

That hardly seemed plausible. I supposed that some of the inmates might have been exposed to the works of Picasso or Stravinsky or T.S. Eliot, as there is little accounting for taste, but it could not be a significant fraction. Other commentators argued, more cogently to my mind, that modernism was more of a symptom of the madness of modern life rather than a cause of it.

The diversity of patients, both in their backgrounds and their symptoms, did not seem to support the idea of a common cause. If there was an infectious agent, a Typhoid Mary of madness, it was well hidden. Certainly, Beltov's brain dissections had yielded little. And Ryan's tiger lay concealed in the undergrowth.

"The whole world is going mad," was Donnelly's straightforward conclusion. "They'll have to build another wing."

The officiating cleric was a vicar from Dulwich in a dog collar so bright it was almost luminous. Some vicars liked to pretend that they were like any other man, and others liked to pretend that they were not. This vicar had settled into the role so that it completely enveloped him. He was probably every bit a vicar in the evenings with his wife, peppering his table talk with fragments of gospel.

It was a full house for Sunday service in the main hall. There was no other entertainment to be had, and any novelty was very welcome. The vicar spoke to Dr Beltov with the slight condescension of one talking to a foreigner.

"My words today come from a greater pen than mine," he said to reassure the doctor. "I'm abridging a sermon from Mr Spurgeon."

Even Beltov had heard of Charles Spurgeon; you could hardly avoid it, given the presence of Spurgeon's College down the road. He was one of the top preachers in the country back in the Sixties, and his sermons still came around regular as clockwork. Not that they were really to my taste.

I have never been a great one for church services. I'm sure it does you good, and there is always something fine about belting out hymns, but the sermons are too long for my liking. The only time I ever thought I might actually want to go to a service was after I received a letter from an American boxer, a coloured gentleman.

My manager had been in correspondence with his, on the grounds of the similarities in the monikers under which we were promoted—I was the "Norwood Titan," and so was he, hailing as he did from the town of Norwood in the state of Massachusetts. As both of us seemed likely to break into the international scene, there was some issue over which of us had prior claim to the title. My idea was that we might settle it with a fight. My manager thought that was far-fetched.

However, the correspondence was terminated when my American counterpart declared that he was leaving competitive boxing. He wrote to me personally to explain that he had a higher calling.

"When the Lord wants you, that's a fight you cannot win!" he wrote in a bold, flowing hand, very free with his capital letters and exclamation marks. "You can duck and dodge, but He sees every move before you make it. You think you're Strong, but your punch is less than a feather-tap, you may be a Heavyweight to Men, but He is a Mountainweight! His jabs are faster than the Lightning, his crosses are Thunderbolts, and his Right Hand is a Landslide. He is Champion of Champions, and the match is over before the opening bell. You cannot resist. Your arm's too short to box with God!"

I wished him luck in his new career. I would dearly love to have been in a revival tent to see him waving his fists and stirring up the crowd with tales of his bouts with Satan. The Church of England is an important institution, but for verve and character, and a sheer ability to keep people awake in their pews, I felt the former Norwood Titan could do better than any of them.

At Beltov's insistence, half a dozen attendants had been turned out, and we lined the walls as though we were ushers. Beltov stood by me, arms folded, as the vicar moved to the front, escorted by Miller—an unlikely, gap-toothed choirboy—and cleared his throat.

"We do not now feel the hand of God as once we did," said the vicar. "Even a century ago, we were aware of Divine Providence, that special ordering of matters which reveals His intention in the world. I have day-books left by my predecessors, in which they recorded diligently every occasion when a man was saved by seeming luck, or when what appeared to be mischance proved to have a purpose. In the twentieth century, we have become blind even to providence. But every apparent misfortune has a purpose, as Scripture tells us. My text is taken from the Book of Job."

The vicar might have had conviction and certainly seemed to believe everything he said, but he lacked fire. I also wondered at his choice of text. The story, with which you are no doubt acquainted, is of a pious and successful man on whom God piles all sorts of suffering. It is not a cheerful tale.

Rows of men in blue uniforms waited dully. Some mumbled to themselves, keeping up a commentary on something invisible to the rest of us. Some watched the vicar with the patient look they gave to raindrops running down the window. Like the raindrops, his words would pass without leaving a trace.

"The path of sorrow has been trod by thousands of holy feet," the vicar assured us. "You are not the first one to sit down and say, 'I am the man that has seen affliction.' You were not the first tried one, you are not the only one, and you will not be the last one. 'Many are the afflictions of the righteous.' So let this be some comfort to you—that you are one of the Lord's suffering children, one of those who have to pass through rough roads and fiery places in the course of their pilgrimage to heaven."

There were a few nods and grunts of approval. This alerted

the less attentive members of the audience that something worth listening to was being said. Heads turned, and eyes opened. It was shrewd to turn the misfortune of the inmates to the vicar's advantage. While the superintendent might think that the place was a sanctuary, it bore more of the aspect of a prison, in which the occupants were unable to understand the crimes of which they had been convicted.

The vicar, gaining strength, spun a potted version of Job's sorry tale. God gave Satan licence to torture poor Job to try his faith, and the Evil One had permission to do everything short of killing the man. Job's goods were all stolen by bandits, and his sons and daughters were killed, before Job himself wound up a beggar covered in painful sores.

This earned him sympathetic murmurs from the audience, each of whom had experienced a fall which was, to him, no less precipitous.

"Interesting that God requires Satan to do his dirty work," remarked Beltov in an undertone. "One might suspect that God did it himself, but wearing a different mask, one with horns."

Nevertheless, Job held on to his faith and refused to complain to God, or to kill himself. Job's friends assured him that his divine punishment must have been the result of some misdeed, for which he needed to atone. They accused him of being a hypocrite, of having committed all sorts of concealed crimes. But Job—like the inmates of the asylum—was completely innocent.

"And even now, some people think you must be a bad man because you have come down in the world." The vicar's gaze travelled from left to right and back. "It cannot be that you are the respectable person they thought you were, or you would not have lost your estate."

That much was true, and there was more nodding and agreement from the crowd. Everyone there had been abandoned by their friends and family, and their presence in the asylum was the consequence. If they had even one friend who could help them, they would not be so incarcerated.

When I caught up with him again, the vicar was saying that it was necessary for some trials that God should withdraw the light of His countenance. For a bit, I was not sure if he was talking about

Job or Jesus, as he certainly referred to the Saviour as one who had suffered, like Job, by God's will.

Having reached a low point, the vicar sought to elevate the audience. He began to speak in a tone of encouragement, as though telling a child about the wonders of Christmas. "Now, lastly, I want to speak concerning the tried believer's consolation," he said. "It is a very sweet consolation. 'When He has tried me, I shall come forth as gold.' No gold is ever injured in the fire." His voice rose, getting ever louder as he worked up to the climax of his speech. "Stoke the furnace as much as you may, let the blast be as strong as you will—pile on more fuel, let another blast torment the coals till they become most vehement with heat—yet the gold is losing nothing. There is not a single particle of it that can be burnt. It is still there, all the better for the fiery trial!"

He paused to gulp a breath then went on, growing even louder. "Corruption, earth, and worms shall but refine this flesh, 'til my triumphant spirit comes to put it on afresh!"

And with that promise of revival, or resurrection, or that perhaps, as Job did, they would have their property restored to them, the vicar came to a close. There was a scattering of applause, cheers, and shouted approval. They had been roused but did not know how to express themselves. Hooper stood on his chair to address the audience. Beltov nudged me, but I was already in motion.

"Though I give all my goods to the poor, and my body to be burned, without madness it profiteth me nothing," Hooper proclaimed.

Before he could get out another word, I had picked him up bodily and turned him horizontal, a move so sudden that he stopped speaking. Vanstone and Miller were holding down an inmate on the other side of the room, and there was another disturbance at the back, with Donnelly separating two patients.

"Peace," said the vicar, holding up his hand in a sign of blessing, as though his word would miraculously calm the audience. He had little experience working with mental patients.

I carefully placed Hooper down against the wall. "Hold your water," I told him.

He belched and blinked, but the urge to preach had left him. He had lost his thread. "Peace," he said, holding his hand in blessing.

"What about the great serpent?" someone was shouting noisily, but he shut up when he saw me headed his way.

The individual conflagrations were extinguished before they could spread, and the rest of the hall was not engulfed. The vicar had taken up an accordion, and started up with "All things bright and beautiful." Perhaps music did have charms to soothe the savage breast, because by the end of the first verse, the audience were all singing along, and all the threat of a major disturbance was gone.

It was a lesson to me. The inmates were a placid bunch, torpid even, but they could catch fire, and the fire could spread. When they were gathered together in a body, they were only one sermon away from a riot.

Afterwards, I saw the vicar beaming and shaking hands with Beltov. From his perspective, the service had been a success. You could already see him working out how he was going to mention it in his next sermon. He could reap credit for coming to the asylum, and no doubt he would either depict the inmates as suffering the inevitable wages of sin, or he could issue a warning, like Job, for his parishioners not to get too high and mighty. I do not think he saw them as individuals who had been unlucky, and the vicar was careful to keep attendants between himself and the Lord's suffering children.

"I hope you found the sermon illuminating," he told Beltov.

"It shed valuable light on the psychopathology of Jehovah," said the doctor.

Chapter Five: The Phantom of the Cinema

There was a note waiting for me at my lodgings, delivered by hand. "From *your friend,*" said my landlady, with a significant look. I did not need to ask which friend she meant. "She looked worried. I do hope it's nothing serious."

She was fishing for information, and I did not reward her with so much as a word, however hungry she was for gossip. My relations with Sally were a private matter and most definitely not for the ears of anyone who was going to spread them around Norwood in every shop she visited in her weekly round.

You could have called Sally my fiancée, but that would be presumptive. There was no formal agreement between us, just an unspoken understanding. I had certainly never made her an offer. Her personal situation—widowed, with a stain on her character from a time spent on the streets and a young son who had been placed with her sister—made it convenient for her to find a respectable husband who could provide for her. She had formed an attachment to me.

Until not long before, I had never entertained the idea there could be anything between us, although I could hardly fail to be aware that she had taken a shine to me. Matters took an unexpected turn when, for reasons related to a case, I was obliged to take her home for lunch one Sunday. To my surprise—which in hindsight was not warranted—my parents warmed to her at once, and she to them. Afterwards, Ma spoke of Sally approvingly; of course, she knew only that Sally now worked at the pickle factory and had assisted me with some cases. It had gotten to the point where I couldn't see my parents without being asked about Sally, and there was an expectation hovering around her name.

My mode of life was hardly conducive to the married state. More importantly, my mother would be shaken to the core if she ever found out about Sally's past. It is a small world, and people know people. If my connection with Sally became an established fact, there was sure to be someone who knew of her previous existence, and it was a piece of gossip too juicy to miss. Sooner or later, word would get back to Ma, dropping from the lips of someone pretending to be a friend.

"Sally? Not the Sally who used to bleach her hair, one of *those girls* hanging around the pub…?"

Sally had repented her earlier life and been washed clean. Christian charity required us to accept repentant sinners and not hold their past against them. Except I didn't know how often it worked that way in practice. To some people, Sally would always be dyed deep scarlet that would not wash off like hair colour.

Equally troubling was the thought of what I might do if some man taunted me with the claim that he'd had her behind the pub for a shilling. I had grown resistant to most gibes, but that would be a hard one to bear.

The ball was in my court, but I was not inclined to play it. I preferred to keep things on an unofficial basis.

So, for the time being, I was allowing things to take their course, willing to see how things turned out. Sally might lose interest, or latch on to another man; or some means might arise to make the thing feasible. I was not sure which of these alternatives I would find preferable.

Sally and I continued to see each other, going to the pictures and walking out in the evenings. Very pleasant evenings they were, too. We had a surprising number of shared interests and passed the time pleasantly together. We went to the pictures and to musical soirees at the Crystal Palace. There was a Saturday afternoon picking raspberries in Musto's Field, and afterwards Carnival Night at the Croydon Hippodrome, where we drank fizzy wine, wore paper masks, and danced, laughed and laughed about nothing that I can remember.

I even met her little boy one Sunday morning. He was living with his aunt and uncle, but Sally was allowed to see him sometimes, and we went walking in Dulwich Park. He was a small, shy boy of four years, who clung to her side.

I squatted down to his height and produced a bag of toffees.

He shook his head emphatically. "Auntie says I'm not allowed."

I looked to the left as though checking to see if we were observed, then looked to the right. I popped a toffee in my mouth and proffered the bag again. "I won't tell if you don't," I said.

He snatched a sweet and disappeared behind Sally's skirts. Later on, I stopped to point out an aircraft droning lazily by, a passenger flight. What a spectacular view they must have from up there, with all of England spread below them. He looked up in wonder, and I felt absurdly proud for having noticed it.

The boy accepted another toffee as a parting gift, with a mumbled "Thank you very much, sir."

"He likes you," she said afterwards. "He asked if you can teach him to box."

"So long as he doesn't call me sir," I said.

It was a rare light moment. My work was grim at times, and my anxiety over the lack of contact from Miss De Vere was starting to gnaw at me. The news was equally dark. It was all talk of Chancellor Hindenburg taking over in Germany and the prospects for another war, which was sounding all but inevitable. There was something new every day. The latest talk was of a Royal Observer Corps being set up to watch out for bombers over our cities. Life needed something cheerful.

Sally and I got on very well, for the present. But my situation was hardly a stable one. It did not need Gillespy's death to remind me of the risks implicit in my position. Any talk of the future was discouraged.

The note waiting for me was a single line from Sally telling me to go to her as soon as I received it. I supposed that she might have preferred to wait there for me, except that female visitors were not allowed. And she could hardly be expected to wait on the doorstep, though the weather was mild enough.

Sally still lived at Mrs Berry's rooming house, in that very room where Mabel Brown had met such a tragic end. That always bothered me, but Sally said it was a nice enough place, and the likelihood of lightning striking twice was low, and besides, Mabel Brown had been messing with things she did not understand. None of that was exactly reassuring. I had seen lightning strike the same spot twice with my own eyes, and not so very far away. And by being involved with me, Sally was also messing with things she did not understand.

However, I had come to a better appreciation of when argument is pointless, and with Sally, it was most of the time. At least her room was pleasant, and the house was conveniently situated.

I was ten paces from the door when Sally came out to meet me, handbag clutched in her fist.

"Hello, Harry," she said. "We've got to go to the pictures. There's something you have to see."

She stuck her arm through mine and led me off in the direction of the Roxy. She was lively enough, but not her usual cheerful self. It was not an outing for a whim, which was more Sally's style—this was something more serious.

"What's the matter?" I asked.

"I can't explain," she said. "There's a strange picture. You have to see it. You'll understand. In fact, you're probably the only one who will understand. It's horrible."

Sally had worked the early shift at the pickle factory and had caught a matinee showing at the cinema. Films were one of our shared interests, but our tastes did not quite coincide, and the *Phantom of the Opera* was more her cup of tea than mine. It had opened that day, and Sally had decided to see it on her own.

I knew the film's reputation. Lon Chaney had made a career out of playing deformed and mutilated characters, from the *Hunchback of Notre Dame* onwards. Strange, perhaps, that Sally, who had experience of real-life horror, would choose Mr Chaney's work for entertainment. But then, I hadn't stopped reading fantastic tales of adventure either, despite of everything. She would not explain what had disturbed her, but I gathered it was not the main feature but something else in the program.

We arrived after the program had started. The usual bill of fare is a balanced blend of serious and lighter pieces: a newsreel, a cartoon, a serial, comedy short, and a travelogue or documentary before the film proper.

"There weren't so many in the matinee," said Sally, shouting over the sound of a beer-hall polka from the cinema organ.

We had to look for seats. I find pushing past others a tricky business, and we settled for two end seats near the back of the stalls.

On the screen, a man was finishing demonstrating the art of glassblowing. An amorphous, glowing blob of material on the end of a tube was transformed into a glass vase, turning and turning all the while so it did not fall out of shape.

"This is it next," said Sally, looking about her. "There're a lot of people here."

The image of the finished glass vase, on a display stand with several others, faded from the screen, and the organ was silent. The submerged buzz of chatter, coughing, and the rustling of sweet papers rose to the surface.

Sally took my arm. "I'm closing my eyes," she said.

The screen remained black, but the organ started a new tune. Less of a tune, more of a whine, like giant mosquitoes.

"The Phantom of the Cinema," announced the title card. Of course, it was a companion piece to the *Phantom of the Opera*. I assumed from the title that it would be a short comedy, with Buster Keaton or somebody burlesquing his way through a parody of the main feature. I could not have been more mistaken.

On the screen was the inside of a cinema, a bigger place than the one we were in, and a full house by the look of it.

The music changed to an ominous rumbling, drumming rhythm. On the screen, hooded men carrying flaming torches raced through a ruined city at night. It was not clear if they were chasing or being chased.

Suddenly, the scene changed to a desert landscape of rocky pinnacles.

Mutters rose from the cinema audience. The transition from one scene to another was too abrupt. The projectionist must have made a mistake.

It was a fantastic scene; the pinnacles were a thousand feet high, and must have been added afterwards by a special-effects artist. Dark birds with jagged wings and curved beaks circled high in the sky. A lone man, a hooded figure who might have been one of those from the ruined city, struggled onwards, steadying himself on a rock. He was dragging a load behind him. His face could not be seen.

He passed a row of people who were carrying out ritual obeisance: standing, kneeling, lying down, and standing again. The object of their veneration was just off the screen, and the shadow which fell across them was oddly suggesting of a living being.

The music changed again to suggest the Orient. Three women in elaborate costumes danced slowly around a gigantic black egg. They circled the egg, stooped, bowed to it, caressed it, circled again. The organ thumped, drumming, as though a huge heart was beating inside the egg.

"What is this?" I asked Sally, but she had her eyes squeezed tightly shut and shook her head.

Then we were back in the cinema again. The film jumped around as though it had been edited by a madman. You barely had time to apprehend one scene before it was snatched away, and you were somewhere else. The cinema audience on the screen leaned forward, clutched their seats, wiped their brows. They were seeing something alarming.

"HE HAS MANY FACES," said the inter-title card.

The hooded men were threading their way through a maze of metal prisms, which turned and shifted as they passed. Pits opened in front of them, and they leapt across, agile as goats. When they came to an open space, you could see that the sky behind them was full of shooting stars, a torrent crossing the sky.

"This is very strange," I said. I felt Sally shake her head again, waiting for it to be over.

Then, the scene jumped to a sailing ship, riding the waves on a storm-tossed sea. The audience was no longer shouting at each transition. It was carrying them along. The clouds were so thick you could not tell whether it was day or night, but there was white water everywhere—what Captain Hall called "white horses" of foam at the summit of every wave. They were such towering waves that the schooner seemed to hesitate with each one, as if it might not crest it but would slide into the water.

The crew clung to the rigging, soaked through from the spray, pointing to something below. Then, the camera pulled back, and confusingly, the waves had become sand dunes in the desert. The desert traveller stopped, got down on his knees, and started brushing at the sand with his gloved hands. He was uncovering something, but we could not see what it was. He stood up and walked several deliberate paces with his hood tilted down towards the ground before stopping again to repeat the act.

The dancers had begun to move more vigorously and less elegantly. They looked as though they had been dancing a long time. Their faces, which had been blank and serene, showed something of panic. The drumming grew louder. The huge egg moved—or seemed to move—and a woman screamed.

"IT WILL BE BORN AGAIN," said the inter-title.

There were a few indignant cries from the audience, and one scornful laugh. People do not like being messed around, and the picture made less and less sense.

"Rubbish!" shouted someone. Nobody told him to be quiet.

The hooded men were streaming into a building. Again, you could not tell whether they were the pursuers or the pursued. Some of them were carrying knives or other weapons. Strange markings were painted on the walls of a corridor they ran through. Then they were in a cinema, too, an empty, deserted one. They ran towards the blank screen, faster than ever.

The ship was still struggling with tall waves, and now you could tell it was night because a full moon appeared between the clouds. The bearded captain pointed up at it.

"THE GREEN MOON DRAWS THEM!"

Heads broke the water, glittering wetly in the moonlight. One turned, showing a big-eyed face that was not a seal or a manatee, or anything else wholesome and natural. People gasped around me.

It was all happening too fast; there was no chance to piece the scenes together or make sense of the film—if it did make any sense.

The next scene was blanked out by smoke or steam, like when a train arrives at a station. You could not make out what was behind it.

"Foggy today!" shouted someone, which drew nervous laughter.

"This is rubbish!" came another shout. "Take it off!"

The desert traveller crouched by a rock pillar, his eyes fixed on something in the distance. Shifting shadows suggested something colossal. The dark birds wheeled around him.

"THE FATHER OF TERROR"

Then, back in the cinema, hooded figures burst out of the

screen. The audience panicked, trying to climb under their chairs or scramble away over others, who sat paralysed. The hooded ones looked odd compared to the normal people, as though their robes covered deformities.

Women were screaming—women in the real-life cinema around me.

The screen showed a close-up of a single hooded figure then went white, the brilliance suddenly dazzling.

I was momentarily confused. A hooded figure ran past, and I genuinely thought it must be one of the characters from the screen until I saw it was just a woman in a shawl, scattering caramels behind her in her haste to get out.

The house lights went up.

The screams had stopped, and there was a gust of male laughter, tension being released. Others joined in less certainly. It was all a big practical joke to scare us, and it had worked a little too well. Some of the women were laughing, too, but friends were crowding round another who had fainted.

"Lie her down," one of them was saying.

"Give her some air," urged another.

I saw a trembling elderly woman make her way out, resting her hand on a seatback at every step. Some of the others looked like they would have liked to join her.

"What a shocker," a man behind me was saying cheerfully. "That was a proper shocker, wasn't it?"

"Nearly made me jump out of my skin," said his companion. "They shouldn't show things like that without warning you."

"You had to see it," said Sally, her eyes open again. "What are we going to do?"

"Well… the first thing is, I'm going to see the manager," I said.

The cinema manager, a silver-haired man in a dinner jacket and bow tie, had his back to his office door, which bore a silver plaque: *Mr J Bellingham BICM*.

Others had arrived before me. The commissionaire, who sported impressive whiskers and plenty of gold braid, was arguing with two men who were trying to get to the manager. Two others had outflanked him and were remonstrating with the manager. The womenfolk stood back at a safe distance.

Others jostled alongside me, all with the same mission in mind, but as soon as I approached, everyone made space and deferred to me, presumably on the grounds that I looked like an individual who would make their complaint forcefully if not physically.

"There are women and children in that audience," a red-faced man was shouting. "You ought to be ashamed of yourself!"

"I was trying to explain—" Bellingham waved his hands in calming gestures.

"It wasn't even on the bill," said another.

"There's two of them fainted in the lower circle."

"Please!" I said, loud enough to cut through the competing voices. "Let's hear this explanation, shall we?"

I said it with enough menace for the others to quiet down and look to the manager, who addressed his reply to me.

"I have been on the telephone with the distributors," he said. "There was some sort of mix-up."

"You!" Someone pushed past me and put both his hands round the startled manager's throat. A second later, the two of them were grappling on the floor.

I stooped and lifted the assailant bodily off the ground. I might as well have been back at the asylum, as it was such a familiar type of assault. The furious cinemagoer still clung on to his victim, and it was only by twisting both arms that I could get him to relinquish his grip and let the poor manager breathe again.

The attacker thrashed and struck out at me with his elbows and heels. I suffered a few bruising blows, but experience and training counted for something. I had him in a secure armlock before too long.

"I'll kill him!"

"Stop it!" I told him. "You'll injure yourself."

His eyes rolled as he tried to struggle, pulling this way and that. There were men at the hospital who were less crazy than he was.

"Him! Him!" he kept saying, grinding his teeth. "I'll kill him!"

As is the way of these things, with all except the most frenzied, the flare-up burned itself out before long, and his struggles subsided. The sudden outburst of violence had shocked the other cinemagoers, and they had calmed down. They were still complaining, but the manager was no longer the target of their wrath.

"You can let go of me now," the man I had pinned down said in a quiet voice.

"Are you going to behave?" I asked.

"Yes, yes. I'm sorry."

I released him quickly and stood back, watching for signs of a renewed outburst, but as he got up, he only rubbed his arms and worked his shoulder joints. He was embarrassed rather than angry.

"Are you hurt?" I asked.

"Nah. Are you?"

I shook my head.

"I'm sorry, I don't know what happened," he said, looking at the carpet, wondering at his own behaviour. "I saw that thing on the screen, and… well, something snapped." A thought suddenly hit him. "The manager, is he—"

"He's not hurt," I said.

"Thank Christ for that." He was genuinely relieved.

"Maybe," I suggested, "you had better slide off now, and we'll say no more."

"Good idea," he said. "Thanks, mate."

The manager was sending away the last of the disgruntled patrons, handing out little red vouchers for free tickets. The commissionaire had returned to his station, judging that the danger to his superior had passed.

"The – customer has gone," I told the manager. I had to force myself not to call him an inmate; it was hard to appreciate that I was not at work. "He won't bother you again."

"I'm very grateful to you," he said, raising a hand to his neck. He had straightened his bow tie, but there were scratches and a livid red mark on his throat. "As I told the others, it was the distributors. They sent us the wrong reel of film. The entire program is delivered in one package, you see. All the projectionist does is play the reels through, one after another."

"It happened in the matinee as well," I said.

"Unfortunately, neither the projectionist nor I was watching it then," he said, a trifle too defensively.

"That seems a bit careless." I would not usually be so forward, but I had saved him some personal damage, and I was more than a little curious to find out what was going on.

"I am extremely sorry, believe me. I've been manager here for twenty years, and nothing like this has ever occurred before."

"I've never seen a film like that ever before," I said. "What was it?"

"God knows," he said with some force. "God knows what it was. I'm tempted to take the celluloid out and burn it. I've never seen an audience react like that before."

"But who made it?" I asked. "And why?"

Seeing that my interest was genuine, and appreciating he owed me a favour, the manager gestured for me to follow him to the projectionist's booth, a short distance down the corridor. He smoothed his hair.

"I've a pretty wide experience of films," he said. "What it reminded me of, a lot, was those Expressionist pictures coming out of Germany. *The Cabinet of Doctor Caligari, Nosferatu, The Golem*—ever seen those?"

"I haven't even heard of them."

He stopped by the door.

"Films like those are not commercial over here, but you have to keep an eye on trends. Modernist filmmaking is all very... weird. Like this."

There was not enough room for both of us to go into the projectionist's booth, but I saw a small, bearded man in silhouette, illuminated by flickering background light, shrugging and gesturing as exaggeratedly as one of his silent film stars. Even from there, I got a waft of hot celluloid from the booth. After a brief but pointed exchange, he passed something to Bellingham, who withdrew a minute later and closed the door.

"Here's the poison," he said, holding up a flat silver can and looking at the label in the light. "Well, that's suspicious for a start. No distributor's name on it. No nothing, in fact."

A plain, typed rectangle, the size of a business card, was slotted into a holder like a luggage label: *Phantom of the Cinema. 8 mins. Reel 1 of 1.*

He drummed his fingers on the film canister thoughtfully.

"The distributors—" I started.

"They denied all knowledge," he said. "You know, I think somebody slipped this little piece of mischief into the program after the delivery was made."

"Wouldn't the projectionist notice?"

"Woods is a good man," said Bellingham. "Dedicated to the cinema. But he's not always the most observant. Bit of a dreamer. And he has to take breaks like everyone else."

I cast about for other clues. "What about the music? Did they give you sheet music to go with it?"

"No," he said, dismissing my layman's ignorance. "For shorts like this, Bobby—the organist—he makes it up. He has a book of standard tunes, for chases and love scenes and whatnot, and for anything else he improvises around the action."

"Your organist has an uncanny knack," I said. The music had seemed to be intended to carry half the effect. Even as I spoke, though, I wondered whether the music was somehow implicit in the images, and the organist was merely more sensitive to it.

"Somebody is playing a joke on us," said the manager grimly, hefting the film can in his hand. "The sort of joke that could lose me my job. Or else..."

I knew then, as I think Bellingham did, that this was more than a joke. Somebody had gone too far and had taken too much trouble, and the effect on the patrons had been far too serious. He was probably thinking about the Germans, and how and why a strange German film could have arrived there. *Might it be a peculiar new variety of sabotage?*

If I had been able to contact Miss De Vere, I would have asked her if it meant anything and if I should get involved, but I was left to my own initiative. What I was investigating left a trail of madness, and this film reel reeked of it. Better safe than sorry.

"As luck would have it, I'm an investigator of sorts," I said, passing Bellingham my Lantern business card. "Insurance, usually, but I can carry out an extracurricular investigation on your behalf."

He eyed me warily, perhaps suspecting a prelude to blackmail. "I can't pay you commercial rates," he said. "I'm working on a shoestring in this place."

"This would be strictly, as we say in the business, *pro bono*," I said. "I'd be interested in getting to the bottom of this, myself. As a matter of fact, I believe it might have some connection with another investigation I'm involved with."

"Oh well, in that case, carry on. 'Another investigation,' you say—do you mean to say that something like this has happened to someone else?"

"Not exactly, but there are, shall we say, echoes."

Bellingham searched my face, but it would not have been prudent for me to say more. For once, I was the one in the know, and somebody else was left wondering. "If we can say we've a man investigating the matter, it would take some of the heat off," he said. "If it goes to the papers or anyone. In the meantime, please accept this as a token of my appreciation." He pressed a book of ticket vouchers on me and took my hand. "I look forward to hearing from you, Mr Stubbs."

I left him contemplating the film reel. Maybe it could have been dusted for fingerprints if he had not touched it so much.

"There," said Sally, once the two of us were back in the lobby. "Could you find anything out?"

There was nobody else around, except the cigarette girl in one corner, counting piles of pennies and ha'pennies. I was deeply reluctant to involve Sally in anything further, but I was here at her instigation. She had a share in it, and it would not be fair to shut her out.

"He thinks it might be German," I said.

Chapter Six: Hydrotherapy

"So, Mr Jenkins, today you begin your hydrotherapy treatment," said Dr Beltov.

Jenkins looked at the bathtub and its canvas apparatus doubtfully, scratching his head.

"I have explained this clearly to you," said Beltov.

"I'm not quite sure..."

"Please, Mr Jenkins, there is nothing to be apprehensive about."

"Don't worry," I said. "It's not cold water."

While there is nothing more invigorating than a cold bath taken in the right spirit, I quite understand why some people view it as a form of torture.

"The warm water will calm your nerves," said Beltov. "We find this is a very effective therapy. It is medically proven."

If Beltov was the patient, that would be all that was needed; he would set himself on fire if some paper said it was medically proven. Jenkins was not so easily persuaded.

"But I don't need a bath," he said. "It's not my bath night."

"Mr Jenkins—" Beltov began, and I could see he was going to start repeating himself. He might have been highly thought of in psychological circles, but he lacked patience in his relations with inmates.

"You're a lucky man, Jenkins," I interjected. "People go to Baden-Baden and pay a lot of money for this exact sort of thing. Spa treatment, they call it there. Very luxurious."

"Don't they have special waters there?" asked Jenkins.

"Unproven," said Beltov, before I could reply. "There is no scientific evidence that the mineral content of the water makes the slightest difference. The critical factor is the temperature of the water."

He tapped the big brass thermometer for emphasis. Yellow and orange bands fanning out around the needle delineated the exact temperature ranges to be applied for different effects.

"There's nothing wrong with English water," I said. "We had Beulah Spa up the road, and that was as good as anywhere in Europe."

"So, it's a spa treatment," said Jenkins thoughtfully, reaching out to touch one of the brass taps. He was already half-won over, perhaps imagining himself as some affluent gentleman in a Swiss resort, reclining among the vapours. We waited expectantly.

"Well, I suppose I'll try it out," he said. "It's just like a warm bath, after all, isn't it?"

"Exactly so," said Beltov.

As Jenkins undressed and I ran the bath, Beltov explained the procedure to me again. I had assisted in hydrotherapy before, but this was the first time I had sole charge.

"I've got the instructions all written down," I said. "Though I can't pretend to know how it works."

It was not even a rhetorical question, but I had touched on a subject close to Beltov's heart, and he felt the need to educate me. "The human brain operates on several levels, each supporting the other, like a house of cards," he said. "There is the physical level, the electro-chemical level, and the behavioural or psychological level. Herr Freud and his disciples think we can do everything on the psychological level, with words and symbols. But this talking cure is useless with psychosis." He emphasised the word *useless* with a gesture of rejecting Freud and all his works.

"The clever German chemists want to cure madness by better regulation of our brain chemicals—with artificial hormones and other substances. And they are very clever." He pulled an enamelled pill box from his jacket pocket and rattled it under my nose. "Acid sodium phosphate. It reduces fatigue and increases concentration by twenty per cent, with no side effects. One day the clever German chemists will find the right formula to regulate our brains as easily as changing a clock. If they don't kill us all with clever poison gas first."

Beltov looked forward to a grand future where every degree of mania or melancholy could be treated with the correctly calibrated doses of pills or injections, where hallucinations could be remedied like headaches. Like his unreliable glass clock, the mind could be corrected as soon as it went wrong. For the meantime, though, all we could do was dose the inmates' evening cocoa with bromide to help calm them and pacify their animal urges.

"But for now, we have crude physical methods. Water changes the temperature of the body. It calms or stimulates the brain—we know this from fevers and hyperthermias, but we are groping in the dark." He looked disapprovingly at the bath, which was almost full. "Now we try this new regime with clocks and tides... This is not science. But if we gather enough data, if we observe carefully—one day. Keep your notes exact. Record the times."

"Can I get in now?" asked Jenkins, shivering in his underwear.

"Yes, yes, Mr Jenkins. Please do so. I will leave you in the management of Mr Stubbs."

I showed Jenkins how to get into the hydrotherapy apparatus. He lay in a kind of canvas hammock in the tub, with another sheet of canvas over him and a wooden lid on top of that to keep the heat in, with only his head sticking out.

The thermometer displayed the temperature to the nearest half degree, but I told him to let me know the minute it became uncomfortable.

"Just lie back and relax," I said, adjusting the taps. Unlike a normal bath, it had a continual slow leak, so it could be continually topped up to maintain the right level of warmth. "Go to sleep if you feel like it."

The pipes swooshed and gurgled pleasantly.

"How long do I stay in for?"

"Half an hour, like Dr Beltov said." I held up the big alarm clock. "I'm timing it on my watch as well."

"What was that he said about tides?"

I tried to gather what Beltov had told me earlier. It was not easy, as there were so many different therapies, but my notebook was in my hand. "You get bathed at a different time of the day, corresponding to the tides," I said. "It's supposed to be more natural that way."

"Huh," said Jenkins. "And what's that over there?"

It was something like an enormous coffin on legs, all carved from teak. The interior, padded with red velvet, was shaped to follow the outlines of a human body. A series of joined metal boxes was positioned around the end which was shaped to fit a patient's head, forming a sort of outsized helmet.

Staff and patients alike—apart from Dr Beltov, who said the word had negative associations—called it the sarcophagus, because of the elaborate carvings, which made it resemble Egyptian funerary furniture. Beltov was right. I looked it up, and sarcophagus literally means "eater of flesh," which is one worse than a mere coffin.

"This is the apparatus for magnetotherapy," I told him. Beltov had explained it to me rather offhandedly. Like the hydrotherapy, it was an old treatment which had been given a new scientific gloss, like putting a lick of paint on an old wardrobe to conceal its poor condition. Magnets did not impress him. "The helmet section contains a series of revolving magnets on springs and wires."

"What does that do?"

Nothing very much, according to Beltov. He thought magnetism was a species of quackery that ought to have been abandoned after Dr Mesmer was exposed a century or two ago. But apparently, he had re-emerged.

"Well, they say the brain is magnetic," I said. "And where there's a disorder, when the brain gets out of kilter, the electro-magnets sort of smooth it back into place. It's perfectly harmless."

It was certainly complicated enough, with an electric motor and mysterious mechanisms in a cabinet underneath. A pen moved on a paper strip, and magnetic wires recorded the machine's actions, presumably as an indication that it had actually done something, as the effects were otherwise entirely intangible. There were several dials and switches; I could not imagine what they were all for, though I resolved to have a closer look sometime. The entire thing was unnecessarily ornate, either to impress patients or the doctors who paid for it. It could have been a stage prop for a Gothic melodrama. I could understand why it provoked Beltov's scepticism more than the unpretentious apparatus for hydrotherapy did.

"I like this better," said Jenkins from his bath. "I must go down to the seas again, to the lonely sea and the sky, the call of the tide and the oceans wide… and that which rises, by and by."

He carried on reciting until the words became slurred and nonsensical. Then, a waft of steam momentarily veiled his face, and for some reason I was convinced that something had happened to him—but as I gawped, the alarm clock came clangourously to life, the steam parted, and Jenkins looked up, startled, wide-awake and quite his normal self.

"It feels a bit strange and dreamy," was Jenkins's verdict as he towelled himself down. "You sort of lose yourself in the water." He looked at his hand as if seeing it for the first time.

That evening, I was to have my first experience of that unusual condition which is known by the French name of *folie a deux,* which in English means "madness shared by two persons."

FitzRoy was one of the more harmless residents. The exact reasons for his being there were lost to history, but he was a portly, middle-aged man with the fixed delusion that he was the rightful king of England. It all started with his name. FitzRoy was the surname they used to give children born to royalty and out of wedlock, but whose parentage was officially recognised. They ended up as dukes and earls and whatnot, hundreds of years ago. This particular FitzRoy had convinced himself that he was something special and, by some genealogy known only to himself, had precedence over our actual royals.

Some years ago, they told me, he considered himself merely the rightful heir to the throne. When the old king died in 1910, FitzRoy elevated himself and crowned himself with tinfoil, declaring himself to be sovereign. His royal ways earned him a certain amount of derision and not infrequent abuse, but his position was immovable. I will always treasure the occasion when another inmate, on being jostled aside, asked FitzRoy who he thought he was. FitzRoy turned around and reeled off his complete list of titles from Defender of the Faith and Emperor of India all the way up to ruler of the British Dominions beyond the Seas. He may have been mad, but FitzRoy was well-rehearsed.

FitzRoy had moved an armchair to the middle of the living area to hold court, as he saw it. This was after dinner; there were no scheduled activities, and the rota had assigned me the task of overseeing. It was considered light duty, as it was generally no more than hanging around, seeing that there was no trouble, rebuking anyone trying to damage the furniture, and preventing squabbles from coming to blows. The inmates rubbed along pretty well, and trouble was rare.

I was standing by the wall, keeping an eye on things. Some of the inmates were watching the glorious orange sunset, with drifts of clouds coloured like an oil painting. Others played dominoes or cards.

"Excuse me, Mr Stubbs, may I trouble you for permission to collect a cup of water?" Jenkins asked me.

"Not had enough water for one day, then?" I joked. He did at least smile back at me. "By all means, you can fetch one."

A minute later, I saw Jenkins bring the tin cup and kneel beside FitzRoy, holding it up like a goblet. FitzRoy took a few sips and then dismissed Jenkins with a suitably royal wave. Jenkins took the cup, still three-quarters full, back to the scullery.

"You don't have to do what he says," I told Jenkins.

"It is my honour to serve the king," he said, with a tone of offended patriotism.

"Well," I said, "just because a man claims to be king, we don't have to believe him."

His look was more one of pity than anything else.

"His majesty is most tolerant with all of his subjects... But really, there's no need for that sort of talk. Not when you are under his roof."

As I followed his gaze, I saw that, to a certain way of looking at it, FitzRoy might appear royal. The institution was certainly palatial. The evening sun had painted gorgeous tapestries on the walls, and even FitzRoy's hair looked gilded. In that light, the garden was as splendid as Hampton Court.

Those around him were, to him, his advisers, courtiers and hangers-on. He issued proclamations as if he were the real king. He was not in charge of running the place, but the king did not manage his own household, either, but was as much a slave to the needs of rotas and schedules as any gentleman who gets turned out of his armchair so the floor can be cleaned. Though in the case of royalty, there needs must be more ceremony involved.

"I have petitioned him, and he is very interested in my case. Next week, I am to be knighted," Jenkins confided to me. "Perhaps even a position in the Royal Household."

He had been imprinted with FitzRoy's ideas, like a blank sheet which picks up newsprint by contact. Nature abhors a vacuum, and queer ideas can be catching.

A man with delusions is like a stick that falls over if you try to stand it up on its own. But two sticks can support each other, and that's how *folie a deux* works. Each of the participants supports the other in his delusion, in return for being supported. FitzRoy had his loyal supporter at last, in exchange for recognising Jenkins's persecution mania. They had found a way of fitting the two together like pieces of a jigsaw, and the two would support and reinforce each other's delusions.

I made a note to mention it to Dr Beltov. Both patients seemed harmless enough, but together they might put each other up to worse mischief than either alone would imagine.

With Gillespy's death and what had happened to Ryan, matters had progressed to a stage where I had to square things with my patron, Arthur Renville. I set out to do that the next afternoon.

Arthur was a figure of some consequence in Norwood. He was a consignment man, one who dealt in shipping cargoes which had been written off for insurance purposes, but which still had some material value. It was a lucrative business, and one which required the mobilisation of considerable resources in terms of manpower, transportation, and storage facilities, for many of the items were in something of a legal grey zone. This meant that he was the steersman for all sorts of activity, some of it entirely respectable, some of it a good deal less formal.

Arthur's position at the hub of things meant he was a coordinator—never a leader, he was always at pains to stress, but first among equals. When a case of pilfering was brought to his attention, the accused would start grovelling; and if Arthur so much as hinted that someone was out of line, then steps were taken to put them in order. Sometimes quite heavy steps.

Arthur was my mentor. He got me out of a jam more than once, and I will forever be indebted to him. I would not wish to inconvenience him by thoughtless action, and it seemed only polite to let him know what was going on. His business hours usually occurred in the hours of darkness, but he was sometimes out in daytime, and that day I found him in the barber shop on the High Street having his fortnightly cut.

It was my usual barber as well, a friendly place, with all-white porcelain sinks, gilt mirrors, and that smell that all good barbers emanate. Giant bottles filled with green and red liquid stood in the window. The three barbers, two brothers and a cousin, worked with brisk efficiency when needed, or at a leisurely pace when the customer was there for relaxation, surrounded by dark Cherrywood furniture and advertisements for hair cream and unbreakable combs. There were two customers waiting; one was leafing through a saucy magazine – there was a low table piled with them – the other a retired gent clearly in no hurry, and they gestured for me to go next.

I was overdue a haircut, one of those things which the busy schedule working as an attendant while keeping up with other commitments had pushed back, and I took the chair next to Arthur. The barber pumped the chair down to a more convenient height, threw a white cape over me and, with comb and clicking scissors, proceeded with the usual trim.

"Stubbsy," said Arthur, genial enough, looking at me in the mirror. "How are you keeping? Working down the local Colney Hatch, I gather."

"I've been obliged to take up a position there for an investigation," I said, "on behalf of that American lady I mentioned."

Arthur raised his eyebrows and waited for me to go on. He probably knew all about it but wanted to hear my version of events. Small locks of hair tumbled over my shoulders, one after the other in quick succession, like autumn leaves.

"A man called Gillespy died in there," I said. "And something happened to an associate of his called Ryan outside."

The barber moved around and stood between us, giving me a clear reflected view of Arthur once more.

"What's going on, Stubbsy? You think there's murder?" Arthur did not like mess and untidiness, and killings invariably brought both.

I had helped bring matters to a satisfactory conclusion, and wittingly or not prevent further disorder, in previous cases. Arthur had come to value my work. Though he remained politely sceptical about what he termed the "hocus pocus" aspect of my work and credited me with an overactive imagination, he respected my activities.

"I'm still very much in the dark on that," I said. "You know I've been involved in some strange cases? Well, this is another one of those."

"If you take my advice, you'd steer well clear," said Arthur. "That place… Well, it has a bad smell about it. A hotbed of buggery, not to put too fine a point on it, and I daresay much other unnatural behaviour besides."

"It's not that bad," I said.

He made a sound in his throat which might have been a growl, and I understood that, as far as he was concerned, being an attendant there was enough to make you complicit, at the very least, in sexual deviancy.

"You don't exactly have a reputation as a ladies' man as it is, even after I fixed you up with that Sally," said Arthur. "I hope she's well?"

"Very well, thank you for asking," I said. I did not see that my love life was anybody's concern but my own. I felt the cool metal as the barber cut around my ear.

"And Stubbsy…" He hesitated delicately. "You don't want to pick up any more crazy notions than you already have."

His laugh was a little forced; mental illness made everyone who was not familiar with it uncomfortable. I had been similarly awkward, myself, a few weeks before.

"The other thing was a strange cinema reel," I said. "Did you hear about that?"

"Everyone's heard about that," he said. "Sending people raving. The manager, Bellingham, is in six kinds of trouble over that. Word has it that the Germans are involved, and that's all I need."

I closed my eyes as the barber combed over my forehead and snip-snip-snipped across.

"There's enough talk of another war already, with all this business over Hindenburg," he said gloomily. "It's bad for trade. People can't stop doing business with people because they're German, or might be German, or because some shipment happens to come out of Hamburg."

"Maybe I can find out where it really came from," I said, "and put that rumour to rest."

"Once they get an idea in their heads, it takes more than a

little thing like the truth to dislodge it," said Arthur. "German infiltrators—I ask you! Still, if you can sort out where that reel came from, it would be a start. We don't need any more disturbance." He closed his eyes as the barber sprayed eau de toilette over him. It smelled sharp, but not unpleasant; it was clean and crisp.

The barber held up a mirror so Arthur could inspect the back of his head. His hair was grey and thinning, but he was still handsome. You would not mind looking so well at his age. He looked at his reflection critically, as if assessing the value of a crate of damaged but still serviceable stock, then nodded.

He stood up, feeling for a sixpence to tip the barber, then patted me on the shoulder. "You need to be on the straight and narrow, Stubbsy," he advised me. "Not in a place like that where even the doctors are a bit funny. Working with those head cases… You'll get tangled up in something that even I can't unravel." He turned to the barber. "His cut is on me," he said, and the other man bowed obsequiously.

My next stop was the West Norwood Library. I did not have an appointment to see Assistant Head Librarian Mr Hoade, but we had developed a sort of understanding.

Hoade was consulting some arcane tables of numbers, but he immediately dropped a leather bookmark between the pages and shut it with a snap when he saw me. "Afternoon, Stubbs," he said, smiling as though I'd brought a gift.

"Afternoon," I said. "I hope you're not too busy."

"Pshaw." He waved a hand at the book he had pushed aside. "It can wait. I received your note the other day." His eyes sharpened. "This would be relating to the disturbance at the Roxy last week, I assume?"

"Yes," I said, there being little point in dissembling. There was no small talk with Hoade; he was straight down to business.

"Quite a puzzle. There are lots of films which are meant to shock and horrify and no shortage of propaganda, but I couldn't find anything quite like it. Nothing deliberately meant to upset the mind. But how does this sound?" He slipped a folded sheet of paper from an inner pocket and declaimed: *"A purely psychological warfare, wherein weapons are not used or battlefields sought… but rather… the corruption of the human reason, the dimming of the human intellect, and the disintegration of the moral and spiritual life of one nation by the influence of the will of another is accomplished."*

"That sounds quite apt," I said. "Who said it?"

"Major General JFC Fuller, writing about tanks in the Great War. His point was that half—more than half—the effect of tanks was psychological. A purely psychological weapon with no physical element might be even more effective. The image of the tank rather than the tank."

"And how far has he got with this psychological weapon?"

"He's a prophet without honour in his own country," said Hoade. "But his theories are well regarded in Germany."

I took out my notebook.

"The other thing that might interest you is that Major General Fuller is a keen student of the occult and a chum of Aleister Crowley. Though, given that Fuller is on active duty in Camberley, and Crowley was last heard of in Tunis, I doubt whether there's a direct connection. But plenty in Germany and elsewhere have read Fuller. And while they're not allowed to build tanks, we can't stop them making motion pictures."

Even as I was taking it down, Hoade was unfolding a second sheet of paper.

"As to your other riddles, the only thing I can tell you is that 'Father of Terror' is what the Egyptians call the great Sphinx at Giza. But I'm looking at the others." I had given him a list of the title cards from the film to see if any of them might make any sense or suggest connections. "Oh, and your robber-ro, robber-ro—I think I cracked it."

That was the phrase I thought Hooper had been saying when he told me about Gillespy being "taken."

"And what's the answer?" I asked, as Hoade seemed to expect prompting.

"It's not robber-ro, its o-robber-o, or rather Ouroborous. It's an alchemical symbol, a snake in a circle, swallowing its own tail." He showed me the word as it was written, and a rather competently executed copy of a picture from a book. "The name is from the Greek, meaning 'tail-devourer.' It's used as a symbol of eternity or infinity, among other things, also the fusing of opposites and the cycle of life."

I could feel myself frowning. I had not expected anything from Hooper to make a great deal of sense.

"Interestingly," Hoade went on, "the symbol first cropped up in ancient Egypt, circa 1600 BC, where it had a protective function. Which makes me wonder if you're now engaged in some sort of Egyptological activity. A British occultist discovering ancient Egyptian mysteries, which are turned into a modern weapon by Germany..."

It was half a question. Ryan had spoken of an "Egyptian Astral," and some of the desert scenery in that disturbing film had looked very much like the Egyptian desert. I could not properly remember whether there had been a pyramid, but it seemed to me that there might have been. Hooper showing some knowledge of Egyptian magic, and a hint of a sphinx, threw me. "It's starting to look that way," I said.

Chapter Seven: The Projectionist's Wife

Eric Woods, the cinema projectionist, lived in a cottage towards South Norwood. I had the morning off, in consequence of having worked a night shift, and wanted to talk to him there rather than at his place of work. He worked in semi-darkness next to a whirring projector, and it would be more convenient to carry out an interview in good lighting and without too much background noise. I felt also that there was a greater chance of his being truthful if there was no chance of being overheard by his boss.

While it was conceivable that an extra reel of film had been slipped into the pile by an outside agent, that called for some stretches of the imagination. An intruder would have to appear at exactly the right time, and I doubted that they could really hang around inside the cinema, waiting for the projectionist to abandon his station for a minute. I wondered how easily they could find where to put it. I had seen inside the projectionist's booth, and it was not a neat arrangement. There were empty film cans, odd reels, and boxes everywhere. While it might sound easy enough, finding anything in another man's working space is never as straightforward as that. Nobody could have inserted another film can in the right place unless they knew his system, and according to Bellingham, nobody knew Woods's working arrangements except Woods.

Unless whoever did it knew exactly where to insinuate the spurious reel, there was no chance of the scheme working. And even if they found the right stack, would the projectionist really not notice, even when he loaded it on to the projector? Did he not check the reels off against a list to ensure they were all present and correct?

And equally damning, had he not watched it himself in the

matinee? The arrival of a new stock of films must be a major event. Even if he did not feel a need to check them for scratches or other flaws, I would have expected him to watch everything out of interest.

I needed to talk to Mr Woods, but already I was forming the impression that he might have something on his conscience. Because, whatever Mr Bellingham might think about the reliability of his staff, the whole business smelled to me very much like what burglars term an "inside job": one carried out with the assistance of someone on the premises.

Woods's bungalow was a dingy affair, with paint flaking off the door frame. If it had been in better decorative order, it might have presented a certain charm, but everything about it suggested neglect. The gate was stuck half-open, its hinges broken. A spade and a fork, both leprous with rust, leaned against a wall. The vegetable patch was overgrown; there would be no harvest this season.

I removed my bowler and rapped twice with the knocker.

A woman with a baby on her hip answered the door. She might have been a rougher version of Sally, more careworn and without Sally's innate good humour. She was untidy and kept her hair hidden under a headscarf. A small girl of two or three years held a doll and peeked at me from behind her mother. The smell of cooking wafted through the open doorway; I had interrupted her in the middle of preparing lunch.

"Sorry to disturb you, madam. My name is Harry Stubbs," I said, the business card ready in my hand, "of Lantern Insurance. I was wondering if I might have a word with your husband?"

"We're with the Prudential," she said, her tone none too friendly. She did not make to close the door immediately, though. Perhaps she was glad for the interruption, and for having another human being to talk to after a long morning with the children.

"I'm not selling insurance," I said. "I would like to talk to Mr Woods—about his work."

She set her mouth in a line. "Is he in trouble?"

"Oh, no," I said, a little too quickly. Chances were that he was in trouble. But I doubted Eric Woods was the man I was really after.

"I'm afraid he's not in," she said. The baby let out a squall, and she bounced him up and down, which seemed to quiet him. The action seemed entirely automatic. Her hands were red from work.

"He's messing with something at the cinema."

"Do you know when he will be back?" I said.

"Half an hour ago," she said. "And he better have remembered the bread, or there won't be any with dinner."

The baby, mollified, had turned to gaze at the bowler in my hands, which was level with his head, as I fed it through my fingers.

"I'll come back tomorrow," I said. "Or—is there somewhere I might find him? A pub, perhaps? I'll send him back your way and remind him about the bread."

"You can come in if you like," she said suddenly. "Wait for Eric."

It was rude to refuse, but I was not sure how Mr Woods would take it if he found his wife with a strange man. Of course, I could look after myself if it came to a physical confrontation, but at the expense of some embarrassment. I half-suspected that Mrs Woods might have welcomed such a scene.

"He's probably at the cinema, fiddling with his projector and his reels. What did you want him about?"

"I wished to inquire about an incident in the cinema earlier this week," I said. "There might be insurance repercussions."

"Idiot," she said, and for a moment I thought she meant me. "It's that phantom film, isn't it? I'll get him to explain the whole thing."

"Did he tell you what happened, then?"

"People fainting and screaming and going berserk? I should think he did tell me," she said. "Not that I wouldn't find out soon enough."

I realised that I was unconsciously rotating the hat in my hands, and that was what was attracting the baby's attention. I stopped. Then, when he looked up at me in confusion, I started rotating it the other way instead.

"It was a rather peculiar business," I said. "Some patrons found it unsettling."

"Unsettling! It was mad. I know," she said. "I saw it." She jerked a head over her shoulder. "He has a projector in the back room. 'You've got to see this,' he says. I said, 'You're never going to show that. They'll sack you.' Daft bugger. Did you see it?"

"I did."

"Lunacy," she said, shaking her head. I had expected a show of protective loyalty to her spouse, but Mrs Woods was well beyond that stage. "So, are folks trying to get compensation from the cinema, is that what this is about?"

I reversed the direction of rotation of the hat again to keep the baby's attention. So long as the baby was calm, she kept talking. "Nothing has been determined yet," I said. "But one thing I did want to ask was where that reel of film came from."

"He made it himself," she said levelly. "Here in the back room. There's no sense in denying it."

"He made it?" I echoed.

There were hundreds of extras, and those huge stage sets, the ruined city and the sweeping desert vista. Some of it was faked with painted scenery and models, but it looked like a full production and not some cheap, homemade work.

"He didn't make it from nothing," she added. "But he did put it all together. He's got a machine for turning the wires into pictures. He did all the title cards himself from scratch. There's special kit for it. He put it all together frame by frame, twenty-four pictures for every blessed second of it. It took him hours and hours with razor blades and tape and glue and everything."

For the first time I detected a twinge of defensiveness, even pride. That film was probably the one thing he had ever made, and there was no doubt it was powerful.

"So where did the original material come from? These wires?"

"A friend," she said, a little too casually. "But Eric says it's like a print shop. The letters, they're gobbledygook until the print setter puts them all into the right order and makes sense of them. That film was all his work."

"Do you know where I might find this friend?" I asked. "Just to corroborate."

"Tom's a photographer. A *real* photographer." She looked down at the baby in her arms, who was bored with me and drifting into slumber. "He comes here every other Sunday morning and brings more film, and they talk and look at what Eric's done with it. He's a very respectable young man. I don't know where he lives."

"That's interesting," I said. "I don't suppose you know Tom's second name?"

"No."

"Well, I'd best be going. Thank you very much for your help,

Mrs Woods. You have a fine baby there."

"Hope he doesn't take after his father," she replied. "And if you do see Eric on the way, tell him not to come back here without the bread."

I replaced my hat on my head, tipping it to Mrs Woods, and left her to her domestic arrangements.

Chapter Eight: Voices in the Dark

When patients were first admitted to the asylum, their effects were catalogued and stored away. Personal possessions were not exactly forbidden, but they caused problems, and few were approved. The usual accoutrements of life—house keys, loose change, wallet, watch—were not needed there. There were no doors to unlock, nothing to spend money on, and no appointments to keep. Jewellery and other items that might be subject to theft were also discouraged because of the trouble that thievery, or the accusations of it, could cause. In any case, cufflinks, tie-pins, and the like were unnecessary. Pen-knives and lighters were of course strictly forbidden; I supposed an inmate might have had a cigarette case, but I never saw one.

Clothing was a standard-issue uniform, as in many hospitals, so patients were relieved not only of their possessions, but also of the skin they wore in the outside world. Their clothes were kept, along with the other effects, in a storeroom.

Gaining access to the storeroom required some subterfuge. Truly valuable items were lodged in an immense safe, which was camouflaged to look like a mahogany cabinet, in the superintendent's office. Even so, the storeroom could only be accessed by special permission, or when checking patients in or out. A good deal of thought went into ensuring that the attendants could not pilfer anything, human nature being what it is.

It was going to be an exceedingly risky business. Getting caught would mean instant dismissal and possibly police proceedings. That would be the end of my mission, and the end of my chances of finding anything out. It would put me under equal danger from both my overlords in TDS and from the opponent whose track I was attempting to pick up. The whole thing had to be managed with some care. If successful though it might give me my first real glimmerings of what I was up against.

It was not without trepidation that I put my plan into action.

I picked a quiet night. There were few regular duties on the night shift, but it was mainly a matter of doing the rounds and being there in the event of any incidents. While there was not much to do, at least three attendants on the premises were required, in case of any contingencies. There was a rota of rounds and checks to be made between ten at night and six in the morning, but the place was often as quiet as the grave.

Miller and I had been sparring, our hands padded with towels as makeshift gloves, at his insistence. He was not a fast learner. I could drill a movement into him with enough repetitions, but as soon as he saw an opening, he forgot everything, dropped his guard, and swung wildly. If Miller ever entered a boxing ring, he would be carried out feet first.

The activity did at least satisfy Miller, and when the half-hour came around, he agreed readily enough to walk the patrol circuit. It would take him fifteen minutes at the least, more if he stopped to talk, or box shadows, or practice headstands in the empty hall.

Miller paused on his way out. "Hey, Harry, what's the second sign of madness?" Before I could reply, he gave the answer. "Hairs on your palms! What's the first sign of madness?"

"Looking for them," I said.

"Looking for them!" he repeated, with his gap-toothed smile. The joke would always be as funny to him as it had been the first time around. He headed off, throwing sloppy punches at imaginary opponents.

Donnelly, the other attendant on night duty, had started playing patience, with the cheerful hopelessness of a man who does not expect it to work out. He did at least have a complete deck—none of the packs in the patients' common room had the full fifty-two cards. Like the patients themselves, I suppose.

I indicated that I was headed for the lavatory. Donnelly barely responded. I was sure I could be out of the room ten minutes without him noticing any time had passed, and it should only take a fraction of that.

I slipped the key from the board. Mindful of the fact that it might be missed if I took longer than planned, I put another key in its place so it was not obvious which key had been taken. Then I made my way upstairs, walking more quietly and carefully than a man with an entirely clear conscience would have done.

That was where danger began. I had no business being on that floor at this time of night. I had brought a pocket electric torch, so I would not need to turn on the lights.

The storeroom was like a cloakroom, or the lost-property office of a large railway station. There were rows and rows of coats hanging up, each with a little number pinned to it. Half a dozen stands sprouted sticks and umbrellas, from which paper tags dangled. Every wall was covered from floor to ceiling with cubby holes for suitcases and brown cardboard boxes. I quickly located the one numbered two-twenty-three, which held the personal effects of Patient Gillespy.

If Gillespy was an investigator like me, then he must have had notes, at least a pocketbook or diary or address book. He had to have had something, at least to say what he had been doing and what he had found out before he went over the edge. Surely he would have kept such a thing on his person. I placed the cardboard box on a convenient shelf and removed the lid.

Somewhere below me, somebody moaned loudly. Other voices joined in, telling him to shut his cake-hole and be quiet.

The shouting increased in volume. Two men were yelling at each other now. It was unusual and could spell trouble. I was going to be needed, and soon. I put the lid back on the box and stood, listening.

Miller's voice cut in, not as loud as the others. I could not make out the words, but I could hear his tone of remonstration. Go back to bed and forget about it, otherwise there would be trouble. He did not know who had started it, and he did not care; the whole lot of them would be punished in the morning if they did not pipe down at once.

Miller had a shrewd idea of how things worked. That type of threat was very effective among men forced to live together. He had experienced it for himself in the army, as I had done. Collective punishment appealed to a universal pack instinct. Anyone who got the whole dormitory punished knew he would be in for it.

There was dead silence. Miller made one last comment. "That's more like it," perhaps.

I released the breath I was holding and opened the box again.

As I did so, I was struck by another thought. What I was holding was the sum of the objects on Gillespy's person at the point when he had been committed, which is to say at the exact time that he had lost his senses. Of course, there was no way of knowing what experience, or what realisation, had driven him out of his mind—I suspect Dr Beltov would criticise me for accepting the view without evidence. I had an intuitive sense that it was a sudden thing.

Perhaps it had been something transient, but perhaps it was something tangible. Two of my previous cases had involved uncanny objects. My former colleague Skinner had hinted at the power of certain writings to affect men's sanity. If that were the case, it was entirely possible that whatever had affected Gillespy's mind was inside the box. To open it was to set off a booby trap.

I hesitated. The world is full of people with an unwarranted faith in their ability to handle things. You might say that the entire sport of boxing is based on the principle that, when two men step into the ring, one of them is wrong in his assessment of their relative strengths. If we all had a clear-sighted view of these things, nobody would ever take on a stronger opponent.

I touched the ring that hung on a gold chain round my neck. I never claimed to be free from superstition.

I opened the box.

Inside, there was a scarf and some woollen gloves. Gillespy had evidently been admitted during a cold spell. Then there was an empty cigarette case and a box of matches. There was also, to my surprise, an electric torch, the twin of my own.

A rolled-up magazine proved to be *Sporting Life*; I flicked through it, but there were no sheets of paper hidden between its leaves, nor were there any notes scribbled in the margins. The scraps of paper in the bottom of the box were receipts from a cafeteria. A flyer from a barber shop offering half-price trims, two bus tickets to Gipsy Hill, and a picture postcard of Crystal Palace, which had not been written on. It showed one of the front elevations, by the water tower. Someone had drawn a circle around the base of the stairs, where the Sphinxes are. Another Egyptian connection, by the look of it.

Perhaps Sherlock Holmes might have reconstructed Gillespy's entire life history from that collection, but I doubted it. My correspondence course had warned me about the dangers of becoming too attached to one particular piece of evidence. Just because a suspect has the address of a nightclub on him does not mean that it is germane to the case in hand.

I was about to put everything back when the torchlight gleamed from something I had not noticed at first because it was in shadow and it was transparent.

It was a glass tube, stoppered and sealed with wax at one end, almost full of clear liquid. From the way the liquid moved, it might have been water, but it might have been something thicker and more syrupy. The tube was perhaps six inches long and an inch and a half in circumference. There was no smell about it.

The sealed end showed every sign that it was meant to remain corked soundly so it could not be opened accidentally. It was as though whatever was in the tube was meant to stay there permanently. It was not likely to be a vial of medicine or poison—it was more like those medical samples that the doctors retained. Or, perhaps a sacred relic? Holy water from Lourdes or some other significant place? Special water had featured in my last case too, but that had possessed a distinct, if elusive, glow. This looked like ordinary water.

I put everything else back in the box and replaced it on the shelf, but I carefully slipped the glass tube up my sleeve, careful not to break it, though the glass seemed quite thick. It might have been something or nothing, but it felt good to have a possible clue.

I headed back to the common room, not forgetting to lock the door behind me. I was even more alert to every noise, and there were always noises. Some rooms echoed with moaning or sobbing, and sometimes it was only snoring, but even that had a disconcerting animal quality when heard from the darkened corridor.

Walking the halls on your own at night could be a spooky experience. You had to keep a firm grip on your imagination and not let it run wild at every moving shadow.

I was back in the common room with Miller and Donnelly, playing a desultory game of dominoes, when we heard the distant sound of a telephone.

"That's the upstairs phone," said Donnelly, cocking his head. "Who'd be calling this time of night?"

"It must be a wrong number," suggested Miller.

The ring-ring kept going.

The telephone upstairs was used only by the superintendent for matters relating to administration. Another phone was at the disposal of the doctors, and might be called on a medical matter, but not the superintendent's phone. Nobody would call that number after office hours, except by mistake.

"They're mighty persistent about it," said Donnelly. "Do you think it's too loud?"

I had the same thought. A sound like that might rouse a light sleeper after a time, and that might mean trouble. One man could wake another, and soon the whole ward is up. It could be difficult to settle them again, and it was vastly preferable for sleeping dogs to be let lie. *One of us ought to answer it.*

The superintendent's office was locked, but we had the keys to every room in the building on the board. There were all sorts of situations where we might need access. I stood up.

"There's a grand man, Harry," said Donnelly.

I slipped the key off its hook and hastened upstairs, wondering if the caller would ring off before I got there.

The superintendent's office was even bigger in the dark, an enormous cavern stretching in all directions. I did not know where the light switches were, but the windows were open, and shafts of moonlight lit up strips of the space, including the superintendent's desk and the telephone. I skated on a rug and nearly fell, but recovered my balance and picked up the phone while it was still ringing.

"Hello, Norwood 278," I said. I was mentally prepared for a wrong number, or some sort of emergency case who had been given the incorrect number for the asylum.

It was neither. "Long distance call for you," said the operator.

There was a rushing sound, the one you hear when you put a seashell to your ear, then some buzzes and clicks. Then, faintly but distinctly, a voice cut through it. It was a woman's voice with an American accent. "Mr Stubbs," she said. "We've been having some trouble getting hold of you." It was Miss De Vere. The beautiful, wealthy, and lethal member of TDS, whom I had met on the Stafford case.

"How did you know I would answer?" I asked.

"I called you," she said, casual as ever. "It's the only channel still open."

"Do you know what happened to Ryan?" I asked.

"I've some idea," she said, which was no sort of answer at all. And also quite characteristic.

"Is he dead?"

The rushing rose to the sound of a breaking wave, as if the Atlantic Ocean itself was sharing the conversation, and blotted out the start of her sentence. "… what you mean by dead."

"Pardon?"

Her voice was lost in static. "…urned the place down."

"I can't hear you."

"…Too late…." were the only words I caught as the hissing intervened and her words were submerged beneath the static. All I could hear was the cadence of her speech, the words as indistinct as faces lost in fog.

"I can't hear you!" I said, desperate. "Speak louder!"

"…with the glass."

"Tell me what I have to do," I said, enunciating as clearly as I could.

Her voice came back suddenly. "He's getting close, and he's *dangerous*." On the last word, her voice altered, slowing and deepening to a bass male tone, like a slowed-down gramophone record.

"Dangerous," said the echo, reproduced by some freak of the telephone system. It sounded nothing at all like her. It was the croak of an enormous frog. "Dangerous."

"Miss De Vere?"

The fizzling rose again, getting louder and louder, closer and closer, rushing towards me like a torrent of hissing snakes, angrily slithering down the telephone line. I had such a sudden fear that they would erupt out of the earpiece that I slammed it down.

Instantly, I regretted cutting the connection. I picked up the handset again, but of course there was nothing, not even the operator. I waited a minute to see if Miss De Vere would call back. A board creaked behind me, and I whipped around. Was something moving in the shadow of the bookcase?

I fumbled for the switch on the desk lamp, picked it up, and pointed it around the room like a torch. There was nobody there.

I locked up behind me and trudged down the stairs again, trying not to look behind me.

"Who was that then?" Donnelly wanted to know.

"A bad connection," I said.

Chapter Nine: A Well-Earned Drink

A day or two later, it being a mild evening, we took a couple of benches outside the Hollybush public house, Donnelly, Vanstone, and me in mufti, and Miller in his white attendant's tunic.

I was still a little shaken by an event earlier in the day. I had been called on to assist with a new patient, a particularly noisy individual who was violent even when straightjacketed. It had been some time before I had recognised the red, spittle-flecked face as belonging to Eric Woods, the projectionist. He screamed obscenities and threw himself around like a wild animal. I could make out no sense in what he was saying.

Nobody could tell me what had happened to Woods. The attendants did not have a great deal of curiosity about admissions, and of course nobody told us anything. If I was lucky, I might be able to get a look at his notes later.

When we left the asylum, we left all that behind us. In the outside world, there was a sense of being all in the same unit. Other people gave us wary looks. We were the men from that strange place, and the miasma of madness still clung to us. We were not quite outcasts, but nobody was ever entirely comfortable talking to us until they had a few drinks, at which everything spilled out and they were all agog to hear what we could tell.

The conversation, which would have been called gossiping if we were women, was generally about work. Away from the doctors, the other attendants, and the patients, we could talk about them freely, expressing opinions that were not safe to say within the confines of the institution.

Of course, there was always a lot of grumbling about which doctors did not know what they were doing, which ones had made a fuss about nothing, and which ones had made us do pointless work. As the newcomer, I was treated to a lot of historical stories, and anecdotes were wheeled out to be shown round.

The chief entertainment, though, was from Donnelly, who took a great delight in turning the world upside down for our entertainment. He could prove at the drop of a hat that the patients, who got three square meals a day and did no work, were the only sane people in the asylum. That day, he was on another tack and waxing lyrical.

"It would be a terrible thing if they could treat madness," he said. "What kind of art, what sort of literature would we have without bards and poets who can glimpse beyond the grey confines of this world to the luminous worlds beyond? Where's your romance? Stubbs, where's your science fiction without visions and hallucinations of other worlds?"

"Madness in small doses, maybe," said Vanstone. "Just a bit of spice on a Saturday night. But raving lunacy's no good for anyone."

Vanstone had a gloomy mien, which made everything he said sound wiser than it was. His undertaker's face was a professional asset; it seemed to reassure patients just as effectively as Miller's perpetual cheer.

"Is it not?" asked Donnelly, and Miller guffawed.

"He's going to tell you what it's good for," said Miller, nudging Vanstone. "Listen now, he'll tell you."

"Poets and painters have to be a bit mad, perhaps," I said. "But as far as practical matters go…"

"You, of all people, should know what madness is good for," said Donnelly to me.

I exchanged glances with Vanstone and Miller, while Donnelly looked on complacently and supped his beer.

"They were some terrible rough times in the old days," said Donnelly. "I'm talking about a thousand years ago and more, back in what they call Dark Ages. The Romans were long gone, society had collapsed into anarchy, and the flickering flame of civilisation was kept alive only by a few monks copying illuminated manuscripts in their cells in Ireland. And maybe a few in England."

"The monks weren't mad," said Vanstone. "They might have seemed eccentric. They were taking the long view. Not mad."

"So they weren't," said Donnelly. "But their labours were interrupted by the Vikings, sailing swiftly o'er the seas in their dragon ships, burning villages and stealing cattle, killing the men and raping the women. The Irish had great warriors and bold men with legendary swords, but we were never a match for the raiders. When shield wall clashed with shield wall, the Vikings always prevailed, and you know why?"

There was a collective shaking of heads.

"The fiercest fighters man ever faced—the berserkers! They fought in the front rank, without armour, sometimes without weapons, naked. The berserkers were madmen, whose madness was fired by the smell of blood. They roused themselves to such fury that they foamed at the mouth and howled like beasts. Some say the berserkers became beasts, wolves and bears, impervious to fire and steel, stronger than bulls, and raging for man-blood. They broke through the shield wall like matchwood, tearing their enemies limb from limb—those who didn't flee from them first."

"Cor," said Miller.

"Madmen, one and all," said Donnelly, "invincible in their battle-fury. The only trouble was calming them down afterwards. The berserker madness, honed to a sharp edge, was the Vikings' secret weapon."

"I hadn't heard of them," said Vanstone.

"Could bullets stop them?" asked Miller, imagining perhaps a whole regiment of berserkers going over the top on the Western Front.

"It might take a lot of bullets," said Vanstone. "You know what they're like. And they wouldn't stop until the last man was down."

"You should suggest it to the War Ministry," said Miller. "But I don't know if any of our lot would be any good. They've got the wrong sort of madness. Like that FitzRoy, he's as barmy as a bandicoot but harmless as a babe."

"But is FitzRoy really mad?" asked Donnelly. "It wouldn't be the strangest thing if by some quirk of history, a secret marriage or a hidden document of disinheritance, the rightful heir ends up in an asylum. Who can say? Maybe your man George at Windsor is a pretender, and we should all be bending a knee to FitzRoy, like Jenkins and Tailor and his other courtiers."

Technically he was correct, though this was dangerous talk. My thoughts immediately flitted to the Man in the Iron Mask and also to the tricky business of determining royal succession, which sometimes proceeds down irregular channels. But Vanstone slapped him down at once.

"We don't need your treasonous Fenian nonsense," he said gruffly, and he was only half-joking. "There's no comparison with the real king. FitzRoy is a crackpot with a wooden spoon for a sceptre and a tinfoil crown under his mattress."

"He's not as bad as Grogan, thinks he's a woman." Miller waved, limp-wristed in imitation of Grogan's girlish manner. "I can't prove who's king, but that's an easy one. I said to Grogan, 'Have you tried looking between your legs, Mister? You ain't no woman, not with that tackle!'"

"Grogan knows what sort of equipment he's got, all right," said Donnelly. "But he's not happy with it. He says he's in the wrong body. To his way of thinking, he's a woman's brain in a man's body."

"That's ridiculous," said Vanstone.

"Why? You say there's something wrong with his brain, but you might as well say there was something wrong with his body," said Donnelly. "If you surgically changed his body into a woman's, then he'd be a sane man—or woman, rather. So maybe it's not the brain at fault after all."

We all laughed at that. I repressed a desire to mention what I had learned of Rosslyn D'Onston and his experiments with exchanging bodies with others. It was unlikely that Grogan might really be the victim of that sort of psychic trickery, but not the impossibility I might once have assumed.

"Hooper, he's proper mad—he thinks he can work magic," Miller persisted.

"He's an umbrella maker," said Vanstone. "Worked in that place on Westow Street, Shelvoke's."

"I gave him a pack of cards and asked him to show me a trick," said Miller. "And he couldn't! He said it's the wrong sort of magic. But couldn't do it."

"Maybe he's the sort of magician that saws women in half," said Donnelly. "You should have given him a glamourous assistant and a carpentry set."

"If there's glamourous assistants being handed out, I'll have mine first," said Vanstone.

We all laughed, but it set me thinking. Ryan had mentioned that Gillespy, my late predecessor, had been investigating an umbrella-maker. I really did need to have a word with Hooper. It would not be easy, zigzagging along with his conversational turns, but maybe he could tell me something.

"What about Ross?" asked Miller, trying to find one patient whose madness Donnelly might admit to. "All that screaming at night."

"Maybe we'd all scream if we really thought about things in the night," said Donnelly. "Maybe Ross is the only one who troubles to lift up his blinkers and see things as they are. And those poor souls staring miserably at the wall see the world clearer than we do." He lifted his glass. "For myself, I'm happy to stay deluded."

Vanstone accused Donnelly of Jesuitical tendencies—meaning, I suppose, that he could talk the hind legs off a donkey, weaving words into fantastic constructions where black was white and mad was sane.

"If you poor prods had to learn about transubstantiation, you'd all have a grand understanding of higher logic," Donnelly said. "Simply because something looks like wine, smells like wine, and tastes like wine to you, it can still be blood as far as the priest is concerned."

"Except priests aren't mad," said Miller.

"I'd no idea you were such a good Catholic boy, respecting our priesthood," said Donnelly with a chuckle.

Miller fumbled, trying to explain that while he did not believe in Popery, he respected religion in general, or at least Christian denominations. But he soon gave up amid the general laughter.

"We're getting a lot of these new treatments now," said Vanstone, perhaps wanting to shift away from religious matters.

"He's a slave to science," said Donnelly. "When science says something works, Beltov has to run after it, like a dog chasing a stick. Now there's this new character, this Nye fellow, putting new twists on all the old treatments, and we have to try them all over again. It's something new every week for poor old Beltov."

"I liked the fruit best," said Miller. "They used to get fresh fruit every day, and there was always plenty left over for us."

"Vitamin therapy," said Vanstone, smiling at the recollection.

"Oranges and peaches and pineapples! And strawberries!" Miller grinned. "That's the sort of treatment I like. Fruit therapy. We never had any trouble administering that one."

"It's all a great waste of time," said Donnelly. "But I've no objection to fruit."

"What do these doctors ever know," said Vanstone. "I knew an old gipsy—old Whately, d'you know him?—who could do more good than all the doctors put together. When people went to him with nerves, night terrors, or seeing things, he'd listen to their troubles and give them two tablets, and that would be it. Cured the next day. The thing is, though"—he paused, looking around for effect—"it was always the same tablets, whatever they had. Whately gave them sugar tablets." He tapped his forehead. "It's the power of the mind, you see. Them gipsies know a thing or two."

Donnelly promptly declaimed:

"Whereat he answer'd, that the gipsy-crew,
His mates, had arts to rule as they desired
The workings of men's brains,
And they can bind them to what thoughts they will."

He dropped back to his speaking voice. "Matthew Arnold, *The Scholar-Gipsy*. A true story, so it is. They're clever, those gipsies."

"They should get Whately in instead of these doctors," said Miller. "Gipsies instead of doctors, that'd be a right laugh!"

"Except they can't get Whately because he just died," said Vanstone. "And they say he was cracking up before he went. He fell down an old well, raving about the Second Coming."

"Should have taken some of his own medicine," said Donnelly.

We all laughed again.

"Better than coming in with us with all these therapies," said Vanstone. "One day, they'll get us to dust off the Faradisation kit. What larks we'll have then, eh?"

The others muttered into their beer.

"What's faradisation?" I asked.

"Torture," said Vanstone, in such a dire tone that I did not pursue the subject.

I had another taste of drink—or rather more than a taste—the next day. I was on the rota for the night shift, so I was free in the afternoon and had arranged to drop round and see my friend Captain Hall, a notable mariner who started his career back when they still sailed tall ships. He had travelled the world and seen the mercantile trade taken over by steam. He was a sailor as full of tall tales as you could hope to meet. Having made a tidy sum at his trade, he had taken retirement here in the city, far from the sea. There was no lighthouse-keeper's cottage or weekend pleasure sailing for him. Captain Hall had his fill of the ocean and left it while he still had strength to enjoy life. He played the part of a local character with gusto.

Before I had even sat down in the Captain's drawing room, the old rogue was holding up two glasses in one hand. His wife was out shopping, and there was no question of a pot of tea with him at the helm. The Captain liked something stronger to loosen his tongue.

"You won't say no to a tot, will you, Harry?"

I was by no means a drinker of spirits, and even if I was, I would not start drinking at that time in the afternoon. But to refuse the hospitality would have been an insult, and the Captain needed my permission if he was to have a drink himself. "I don't mind if I do," I said.

"Ha-ha!" He chortled as if I was an old dog for suggesting the idea, but that he would indulge me. The Royal Navy took to diluting its rum with water years ago, but the Captain was a merchant seaman. He disdained the foibles of the uniformed service and never had any truck with anything less manly than neat spirit. The Captain filled both glasses to the brim with clear brown liquid in a twinkling. He might have been an old man, but the Captain had an impressively steady hand.

I took a preparatory sniff. The fumes rose off it, stinging my nose.

"Your health, Harry!"

"And yours!"

The room had a few odds and ends to remind one that this was the house of a former sea-captain, including a couple of prints of sailing schooners, a framed Master's Certificate, and a brass clock on the mantelpiece that was decorated with anchors of assorted sizes. But more important was the parrot, a great scarlet bird who occupied a rail running along one side of the room at head height.

It sidled over towards me on scaly dragon's feet and cocked its head, blinking in that disturbing way they have. The Captain's parrot is famed for its command of invective and can swear in a great many languages. But after looking me up and down, it only said, "Ello!"

"And hello to you," I said politely.

"I hear you've been getting into all sorts of adventures," said the Captain, admiring the colour of the rum against the light. "I can't thank you enough for sorting out that business with Yang's nephew."

"That was all Arthur's doing," I said.

"Not the way I heard it," he said. "But I won't ask no questions, and you won't have to tell me no lies, eh?"

The rum was fiery, but the burning subsided almost instantly, leaving a pleasant warmth and a long, smoky aftertaste like burned sugar in its wake.

We chatted about general matters for a bit, but he was impatient with my attempts at small talk. "Come on, Harry," he said. "You tell the Captain what's on your mind now."

"As a matter of fact, I have a question for you. It's a bit of a long shot, but I thought I remembered something from somewhere."

It was disingenuous. I wanted to ask someone I could trust, and someone who could keep his mouth shut. Also, the Captain was a tough old bird, who on his own account had survived enough serious scrapes to kill any six other men. I did not feel I was endangering him.

I produced the glass tube from its newspaper wrappings and passed it over to him.

"I need to identify this contrivance," I said. "I believe it might have some significance for a case I'm working on."

The Captain extracted horn-rimmed reading glasses from an inner pocket and placed them on his nose. "That's a funny inscription, there," he said, squinting at the green wax seal on the end. "I haven't seen one quite like that before."

"Do you know what it is?"

He passed the tube back to me. "Of course I do!" He stood up. "But that one's just a toy. I'll show you what a proper one looks like.

And while I'm on my feet, I'd better recharge the glasses," he added. Mine was still half-full, his considerably less so.

A minute later, the Captain was back with a mahogany box with brass fittings. Inside, nestling in green baize compartments precisely mounded to their forms, were a set of instruments. *Captain's Meteorological Instruments* appeared on a sheet pasted to the inside of the box lid, above a lot of instructions in small print.

He placed an instrument in my hands—a glass tube on a mahogany base, with brass fittings. It looked very much like some sort of nautical instrument, but I would not know a sextant from a plumb line.

"Now that is a proper FitzRoy Storm Glass," he said. "Not so much used these days, but plenty of captains swear by them. That can tell you what weather's coming when the barometer fails."

"How does it work?"

"Hmm, well, there's nothing to see now, as it's set fair for days to come. But when the weather starts to change, so will the glass. If there's going to be cloud, it turns cloudy, and there're different signs for the different winds."

From the lining of the case, he produced a slip of dry, brown paper with illustrations of the storm glass in various weather conditions.

"'A north wind produces crystal growths resembling fir, yew, or fern leaves,'" I read.

"That's right," he affirmed. "I've seen that many times."

This sent an odd chill down the back of my neck. "Is there vegetable matter in the mixture?" I asked.

"Camphor oil," he said after a moment. "Camphor's a tree. Not here, but I've seen them growing in Japan."

I had previously encountered the phenomenon of palingenesis, where the form of a living thing could be recovered from its powdered ashes. I had seen photographs of a rose recreated from its dust. I had also encountered the considerably less harmless exercise of reanimating a human being from grave soil. The operation of the storm glass seemed altogether too similar. "It sounds more like magic than science," I said.

The Captain shrugged and took a good swig of rum. "You don't know what a storm is," he told me. "A landsman, living in a city, all a storm means to you is you lose your bowler hat, and maybe a roof tile or two goes flying. Storms don't mean anything in London, but at sea—that's another matter."

"I've heard you tell of storms at sea," I said.

"A storm glass can save your life," he said. "One time, when we were at anchor in Maldonado Bay—that's South America way, on the coast of the Argentine—the barometer dropped, and the storm glass grew leaves, like it says there. Now, that was strange, because the wind was in the southwest, and no sign of bad weather. But Captain King, he was a wise man. Here." He leaned forwards and topped up the glasses again, raising his. "Here's to Captain King, as wise a master as every ship should have."

We gravely clinked glasses, and I ingested another slug. It was easier to drink with every swallow, the trail having been blazed, so to speak, by the first glass.

"Captain King reefed the sails and ordered the watch doubled, and it was lucky he did," said the Captain. "We had one of those blows the locals call a pampero, a storm that blows over the plains and brings a squall line with it. Well, was four bells on the first watch, and the wind veered to southwest and strengthened so quick that there was no time to do anything, and before you knew it we were broadside on, with two boats washed away.

"Captain King was on deck in a heartbeat—he'd never taken his boots off—and he picked up an axe and cut through one of the anchor cables. That brought the head of the ship into the wind, and he let the other anchor drag as we were carried clean out of the bay and into the open sea among foaming whitecaps that came out of nowhere.

"Now, I had gone to my hammock when it was all peaceful, exhausted as always from all the running about they put you through. I was practically thrown out of it when the storm hit. Half the lanterns were out, and hands were rushing about everywhere, and the ship heeling more violently than I had ever seen. I didn't know where I was or what was happening or what I was supposed to be doing until the bo'sun slapped me about the face and sent me to help with pumping."

I missed some of the technical terms—all of them, in fact—as he explained what the storm did and how it damaged the spars and why they could not get the ship under control, but fifty years later, the old man was still in the grip of the boy's fear and disorientation that night.

"If it hadn't been Captain King reading his storm glass, the ship would have been lost," he said, contemplating the instrument fondly. "People don't use them anymore. It's because it's not scientific like a thermometer or a barometer, where it's just a matter of reading numbers. A FitzRoy Storm Glass calls for judgement. It takes an experienced eye to read it properly, but a storm glass can warn you when nothing else can. I don't care what His Majesty's blasted meteorological office has to say about it. They ought to issue 'em again."

"What puzzles me is what Gillespy would want with one."

"Gillespy?"

"The man I got it from," I said, my tongue thickened by the rum. "But, in London, who cares about storms? There's a daily weather forecast in all the newspapers, so why does anyone need a storm glass?"

"It's not an ordinary storm glass, though, is it?" observed the Captain, picking it up again and looking at the clear liquid, then at the seal. "This one is made different. The water's thicker, and there's a green cast to it."

"What does that mean?"

"Blessed if I know!" he said cheerfully. "Have another drink."

"Have another drink!" ordered the parrot.

So I did. And that was the last word we said about storm glasses that afternoon. The funny thing is that I cannot even remember whether we finished the bottle, but I do remember our parting, when we slapped each other on the back like old shipmates, and I walked off rather carefully, as a man will on the deck of a ship pitching in a heavy sea.

Chapter Ten : Questions And Answers

The Woodlands, a substantial building housing a number of purpose-built flats with a fine view across Croydon and the green fields of Surrey, was only a few years old. The fields had grown quite brown, after the long dry spell in what seemed to be an endless hiatus, during which summer had finished and autumn had not begun.

A car park outside the building showed off quite a selection of motors, many of them sporty models. I should say that the block was inhabited largely by younger people of a certain class, enjoying the opportunities that their position presented before they settled down to houses and families.

The hall carpet was thick and velvety, with strips of parquet showing on either side. Niches on the stairs held tall glass sculptures in the style that they had begun to call art deco. I tried and failed to imagine what it would be like living there instead of the rooming house that had been my home for the past few years. The uniformed porter looked up at me through a glass half-window in a way that made me wonder if there was a tradesman's entrance I had missed.

"Mr Harry Stubbs of Lantern Insurance, for Miss Ellen Bentham," I said, handing him my card. My suit was fresh back from the cleaners, and I felt smart and professional.

"In-sur-ance," was all the porter said before he dialled up for her. He held the handset up so I could hear it ringing with no reply, and he was in the process of hanging up when the sliding cage door of the elevator—an elevator for those who could not be bothered to walk up four whole flights of steps—opened, and a lady stepped out, leading a Pekingese.

"Visitor for you, Miss Bentham," said the porter.

"Harry Stubbs," I said, tipping my hat. "By appointment, as arranged."

"Oh, I'd forgotten," she said offhandedly. "Still, we can talk while we walk, can't we? He always has his walk this time."

Miss Bentham had set the time for the meeting, but for some reason she did not want me in her apartment. The dog sniffed tentatively at my trouser cuff; I squatted and let it lick my hand.

Walking side by side gave me little opportunity to examine Miss Bentham. I registered that she was wearing a grey cashmere cardigan, and her skin had that almost translucent paleness. She would have been called pretty, I suppose, except for a certain firmness about the jaw and a manner that indicated she was not to be trifled with. The one thing I could see without being too obvious was an engagement ring twinkling on her finger.

We exchanged a few remarks about the weather. I had not quite thought about how I would introduce the subject of her fiancé, Ross, being in a mental institution and why she had felt it necessary to have him put there. It was a delicate matter. Beltov had assumed, perhaps correctly, that he lacked the tact for it. For some reason, he thought that I could do better, though in fact Miss Bentham raised the subject herself.

"How is he?" she asked abruptly when we were twenty paces from the door.

"Mr Ross is in good physical health," I said. "And mentally speaking, he is both lucid and co-operative. In fact, he is fully as well as can be expected, under the circumstances."

"You must think it strange that I never visit," she said.

"It's not my place to judge, Miss Bentham," I said. "I can quite understand why a lady like you would not wish to enter a place like that, and I'm sure you have your reasons."

"Yes, but what are you doing here? What's changed? What does it have to do with insurance?"

"The insurance business is a cover," I said easily. "Dr Beltov believes that Mr Ross may be approaching a fork in the road, so to speak, and he wanted to know more about his background."

"I suppose you can't ask him. But surely you're not a doctor yourself?"

"Oh, no, but you can check my credentials with Dr Beltov."

"I did, or I wouldn't see you. Not that you look like a journalist."

Beltov had ambushed me a few days before. I had left a message from Dr Hamilton on his desk and was just standing there, admiring the workings of the glass clock. The mass of gears and cogs and springs were all moving round, meshed together in ways I could not fathom. Seeing the workings laid bare like that made me realise what a complicated mechanism a clockwork really is. Beltov was convinced that it could keep perfect time if properly adjusted and not over- or under-wound, but it was five minutes fast.

What did all those cogs do? My admiration for watchmakers was increased considerably.

"Ah, Stubbs."

I started guiltily, but Dr Beltov was pleased to see me. "This is really quite convenient. I wished to have a word with you."

Something tightened in my stomach. "Yes, sir?" I said.

"I would like you to do a little detective work for me," he said.

"Me?" I said. Not perhaps the most intelligent of responses, but the question had caught me off guard.

"You are, I believe, some sort of detective," he said, holding up a hand before I could reply. "Please, there is no need to deny it. The notes you are always taking, your interest in certain of the cases... Please, do not insult me and embarrass yourself."

He had been watching me more closely than I realised, and my eavesdropping had been noted.

"The subject of your investigation here is of no relevance," he went on. "If there is a malpractice here, I hope you expose it. If there is no malpractice, I'm sure you will still be well paid. For myself, I have nothing to hide."

"Of course not," I said.

"I have no intention of exposing you. But I do find that you present a certain opportunity. I find I am in need of some external data that can only be supplied by investigation. This is unorthodox, but this is a new field and orthodoxy means little, as my colleagues often inform me."

He was writing in a notepad with a mechanical pencil as he spoke, and he ripped off the page for me. "This is the address of patient Ross's fiancée. We have no other personal details about him at all, and I do not find this situation satisfactory." He had been genial, but now there was grit in his voice. "The circumstances around his admission are ambiguous, and if you are looking for malpractice, then this is where to start."

"What do you want me to find out?"

"Tell me why Ross is here," he said. "Perhaps I am myself becoming paranoid, but at times I doubt the good faith of my colleagues."

"Who?"

He shook his head. "Find out why Ross is here. I feel this might be beneficial for both of us. Please do not tell anyone else. This is between the two of us. A 'gentleman's agreement.'"

I had been called many things before, but never a gentleman. Beltov did not perhaps grasp the niceties of English class distinction, but he meant well.

Ross suffered from acute night terrors. For some reason Beltov did not think this was an adequate cause for Ross to have been admitted. It belatedly occurred to me that the night terrors might not have been the cause of his admittance, but an effect.

And so there I was, interviewing Miss Bentham on Beltov's behalf and wondering why a journalist would wish to talk to her under false pretences. The walk was a slow one, because of the Pekingese; we would go ten paces then stop for the dog to sniff at a tree, a hedge, or a lamp-post.

"Perhaps you could tell me a little about Mr Ross," I said. "We have no other family members recorded for him."

"He doesn't have any," she said. "He has a sort of foster mother, but he hasn't seen her for years."

"I see," I said, thinking that already it would be fertile ground for Dr Beltov.

"He's always been quite highly strung, artistic, imaginative," she said. "You know, all those words people use for people who aren't quite conventional enough for their taste. He was intense, but not neurotic – not by the standards of some of the people we know!"

Her laughter was nervous and cut off quickly. The dog looked up at her.

"It's become very fashionable to be neurotic now," she said. "Tom was never like that. He had some queer ideas, but then I think all of us have our little peculiarities, don't we? Our own little superstitions about things that we never let on to strangers. Tom has had more exposure to the wide world than most, so he's picked up more strange ideas."

"How do you mean, 'more exposure'?" I asked.

"He was out in the Middle East," she said. "He loved it."

"When was that?"

"Most of the War," she said, as if it was obvious. "He wrote long, rambling letters about every detail. The souks and the Arabs and the architecture. Archaeology—old remains everywhere. Fruit sellers with wooden stalls leaning against crumbling walls two thousand years old. The call to prayer at sunset echoing from all directions. And lots and lots about wind speeds and sandstorms and thermals. And the efreet winds—that's what they called whirlwinds. They always had a lot of those."

"Where, exactly…"

"I forget the place names; they were always so difficult. But he was in Cairo mainly."

"That's Egypt, isn't it?"

"He kept sending back curios he bought from tremendously shady backstreet dealers. He always fancied they were tomb robbers and he was getting a fantastic bargain, but at least half the things he picked up were made in Birmingham. Then he started buying old papyrus scrolls and trying to decode them with a dictionary of hieroglyphics…" She broke off, shaking her head. "If only he wasn't so intelligent," she said. "He thought he was getting somewhere, but then he met that old man and there was this dance… I couldn't really follow it, but that was where it started. His Christ complex."

"I see," I said. I was vexed that I could not walk and take notes at the same time. It was all piling up too fast for me to keep track. If Ross really did have a Christ complex, assuming that was what it sounded like, it was the first I had heard of it. "And the night terrors?"

"Oh no, he never suffered from those, but he was convinced that he was the only one who understood ancient Egyptian texts—the *Book of the Dead*, is it? Something like that. And that he had to save the world."

It was beginning to sound ominously familiar. You do not need to encounter the same pattern too many times to recognise it, and I could tell it easily enough. An educated young man picks up an interest in occult matters, which spirals into an obsession. Powell, the vagrant scholar in the Upper Norwood library, who was obsessed with the legacy of a dark occultist. The ruined Oxford professor who died, mocked by his colleagues for his absurd beliefs about the reality behind *Arabian Nights*, which turned out to be all too true. The members of the Theosophy Circle, whose dabbling in the alchemical art of palingenesis had such disastrous results. Randolph Stafford, the amateur astronomer… I could not help but conclude that anyone and everyone who was drawn into this pattern would end up the worse for it. It was not that they were wrong in their beliefs. If they were wrong, they would be mere harmless eccentrics. The problem was more that they were right, and they were prodding and poking at things that could explode in their faces.

"And so it became necessary for him to be confined, for his own good," I said.

"Absolutely. There was no other way."

The dog had paused to sniff a lamppost, and Miss Bentham jerked it forward impatiently.

"Was it Ross's own doctor who signed the certificate?"

"No, it was a friend—the friend of a friend. Tom could sometimes go overboard at dinner parties, telling people about… things… and after one party, a man approached me and asked if Tom needed help, because he was a psychologist. Quite young, but very professional. Foreign-looking, but English." She frowned slightly. "I'm afraid his name has flown out of my head. It must be on the paperwork."

Some of the doctors say that our minds deliberately forget the things we do not wish to remember. I did not think Miss Bentham wished to remember the doctor who had colluded with her to imprison her fiancé.

"It's funny," she admitted. "I met him several times. His interest was… rather intense. He made me quite uncomfortable, and I eventually refused to see him. But I can't recall his name. Something Jewish, was it? I don't remember."

Miss Bentham was Ross's only family member; it must have been entirely at her instigation that he was certified and incarcerated, aided by this friendly doctor. I was still working out this conclusion, but she took my pause as an accusing silence.

"It's been very difficult for me," she said, "in my position. I work with Marie Stopes, campaigning for birth control."

This was an area on which my knowledge was hazy to say the least, although I had seen the stories about Mrs Stopes, who was often in the headlines for her controversial views. "I didn't know," I said.

"We have to limit reckless breeding. Everything depends on it. Good breeding can turn the ravening wolf into a fit and civilised companion." She paused to smile at the little dog. It had stopped to look up at her, with that sense dogs have for when they are being discussed. "Its opposite will turn the civilised back into animals. It's nothing but science, but it's a stance that invites hostility from all quarters. The newspapers will take any opportunity to attack us, stooping to any low tactics. So, if it was known that my own fiancé was..." She stumbled over her words for a moment, but recovered quickly. "If it was known that he was tainted, they would splatter the mud far and wide."

"Your concern is that his condition is a hereditary one," I said.

"We have no idea who his family are," she said. "There might be any number of mental cases in his family tree. But a girl doesn't always think of these things, not until it's too late. I should have been more rational."

That would certainly account for why Miss Bentham did not wish our conversation to be overheard, and why she lived in fear of journalists. And, indeed, why she had found it so imperative to have her fiancé shut away from the world. "Some psychologists talk about the degradation of the race," I said, to see how she would respond.

"Reckless breeding," she said. "If we cannot stop the undesirables from multiplying out of control, our race will devolve into something worse than animals. Birth control is the only way. Women must have the means for contraception and abortion. And legal sterilisation of defectives. It's the only way to stop reckless breeding."

It could have been Miss De Vere speaking, my putative employer, who was so obsessed with protecting the human race from alien influences at all costs. She was scathing about Jews and gipsies and other inferior types; for some reason they fell short of her mark of what constituted humanity. She was a hard woman. "There are other causes of insanity besides heredity," I said. I hesitated to mention syphilis, but there were other possibilities. "Shell shock, for example, can manifest itself years later in unexpected ways."

Instead of answering, she suddenly burst out sobbing, like a small child might. Another man would probably have put a reassuring arm around her, but that is not a gesture which I have ever mastered. I did not even know the right comforting words to say, so instead I maintained what I hoped was a tactful silence while she recomposed herself.

"I'm sorry," she said at last, after she had produced a handkerchief from her bag and sniffled into it. "Do you mind if I smoke?" She lit a cigarette while the little dog waited patiently, and we walked on. "I don't know what else I can tell you," she said.

"Do you know anything about his war service?"

While Easton's suggestion of shell shock seemed unlikely, it was an avenue that nevertheless required exploration. Shell shock was such a common condition among those who had returned from the war, even though it was not often spoken of, that Miss Bentham must have been aware of it.

"He never talked about it, so I never asked," she said. "The usual sort of thing, I suppose. He was in the same unit as Humphrey Rowe. Miss Stopes's husband was how we met, at an Army occasion. I mean her second husband, not that Canadian. Humphrey is her secretary. He's a great support to her. They both looked so fine in their uniforms! He helped me, too, but..."

Her little shrug expressed frustration and resignation, but also something else. She would continue with her mission with or without her fiancé.

"No reason why you should know about his war service," I said. "I shall leave you to enjoy the rest of your stroll. I have another appointment, and the shortest route is this turning. Thank you very much for your help."

"That's quite all right, Mr Stubbs. You will let me know if there's anything—"

"Of course."

I left her walking her Pekingese. She was a pretty woman,

and healthy, too—good breeding stock, as far as Miss Stopes was concerned. There was no doubt about her determination and dedication to the cause of eugenics. I was pleased that she had tears to shed over her fiancé, and that Miss Bentham was not so very rational as all that.

My next errand took me back to the bungalow of the unfortunate Eric Woods. It was not a long walk, and it gave me a little time to contemplate my next move which might involve a degree of coercion.

The place was as before, and the sound of a child crying told me that Mrs Woods was in residence. However, she was not the subject of my interest. I stationed myself across the road at a nearby bus-stop where a man could wait without attracting attention.

Mrs Woods had mentioned that his friend visited at fortnightly intervals, so I had determined to intercept him. He was on a bicycle, with bicycle clips to keep his Oxford bags from flapping and being caught in the chain. The saddlebags bulged with what I took to be photographic equipment.

As I approached, he looked at me with concern and then alarm. When I was a few paces away, he mounted up and started to pedal away furiously.

I put on a burst of speed that surprised him. He wasn't the first person to decide that he preferred not to engage in conversation, and I had a turn of speed when I was put to it. I got hold of the rear mudguard with both hands, and the disparity in our weights meant I had little trouble slowing him to a halt.

"I'm sorry to trouble you," I said. "All I wanted was a word."

"What about?" He had the alarmed eyes of a rabbit, looking left and right for someone who would save him.

"If you stop pedalling, sir, I'll explain," I said.

It was an absurd situation. The fact that I was clinging on to the bicycle and not assaulting his person must have made some impression. And he rightly judged that he was not going to get away.

"Awfully sorry about that," he said awkwardly, concluding that I was not in fact an assailant and stepping off the bicycle. "But you gave me quite a scare."

"I do apologise," I said. "The fault was all on my side. I was anxious that you might go off without talking to me."

He was a good height and younger than I had first thought, no more than twenty. His features were strong and regular, and his reddish-brown hair was long, the way all the university types wore it in those days. I could see how he might have charmed Mrs Woods.

There was something about his eyes, though. He had an unconscious way of looking at things as though through a lens, as it were, and drinking in details wherever he looked. His was not an intense gaze, but the frank and interested look of one for whom everything was fascinating. In a moment, he had changed completely from apprehension to cordiality. "Tom Reynolds," he said, and his handshake was firm and manly.

"Harry Stubbs," I said. I would have fished out a business card, but it seemed that we had passed beyond that.

"Harry Stubbs? My godfathers," he said, surprised by the name. "I suppose there's only one Harry Stubbs? You were a friend of Lavinia's, the lady that runs the Theosophical circle?"

It was my turn to be astonished. "I was," I said.

"And you saved the day when that séance turned nasty? I was so sorry I missed that. I must have heard that story from six different people. Well, well, well, I am pleased to meet you, Mr Stubbs."

"Likewise," I said, placing him. This Tom Reynolds was Tom, the student photographer who had created a photographic record of the Theosophical Circle's activities to encourage patrons. His pictures of a phantom who rose from ashes had been crisp and clear, not like most of the images you see of supposed psychic phenomena. Unfortunately, this had done nothing to avert the tragic events that broke up the Theosophical Circle.

He looked towards the house and started unbuckling the straps on a saddlebag. "Look, I have to see a friend now, but if you're free—"

"I'm afraid Mr Woods is not at home," I said. "His condition required him to be institutionalised."

He stopped mid-gesture, reinterpreting my appearance in light of the new information, and apprehending that events had taken a turn for the worse. Interestingly, he did not seem keen to talk to Mrs Woods. "Let's walk to the park," he said soberly, already wheeling his bicycling along. "You can tell me what's happened, and I'll do my best to answer your questions."

Reynolds had been away at university, and had only come down to London on the morning train. He had not heard from Woods, and had come to make their fortnightly appointment as usual. He had no idea that Woods had displayed his work to a cinema audience, and he groaned when I described the response.

"What did he think he was doing?" Reynolds was baffled by Woods's action. "This is an experimental scientific study. It's not something for a suburban matinee audience. What did he expect, a round of applause? He must have had a nervous breakdown."

"So, you were aware of what he was doing?"

"He was helping me with a photographic experiment," said Reynolds. "It's not a movie. Just a sequence of unrelated images."

Reynolds was looking ahead down the street, framing the view above the handlebars and under the trees as the pavement scrolled by beneath him. Bicycle wheels turned like film in a projector.

"It looked like a movie to me," I said. He had not seen the finished product, and I described the *Phantom of the Cinema* as well as I remembered it. Reynolds nodded at the sections he recognised, puzzling over the surtitles that Woods had added. When I finished, there was the sound of the wheels going around and the rubber tyres crushing the ground.

"I wish he'd confided in me," said Reynolds. "But he was obviously inspired to share it with the world first. I thought he trusted me."

"I think you had better explain from the beginning," I said.

"I've always tried to push photography beyond photography," he said. "Pictures of things that have never been pictured, things that nobody thought could be pictured. Infrared, ultraviolet, making visible colours invisible to human eyes. Electrophotography." He picked up a plane leaf, turning it by its stalk. His gaze swept the park. He was taking in, perhaps, the microscopic insects feeding on the fallen leaves, the geometric arrangement of each leaf, the path through time from leaf to leaf-mould, to bud and bursting into leaf again. "We can see inside bodies with x-rays and other radiations, but seeing inside minds is another matter. The optic nerve turns an external image into a visual impression, so why not reverse the process and turn thoughts back into a pattern of light and capture them on a photographic plate?"

I had no idea how to begin to answer such a question. He might well have asked me how I would go about distilling moonbeams or catching unicorns. I needed to take a step back. "So those pictures in Woods's film," I said carefully and slowly. "Those were pictures of his mental images?"

Reynolds screwed up his face.

"It's difficult to explain to a layman," he said. "The process involves a certain amount of manipulation. It's as much an art as a craft, and that's why Woods was so good at it. But that is the essence of it, making mental images visible."

"And this is your technique?"

"Oh, no, not mine. I'm no more than an interested amateur having a go at it. You see, you can record what happens at the optic nerve, but it's just electric snow. We can't directly recreate it; we have to match the pattern with what it means. It's like decoding a cipher, but with pictures."

"I don't quite follow you," I said.

"Woods had a whole library of images. He had shelves and shelves of films, and an absolute genius for finding what chimed with a particular brain recording. With a bit of fiddling, he could take a stock image and revamp it to match the mental image. He built his own machine, which uses an interference pattern to warp an original to match the input when I only got snowstorms and blurs. He's a wizard."

"This library of films that he started with… Were they mainly German?"

"*Universum*," he said, nodding. "Cheap, and with plenty of surreal images. The result was usually blurry at best, but he was getting better and better."

"Let me get this straight. A machine captured Woods's brainwaves, and he turned them into pictures."

"Not his own brainwaves," said Reynolds. "They're wire recordings of mental activity wires. The apparatus isn't nearly sensitive enough to pick up most people's thoughts. It's only certain people with a special aptitude, who generate powerful-enough imagery to show up through the static."

"People like psychic mediums?" I asked.

Reynolds licked his lips. "I told you, this was a research project. There's a doctor who makes the brain recordings and sends them to me. They come from…. certain mental patients."

As he spoke, I could see the Sarcophagus, the electro-magnetic-therapy machine with the oversize helmet that fitted around the patient's head, and all of those baffling controls. The patient went into it, and the magnetic waves were supposed to damp out their nightmares and their attacks of madness. The record of it was captured on magnetic wires, as though their exhalations had been bottled.

"It's supposed to be a diagnostic tool," said Reynolds. "It can show psychologists what is going on in someone's head."

"Madness made visible," I said. "I suppose viewing it would be safe in small doses."

"I had no idea it would affect Woods like that," said Reynolds unhappily. "He was always so stable, so focused. I didn't think he cared about the content. He was just so happy when he could get a clear image."

I nodded slowly. Eric Woods possessed the gift of being able to decipher the dream-images and throw them onto a screen. And madness piled together upon madness made it crystal clear and showed it to people… It was no wonder it had such a powerful effect on the audience. While it might have been intended to open a window into disturbed minds for clinicians, the images were likely to provoke reactions in those with their own latent psychoses, stirring up things that were better left undisturbed. I could hardly imagine what effect it could have had on Woods himself. "This doctor who you're dealing with," I said. "Who is he?"

"I can't tell you his name," said Reynolds. "Not until I've informed him. Oh, God." The implications of what Woods had done seemed to be sinking in.

"I think he has some idea already," I said. "It wouldn't be a Dr Beltov?"

Reynolds sighed heavily, then nodded.

"I think we'd better go to the cinema," I said.

The Roxy was shut, but the commissionaire saw us looking in and swept the door open. He was a man of few words but grand gestures. "Enter!" he commanded.

I might have wondered if he was quite sober, but there was no smell of drink on him. As far as he was concerned, it was show business, and he was the gatekeeper to a magical kingdom.

Reynolds and I stopped to look through the little glass window into the projection booth. There was a new man in there, a pimply youth with a scraggly beard. The lights were on, and he was carrying out some sort of maintenance with a whole set of screwdrivers of different sizes beside him.

Mr Bellingham seemed pleased to see me. I introduced him to Reynolds.

"I believe I have identified the source of that disturbing *Phantom of the Cinema* reel," I said.

"As a matter of fact, Woods told me himself," said Bellingham. "He confessed everything, told me that he had created the film himself."

"So, you know already," I said. I wondered how long he had known, and whether he would have shared the revelation with me.

"Remarkable, isn't it?" he said, more wondering than appalled by what Woods had done. "He has hidden depths, that Woods. A pity about his nervous breakdown. It's the artistic temperament."

"I'm not sure about that," I said, but he brushed me aside.

"He's not in a good way just at present," he said. "But he has a remarkable future ahead of him. Making pictures, not showing them."

"We need to talk about that film he brought in," said Reynolds.

"Absolutely! Have you seen it? You must. We're having a showing before we open for business, just for the staff. You need to keep seeing it. The first time, it floods the system. It's too much. It's like eating a whole box of chocolates at once. You can't appreciate it."

"The audience certainly found it troubling," I said.

"Didn't they, though?" Bellingham was triumphant. "I have never, not in twenty years, seen an audience react so strongly. It's a genuine breakthrough. This is the real future of films. It's not colour, not talkies, but what you saw right here on that screen."

"It could be damaging to those who see it," said Reynolds, but Bellingham's enthusiasm was unstoppable.

"You know they rioted the first time Stravinsky's *Rite of Spring* was performed? And when Duchamp displayed his Fountain? There's never been anything like it in cinema until now."

"It sounds," I said, "as though your view on the work in question has turned around."

"Films can seem banal the first time you see them. Their true worth only shines through after you've seen them a few times. But the *Phantom of the Cinema*—that's not its real title, of course. That was something that Woods added when he saw the Lon Chaney was coming up. It's something else. I'm trying to arrange a screening for an invited audience."

"I don't think that's advisable," said Reynolds.

"I don't care what you think, young man," said Bellingham, who was losing his patience. "This is my cinema. I'm making history. That film is mine now."

"But—" I started.

"I appreciated your help very much, and I wish a very good day to you, Mr Stubbs and Mr Reynolds."

"We'll be on our way, then," I said, donning my bowler. "Thank you for the free tickets, Mr Bellingham."

I could hardly tell Bellingham to his face that he was deranged, or that repeated viewings of the film had disordered his mind. But I could not allow him to start showing that reel to more people. I stalked down the carpeted hall, wishing I had some help.

"Exit," said the commissionaire, flinging open the door for me, his eyes glinting.

Chapter Eleven: The Electric Cure

I needed to have a private conference with Dr Beltov about the Phantom of the Cinema and what should be done about it. I also wanted to find out who the doctor was who had incarcerated Ross, and to discuss a few other matters, as well. Unfortunately, I had no time for that, as I was on the rota to assist Dr Easton in the Rose Room.

I went to collect Jenkins from the day room. He was just finishing a game of dominoes, and rather than being heavy-handed I allowed him to conclude his play. Then I felt something unaccustomed in my pocket. Taking it out, I saw that my little storm glass, which had been completely clear, was clouding over; dark billows occupied the upper half. The forecast was for a continuation of the long, dry, unseasonably warm spell we had been experiencing. There was no way of knowing what the glass was responding to, but it seemed to me that it was a different sort of weather.

"Turning nasty," observed Hooper, as though he knew what the glass meant. He made that spiral gesture again with his finger, the Ouroboros. "Turn, turn, it all turns."

"You've seen one of these?" I asked. I had been meaning to talk to him and now I had my opportunity.

"I've had my turn," he said, and his eyes suddenly filled with tears. "It's another turn of the screw, a funny turn for me and you. The world turns, but what does it turn into? I'd turn my coat, if I was you, Mr Stubbs."

"Hooper, I wanted to ask you about something," I said.

"Turn and turn about," he said sadly. "Turn and turn about."

I could not tell whether he was responding to me, or just killing his half of the conversation with the first words that came to him.

"You knew something of the occult."

"I turned over a new leaf, turned to books, turned the pages," he said, and it was a sort of answer to my question. "A turn-up for the books. But you can't stop the world turning, and I'm turned out!"

"What is the matter?" I asked, but it looked like the moment of clarity had gone.

"Turn away while you can," he said in a choked voice. "It's a long road that has no turning wheel – wheel – wheel not meet again, Mr Stubbs. The end is nigh. The end is nigh!"

"What do you mean?"

Hooper was crying now, and Jenkins tugged my elbow. His game was over.

"I'm ready," said Jenkins. We were already late. Reluctantly and I led Jenkins away, still wondering what Hooper had been saying.

"Isn't it hydrotherapy this time?" he asked, seeing that our destination was different to the previous treatment.

"I don't know what it is," I said. The Rose Room did not have the plumbing for hydrotherapy, so whatever it was, it could not be that. But I did not want to disturb Jenkins unduly. "Dr Easton is in charge."

Jenkins checked his pace a moment, and I thought he might give me some trouble when I saw he had stopped for an ant on the floor. The place was not so very hygienic, and pests were not uncommon. Jenkins placed a foot over it and very deliberately crushed it into the floor then smiled as though he had done something clever. I said nothing, but could guess his motive. He might be a helpless patient, but to that ant he was a vengeful god. Being able to crush others is a godlike thing, even if they are only insects.

The Rose Room had the same cream-painted walls as the rest of the place, but the ceiling was decorated with garlands of plasterwork roses, painted in red and pink. Easton greeted us with the bluff cheerfulness of one meeting his companions for a good game of golf. I suspected that he was not quite as confident as he would have wished to appear.

There were a couple of tables occupied by an untidy arrangement of wooden boxes connected by wires. The room was wired for electricity, and a long cable snaked across the room to the outlet socket.

"Secure Jenkins into this one, will you." Easton patted an armchair fitted with stout leather straps for the restraint of patients' arms and legs.

Jenkins gave me a look of alarm, as though he were an animal entering the slaughterhouse, scenting its own blood. Easton ignored him, busying himself with the equipment.

"This is all part of the procedure," I told him as I buckled up the straps. "You sit here now and listen to what the doctor says."

"Is he secure?"

I nodded affirmation.

Dr Easton, clucking to himself, leaned over Jenkins, attaching wires to his ears and wrists with clips. "There we are," he said.

"What is this?" asked Jenkins.

"This is the long-overdue first step on your road to recovery, Mr Jenkins," said Easton. He pulled up a chair and paged through a sheaf of handwritten notes.

"You sit there, Stubbs," he said. "I will need you to operate the apparatus for me while I conduct the interview."

"I'm afraid I'm not familiar with this equipment," I said, surveying the dials and Bakelite knobs.

"There's nothing to it," he said. "You just turn that knob when I tell you to. See the numbers round the circumference here? That's the setting. And throw that switch"—a big wooden handle like the ones in a railway signal box—"when I tell you to. Is that clear?"

"Quite clear, Dr Easton."

"What do I do, Doctor?" asked Jenkins.

"You will take your medicine," said Dr Easton. "It is an electrical medicine, administered through these wires. It will correct those defects in your brain which have muddled your thinking."

"How does it do that?" asked Jenkins. He was stalling for time, trying to keep the doctor talking.

"Well… let's see, shall we?" said Easton. "I have a list of questions written here, and I'd like you to answer them as quickly and honestly as you can."

"Is that all?"

"Quickly and honestly." He looked intently at Jenkins. "First question—why are you here?"

"I don't know."

Easton shook his head and made an X on the page in front of him.

"This is Faradisation therapy," said Easton. "The workings of the brain are electrical in nature. By applying electricity, we work to correct the faulty brainwaves which are causing your condition. Stubbs, turn the dial to forty volts and throw the switch, if you please."

The equipment was comprised of a series of mahogany boxes, some with protruding glass domes and tubes, and interconnected wires. More wires went to the dials and meters in front of me, and to the connections on Jenkins's arms. The control in front of me was simple enough, though, and Easton could have managed it himself. But for some reason that was not how it was done.

"Dial set to forty volts," I affirmed.

"Excellent. Now pull the switch," Easton ordered.

With some trepidation, I complied. Jenkins jerked violently, throwing himself backwards and forwards in the chair, an agonised expression on his face. After a few seconds, Easton signalled for me to turn it off again.

"God alive!" said Jenkins.

"It seems to be in working order," said Easton, in the tone of one who has set off a firework more powerful than he had realised but does not wish to alarm the spectators. "I should mention that there is a danger of biting your tongue, Mr Jenkins. It's best to try and keep your mouth shut when the current is being applied."

"It hurts," said Jenkins.

"Yes, that's quite normal," said Easton, nodding. "Now then, let's try the second question. Do you believe you belong in this institution?"

"No, I don't," said Jenkins.

"Another clearly erroneous belief." Easton slashed a large X on the paper in front of him next to the question. "Set the dial to sixty volts and activate."

I hesitated.

"Come on Stubbs, we haven't got all day."

This time there was an audible crackling sound from the machinery. Jenkins thrashed about again, and a groan escaped his lips as the current racked him. Easton watched with professional detachment and made a small note, then held up his hand to me. I cut the electricity at once.

"Are you starting to feel any different, Jenkins?"

Jenkins took a second to recover himself before replying warily. "I-I don't know. I don't like this. It's very painful."

"Medicine is rarely pleasant," said Easton complacently. "You see, sometimes it has to have a nasty taste if it's to be effective. Your brain is set in the wrong pattern; we must tear up that pattern and replace it with something healthy. Now, tell me, do you think people are conspiring against you?"

"How do you mean?"

"It's a simple enough question," said Easton. "Do you believe that people are talking about you behind your back, watching you, plotting against you?"

"I don't know." Jenkins was wary of giving the wrong answer, not sure which way to go.

"You've said your wife was 'plotting against you'—your exact words," said Easton. "Many times."

"I thought she was," said Jenkins. "But…"

"I see." H slashed another X on the page. "Please continue, Stubbs—one hundred volts."

That did not seem fair. Jenkins sounded as though he had doubts, as though he was ready to recant, only he had not expressed himself very clearly. "But he didn't say yes," I offered. "I think he means no."

"We have to follow the protocol, or the whole thing is useless." He tapped the paper in front of him with his pen. "The treatment requires you to continue. One hundred volts."

With a regretful look at Jenkins, I turned the dial and threw the switch. The boxes crackled and spat, and current flowed. Jenkins jumped like a landed fish, arched his back, then stayed in that position. Long seconds passed, and it seemed like an eternity before Easton, who was silently counting off the seconds to himself, raised his hand for me to stop.

At the end, Jenkins slumped forward, breathing heavily but not moving or raising his head.

The setup was starting to make some sense to me. Easton could not have inflicted the shocks himself, but he could bring himself to do it by proxy. In persuading me to throw the switch, he had to persuade himself. And I, compelled by his authority, had to comply. I was concerned though about how much farther up the scale we would progress.

There was a red band on the dial at the setting for a hundred and twenty volts, and the voltages continued all the way up to a hundred and fifty. The word DANGER was spelled out along the length of the red band. I resolved that I would not turn the voltage up any higher, not after seeing the effects of the hundred-volt jolt.

"Some signs of positive response in the patient," said Easton, speaking to me. "It's not easy, but it gets results. You can have madness, or you can have treatment. A bitter pill, but a potent one. We have no choice but to continue. Now, Jenkins—can you hear me, Jenkins?"

Jenkins did not respond.

"I'm not sure if he's conscious," I said.

"His conscious mind is not necessary for the process," said Dr Easton. "Jenkins, do you think that your neighbours were trying to poison you?"

We heard Jenkins breathe, in and out, twice, and Easton looked up at me.

"One hundred and—"

"No," said Jenkins weakly, still without lifting his head or opening his eyes, and Easton smiled.

"Are you sure about that?"

"I'm sure," said Jenkins, still not moving, his voice no more than a mumble. He swallowed and spoke up. "They never tried to poison me. I imagined it. It's all my own fancy, a mania that was all in my head. Just paranoia. My neighbours are perfectly decent people. They wouldn't hurt anybody. I have paranoid delusions of persecution."

Those were the words and phrases that the doctors always used when they were talking to him. I never knew he even heard them, but they must have been stored away somewhere.

Dr Easton made some notes and waited to see if Jenkins would say any more.

"I imagined the whole thing," said Jenkins. He opened his eyes to appeal to Easton. "Made something out of nothing. They never tried to poison me. Nobody tried to poison me. Not out there, or in here, either."

Easton was pleased. These were the answers he wanted to hear. A patient was recovering before his eyes—or, at any rate, had been coerced into saying what the doctor wanted him to say. From Easton's perspective, compliance may have been the same as recovery.

"Very good," he said, turning to me. "Clearly the treatment is beginning to work! Set to one hundred and thirty volts, and throw the switch, Stubbs."

"Is it really—"

"It's the protocol. You have no other choice but to continue," he said.

"Yes, Dr Easton," I said, but I hesitated a long second before I threw the switch.

Apart from a loud click, nothing happened. No electrical sizzling, and Jenkins remained slumped as before. I worked the switch to and fro a few times, to no effect.

"What's the matter?" asked Easton.

"The fuse has probably blown because of the high voltage," I said. "The plug in here isn't meant for heavy-duty equipment. It's only rated for lamps, wireless sets, and that sort of thing."

"Oh, that is a shame," said Easton, though he did not sound so very disappointed. Fixing a main fuse would mean calling out the electrician; it was not something any of us was qualified to deal with. "There isn't another room in this section with an electricity supply, is there?"

"The patients' common room might have one," I said.

"Oh well," he said, knowing as I did that we could hardly clear the place on short notice and move the whole apparatus over. "I think we've made excellent progress for one day, don't you? Stubbs, disconnect Jenkins and take him back to the ward."

There was something more beneath Easton's hail-fellow-well-met demeanour. He was pleased at the success, but beneath the surface he seemed as alarmed as I was at the torture we had inflicted. He had been compelled, as was I, to carry it out.

Dr Beltov was a stickler, but he was humane. Or so he seemed. Donnelly had called him a slave to science, unable to resist its remorseless logic. If science said that electrocution was a proven, effective way of curing patients, Beltov would obey science, according to Donnelly.

Jenkins did not say a word to me the whole way back. I patted his shoulder as I left, but he shrank away from my touch.

I did not tell him the reason the treatment had ended was not the fuse. While Dr Easton had been looking at his notes, I had stealthily tugged the leads to one of the boxes until I heard them snap inside. The sabotage would be discovered soon enough, but it had bought Jenkins and me both a little time.

Chapter Twelve: Stormy Seas

To my great frustration, I did not have a minute to myself the rest of the day. Circumstances seemed to conspire against me, and every time it looked like I might be able to get a break to confer with Dr Beltov, there was another interruption.

My problems were trivial ones, though, within the larger context. The triggering event was the sudden death of Hooper, the word-tangled patient who had always seemed so amiable. He had said the end is nigh, and it was for him.

He had shown increasing levels of disturbance and had been placed in the segregation section. Restraint had been applied. Hooper had appeared to calm down, but in the interval between checks he had killed himself. His arms and legs had been securely fastened, but he had thrashed about violently enough to snap his own neck.

This form of self-destruction could not have been anticipated. In the experience of all the attendants, some who had been working in asylums for twenty years, it was unprecedented. Miller, who had been on duty, was distressed but resigned. "It's like a curse on me," he said. I had forgotten how he had been the first to discover Gillespy, likewise dead in one of the segregation cells.

As with Gillespy, there was no question of murder: Hooper had been in a locked cell. But I could not help but recall Ryan's remark that a tiger will kill a victim by breaking its neck.

They told me after Gillespy that deaths always put a strain on the place and raise the psychic temperature. Patients became unruly, and accidents happened. Something occurred during a hydrotherapy session that Vanstone was supervising, and he came back with red welts across his face which he did not wish to discuss.

The patient, Collier, was evidently distressed as well and had to be put in segregation, requiring assistance, all of which took up more time.

Then, I was drafted to supervise a basket-weaving session for a dozen of the patients; Miller was rostered for it, but he was being given the third degree by Beltov on the circumstances surrounding Hooper's death. Miller was co-operative, but I doubted whether the speed or details of his answers would be sufficient for the exacting doctor, and it was likely to be a long session.

Tempers were frayed, and that made everything worse. Even Donnelly was talking about rubber truncheons and sedating the lot of them, and Miller's jokes wore thin indeed.

I did glean one piece of information. FitzRoy was among the group of basket weavers; the royal personage found this occupation relaxing. No stranger, I suppose, than our real king, who was said to spend his spare hours engaged in philately, endlessly sticking depictions of his own crowned head into albums. As Donnelly said, it's a finer line than we sometimes cared to notice.

FitzRoy sat at the head of the table, the others disposed around him like a court. Grogan, demurely quiet, was among them. His, or her, peculiarity had been accepted in exchange for recognising the monarch.

I showed FitzRoy the storm glass, hoping that he might know something about it.

"I believe this was invented by a relation of yours," I said. "Vice-Admiral FitzRoy of the Meteorological Office."

Some of the others glowered at me. A growing number of them now accepted FitzRoy as their monarch, and they viewed my attitude as being excessively forward. Or perhaps they suspected me of mockery. But FitzRoy himself was in good humour, buoyed up by the attention he was receiving from his subjects. He was no longer bothered that some of us did not address him as "your majesty."

"A rather unstable branch of the family," he said lightly. "The vice admiral thought he was a prophet who could predict the weather. Sheer madness! Chaos cannot—will not—be foretold by any man, whether he claims to be a scientist or a magician." He laughed, and the others all laughed with him.

It gave me a most peculiar feeling, as though I should laugh along and agree that weather forecasting was a species of lunacy.

"My great-uncle – the old Duke of York, you know – told me the vice admiral experimented with all sorts of alchemical toys for prognosticating wind and rain and whatnot. Nothing was too absurd for him." He shook his head. "Poor Robert FitzRoy couldn't stand all the mockery about his weather prophecies. They laughed at him in the House of Commons. And the newspapers were merciless."

"Is that so?" I asked.

"In the end, the poor fellow killed himself. Cut his throat with a straight razor. Quite mad." FitzRoy spoke with cheerful contempt. "They gave him a decent plot in All Saints' Church, anyway."

He held up the glass to the light to study the murky green liquid. "A curiosity. Maybe it changes with the winds from the moon, or the earth's magnetism, or the dances of the angels on pinheads. Here. A little thing for little minds."

"I dare say you're right," I said, pocketing the glass again.

"The worst of it," FitzRoy went on, "is that it stains the family reputation. That wretched doctor…tried to imply there was something wrong with my brain…he calls it a medical opinion, I call it treason. George III's doctors…"

He trailed off into an irritable mutter.

"That's just your Dr Nye," said Grogan sympathetically. "He sees madness everywhere. Those doctors should try looking in a mirror."

The conversation moved on. I was not going to learn anything more, but it seemed to me that this particular glass was not meant to foretell the weather, that it had been made sensitive to other sorts of current. Given that it was in Gillespy's possession, my guess was that it was a sort of tiger detector. Not that it had done him any good.

At the end of the working day, I was rostered on night shift. I was drowsy after the evening meal and resolved to take a nap to fortify myself before taking further steps—specifically, having a look at patient Ross's notes and writing a letter to Dr Beltov so that even if I did not see him, he would be able to advise me.

You were not supposed to go to sleep on duty, but everyone did. The pattern of shift work practically guaranteed it, and since there was only enough occupation for one of three men on duty at any one time, all that mattered was that you were there to be roused when the need arose.

I was stretched full-length on the floor, the couch being too short to accommodate me, with my head resting on a seat-cushion. Not the most comfortable billet, but fatigue makes the hardest floor into a feather mattress. Except for one thing; the solid lump digging into my side was the storm glass in my pocket. I took it out: filled with dark clouds.

Sleep overtook me in a rush. It was more like that groggy, dizzying experience of unconsciousness that you fall into at the extremes of fatigue or physical hardship, something I had seen enough times in the ring. Your body gives up on you, and your mind pitches into the dark. That time, I seemed to be dragged down into it by innumerable shadowy figures clutching my arms and legs.

I was wandering through a desert in the dark, under a night sky full of shooting stars. I did not know where I was going or why, but with the logic of dreams, I knew I had to carry on.

Then, the ground lurched, and the sand-dunes turned into breakers. I crawled through a porthole—it was a tight squeeze—into a ship's cabin, then fastened the portholes behind me with metal screws. Somehow, I knew they were called "dogs," something I never knew before, and I knew they had to be fastened tightly or the seawater would come flooding in. In fact, at every wave the porthole was underwater and showed a strange underwater world full of drifting seaweed.

The motion of the ship was violent, pitching first one way and then the other. I wondered if I was going to be seasick.

The strange thing was that at some point I knew I was dreaming, but I was puzzled to know whose dream it was. It did not seem like one of my dreams at all: surely, it was one of Captain Hall's dreams.

"If it's only a dream, it can't hurt me," I said to myself, and even as I was flung against one of the wooden walls—which were bulkheads, I knew—the impact was muted and muffled, as things are in dreams.

"It's tedious enough, though," I said.

The next roll took me to the porthole again, where I looked down towards the bottom of the sea, which was lit in a strange green, although it should have been dark.

A face stared back at me. I recoiled violently. Dream or not, I did not like that face.

The dogs fastening the porthole rotated, and I stared as the thing sprang open and a torrent of green water laced with seaweed gushed through, soaking my feet and ankles.

The shock woke me up. But instead of being back in the hospital, I was still on a ship.

As the ship rolled, I landed on the floor, or rather the deck, and as often happens in these things, the shock of the impact woke me up, and for a second I was glad to be back in the hospital and out of that dream. But the storm was still roaring outside, and as the ship lurched over I was rolled bodily into a piece of furniture.

I could not wake; the dream had dragged me back in like a whirlpool. I did not know what would happen if I drowned in the dream. Would I wake up properly, or would I die, as they say dreamers do at the moment of death in their dreaming if they do not awake in time? I was not bold enough to find out, and at the sound of water surging below me, I clambered to my feet, steadying myself against the wall with the roll of the waves, and staggered towards the pale outline of a doorway.

I rushed up some steep stairs, but found I was trapped. There was no way of getting up through the deck.

There were figures moving about me below, big, slope-shouldered figures with long arms. I had a hunch about them. It was Captain Hall's nightmare, and those were his sea-demons, smelling of weed and seabed slime.

There was a hatchway above, but no ladder to reach it. The heeling of the ship almost sent me tumbling back down the stairs and into the arms of those creatures down there. I held on and, putting a stool on a table, launched myself upwards to the hatch, even as the table splintered beneath me.

It was even darker up there, in some 'tween-deck space, with a cramped low ceiling. I had gone wrong somewhere; it was not the way up to the deck. It was a storage room. But it was a wooden ship, and desperation is a powerful motivating force. Bracing myself against the motion of the vessel, which was as violent as ever, I felt around for an instrument. My hand closed around a wooden rod or staff. Taking it in both hands, I thrust upwards. The rod broke after the second blow, but the shortened stick was easier to use in the confined space, and something gave way above.

I bashed upwards again and again, widening the hole, falling over once in the process as I could not keep my balance. Rain splashed my face; it was the way through to the deck. I redoubled my efforts, and the pieces of decking broke away at every blow, until the hole was large enough for me to crawl through.

As I squeezed through the aperture, desperate that I should not get stuck and be dragged back by the things below, I looked around, expecting to see the masts, the rigging, and the storm-wracked seas around me. But the scene was not at all what I had expected.

There is a celebrated woodcut from medieval times of a man who has reached the edge of the flat Earth and succeeded in sticking his head through the dome of stars that surrounds it. He is stopped by wonder, looking at the great mechanical clockwork that moves the sun and the stars on their courses, seeing the deeper reality behind the familiar world. He could not have been more astonished than I was by what I saw.

The dark and the rain impeded my vision, but there were electric lights which gave fixed points. The ship no longer rocked, although I felt a residual motion within my body. What had at first looked like waves resolved themselves into trees waving in the storm winds. There were no masts about me, only chimneys. I was looking out across the roofs of the hospital.

It was a gradual awakening rather than an instantaneous one, as the last vestiges of the seascape dissolved into the everyday world. The shift in perspective was baffling, and I was stupefied by the transformation, which had no parallel in my experience. Everything had changed, but it had not changed.

I realised that I must have been sleepwalking in my dream, imagining the surroundings... but my imagination had not actually put nautical fittings in the hospital. It had merely changed the way I saw things and my assumptions about them.

My shirt was soaking wet, and for the first time I noticed the voices below. They must have always been there, but I had not paid them any attention. As in the boxing ring, when your mind was focused on the movement of your opponent's fists and body, the tilt of his head and the movement of his muscles, the words of the crowd all mingled into background noise that was no different from silence.

I picked up a broken roof slate, still struggling to comprehend what I had done. In my other hand was a broken piece of wood that looked like a billiard cue.

"It's Stubbs," someone was explaining.

"What the blazes is he doing up there? What was all that smashing about?"

"I don't know."

"Stubbs!"

Awkwardly, I withdrew back through the hole I had made, into the loft space. Six feet away was a square of light where I had entered. "I'm up here," I said.

"What are you doing?" Vanstone demanded.

"I'll explain later," I said, surveying the damage. Rain was already soaking the floor below the hole. I needed to try and patch it up at once. Proper repairs would have to wait till the morning and would take a skilled roofer. "I'm coming down."

I lowered myself gingerly and dropped the last couple of feet. Next to me was a broken table and an overturned stool. Miller and Vanstone were staring up at me, astonished. I smoothed my hair. "I thought I saw one of the patients on the stairs," I said. "I couldn't see anything, but then it sounded like they were up there, moving about in the eaves, so I went up after them."

"And what was all the bashing about?" Vanstone was peering up through the loft hatch, which I had left open.

"I hit my head," I said. "And I thought I was being attacked, so I hit back."

"Bloody hell," said Vanstone.

"Only the noise from the plumbing," said Miller. "There's nobody up there. Nobody's missing from the wards."

I had heard of people sleepwalking, not knowing where they were. Maybe that was what had happened to me, though I had never sleepwalked in my life. And I had never heard of a sleepwalker who climbed into a loft space, nor one who smashed a hole in a roof.

"Ghosts," said Vanstone, looking at me strangely.

"We thought you'd gone mad," said Miller, grinning, as we descended the stairs. "Couldn't think what had got into you. 'He's gone mad,' I said."

"This place does affect people," said Vanstone. "How did you get wet? Is there a broken pipe?"

"I don't think so," I said. "It was dark, and I was panicking."

"Don't worry," said Miller, patting my shoulder. "Accidents happen. We'll have a proper look, get it fixed in the morning."

I was more shaken than I cared to admit. I could not understand what had happened, how the line between sleep and waking had been crossed, and I could not let on to these two. They were friends, but I was still the newcomer who was not tried and tested like they were. A man who might see ghosts, who the place might get to.

"I just woke up," I said. "Maybe I dreamed seeing someone on the stairs."

"Most likely," said Vanstone. "You've got something stuck to your face."

I pulled off a small dark-brown square, no bigger than a postage stamp. Some piece of debris I had picked up while smashing about in the roof space.

It looked like seaweed, but that could not be so. A dream was a dream, and reality was reality, and if the water on my face was salty it must be from sweat. It was all a sort of delusion or hallucination, and I had to be clear what was real and what was not.

Really, though, I'd had a lucky escape. If I had seen Miller and Vanstone in my confused state, and lashed out at them thinking they were those fish-eyed things, maybe I would have caused one of them serious injury... And maybe I would be shut away, under heavy sedation in one of the cells downstairs.

"You should go home," said Vanstone, a hand on my shoulder. "Get some kip in your own bed."

"A night's sleep and you'll be right as rain," said Miller.

I protested, but the others insisted. They would manage the rest of the shift without me. I felt I was being condescended to, and there was a little too much in their voices of that tone you fall into when addressing an agitated patient. But it was my welfare they were concerned for, and the least I could do was follow their advice.

It was no longer raining when I tramped home; there was no sign, in fact, that it had rained at all, or that there was any storm. On an impulse, I pulled out the storm glass and held it up to a streetlight. It was clear as water.

Chapter Thirteen: The New Physician

I arrived early the next morning, full of purpose. A good night's sleep had helped persuade me that I was not cracking up, and that Hooper's death meant that I needed answers more urgently than ever. Things were coming to a head.

I managed to avoid being collared for any duty and headed straight for the patients' medical records, which occupied an open area next to the doctors' common room. I wanted to find out the name of the doctor who had authorised Ross's confinement. Then, I wanted to talk to Dr Beltov about a number of matters, chief among them being that reel of film.

The first task was easy enough.

"Doctor Nye," I said, taking it down in my notebook. Why did that name seem familiar? He was not on the staff there, not even as an occasional visitor. As soon as I spoke the name out loud I was troubled by a presentiment of danger. I had a feeling that I was too late. I checked Hooper's admission record and Gillespy's and the same name came up both times: Doctor Nye. The hairs on the back of my neck prickled.

Unusually, there was nobody in the common room; usually the doctors were there, having their coffee and the first pipe of the day before getting to work. I started going through the indexes to bound journals, and found my answer soon enough. Dr Nye was a rising star with many citations to his name in medical literature, having pioneered a whole host of new therapies of unparalleled effectiveness: the magnetic therapy we called the Sarcophagus, the new version of hydrotherapy, and the improved variety of Faradisation therapy had all originated with him. There was even a piece suggesting that the wires from the Sarcophagus might be used to reconstruct a patient's visions: a trap for the unwary who might inhale the fumes while working too closely with the stuff of madness.

I arrived at Beltov's office to find Dr Hamilton already at the door.

"You may prefer to come back later," he told me. "Dr Beltov won't be available this morning."

He knocked, a quick double rap.

"What's happening, Doctor?"

"You hadn't heard? There's a notice up in the attendants' common room. Dr Beltov is no longer in charge."

The world lurched under my feet. It must be a consequence of Hooper's death, though what that had to do with Beltov was beyond me. There had been deaths before; they were unavoidable. Dr Easton made occasional efforts to undermine Beltov's authority, but I could not believe these would have any effect. "But he's been here for years," I said.

"We're all behind Dr Beltov," said Hamilton. "He's an outstanding clinician, and there's no suggestion of negligence or malpractice. Privately, I fear there is politics at work. This new doctor is the coming man, a shooting star. More appealing to the board than a fusspot like Beltov."

"Isn't Dr Easton taking over?"

Easton was nominally the second in command, but Hamilton shook his head. "Dr Nye is taking over as senior physician, effective immediately. He'll be here shortly."

He knocked on the door again, with three loud raps. I was still working out what it meant, impatient with Beltov's ignoring his knocking, when Hamilton swung the door open. "Beltov! My God!"

I smelled it before I saw anything. My nostrils were filled with the familiar aroma of fresh blood. I worked as a butcher's boy in my father's shop, so I had plenty of opportunity to see animals killed and bled. You can get a bucket of blood out of a pig, and they say a man has a gallon of the red stuff in his veins. Blood looks very different, though, when you spread it about a room, pint by pint; you can hardly believe the quantity. Beltov's exsanguination was a thorough one, his body squeezed dry like a sponge.

I will not readily forget the scene inside. The floor was covered in glass and blood—extremely fresh blood, forming a pattern of rivulets across the carpet. As though a tide of blood had risen and fallen.

Dr Beltov was seated at his desk, his head thrown back, his neck opened by a broad gash from which blood still oozed. The gore made a pool on his desk, with the rectangular outline of the blotter forming an island. A crimson waterfall, dripping like a rain gutter into a puddle on the floor, fed the rivulets stretching to the very edges of the room.

He must have been recently dead—a matter of minutes—for the blood still to be flowing so freely. There was no doubt that he was dead, even though Hamilton rushed over to check, his feet crunching the glass shards and leaving bloody footprints as he went.

I was no stranger to blood and death, but some squeamishness held me back. Or perhaps it was something else; a part of me was surveying the room, taking in details. A dial lay on the floor, a clock face. Near it was a big chunk of brass gears and rods, the internal working of the glass clock which had been shattered. Beltov would never get it to work properly now, never find the secret of perfect regulation to keep the clock running in perfect synchrony with reality.

Beltov's hands were open on the desk in front of him in the blood. A pen lay nearby, as though he had written something in the minutes before he cut his throat with a shard of glass from the broken clock. If he had left a note, his words had been obliterated by the red flow.

Beltov's wire letter tray, which stood clear of the desk, was untouched and held half a dozen letters that would forever be unread. At the top was a thick cream envelope with nothing on it except Beltov's name. That would be the letter from the superintendent's secretary, a letter which he had not opened. Perhaps he had found out about his dismissal through some other means.

"Double incision," said Hamilton, thinking out loud. "He must have cut once, then cut again deeper. Dear God in heaven!"

Beltov had killed himself. But the double mark made it look as though he had been swiped by sharp claws. The location of the office made it impossible that anyone could have been in and out without being seen, unless they could climb in and out through the window then lock it behind them. Beltov's professional ruin and his own obduracy made a verdict of suicide inevitable, even without lack of physical evidence for any other possible explanation.

"What should I do, Doctor?" I asked, still standing in the doorway.

"Get back to your job," he said promptly. "Make sure that everything keeps running smoothly. The patients have had too much disturbance already."

He held up a bloodied hand, his sleeve dipping, trying not to show dismay.

"Everything must carry on as normal. Dr Nye will arrange everything when he gets here, I'm sure of that."

"Very good, Doctor," I said.

It's over, said a voice in my head. *Dr Nye is coming. You have no answers and no allies. It's time to face the inevitable.*

It could have been Ryan speaking to me with the voice of well-reasoned despair.

Things were moving too fast. The whole world seemed to be closing in on me from all directions. Or rather, the floor was disintegrating under my feet, plank by plank. Things were spiralling out of control, but I had not quite run out of options.

I found Donnelly in the east wing, leading Ross away from his cell.

"Top of the morning to you," Donnelly said with exaggerated cheerfulness, rolling his eyes to express the craziness of it. "Ain't this place a madhouse today though?"

"Where are you taking him?"

"We're off on a little excursion to see Dr Easton in the Ivy Room," said Donnelly. "Trying him on the F-therapy." Donnelly did not like the Faradisation treatment any more than I did.

"I'll take him," I said, too quickly.

"You will not," said Donnelly, unfolding his arms. Donnelly has an acute sixth sense when it comes to judging intentions. He had seen what I planned to do almost before I had myself. "What are you up to, anyhow?"

"I have to take him somewhere else," I said.

Donnelly leaned in close, his voice dropping to a whisper.

"I don't like it either," he said. "But you're not Lord God Almighty, you're only another bloody attendant, like me. Now will you let me do my job before I get into trouble."

Donnelly was a solidly built man, considerably shorter than I and somewhat lighter, but with a good amount of meat on his bones. He was well experienced in the art of unarmed combat. If it came to it, he would put up a fight, and a fight was the last thing I wanted.

My uppercut caught him completely off guard. His own fault, really, for leaning so close and giving me the idea. He fell back heavily against the wall, not quite knocked out but at least stunned.

They key was still in the door to Ross's cell. I opened it and shoved Donnelly inside; he tried to grab my arm, but I chopped his hand away, and the closing door forced him inside before he could get a foot out to stop it. I turned the key, once, twice.

Ross looked at me, agape.

"What are you doing?"

"Rescuing you."

His response was interrupted by a hammering on the cell door beside him. Donnelly had not taken long to recover and fully appreciate the situation.

This was not the time to have a discussion about Ross's psychological state and the merits or demerits of an unscheduled departure from the institution. I marched him forcibly down the corridor and into a hallway. Two of the older patients were playing draughts in one corner. All they saw was an attendant leading a reluctant inmate, nothing to raise the alarm about.

A door marled Authorised Personnel Only opened to my key. It led to the sections forbidden to patients, but nobody saw us slip through. Escape would be much easier from one of these sections.

I had previously noted that the side corridor leading to the kitchens had sash windows with no bars over them. These windows were never opened; they had been painted over, and there were locks on them. Such a window would be impossible to open from the outside, as a locked window should be, but inside you could get some purchase on the window and give it a good heave.

For a moment, I wondered if the thing was going to break apart and I was going to be left holding a piece of window frame, but with a loud squeal the lock gave way and the window opened for the first time in decades. There was nobody else in the corridor, but it was too much noise.

"After you," I said.

Ross stepped through the window readily, and I followed and closed it behind us. I did not think we would be observed; the only windows that gave a good view of us were in the kitchen, and they were partially steamed over by preparations for lunch.

There are three gates, and I headed straight for the side gate used for deliveries. It was not the most convenient, as reaching it took us past the entire north wing, but there was no help for that.

White faces appeared in the windows of the common room. They were always quick to notice anything from a pigeon on the grass to a laundry van, and the sight of the two of us aroused instant interest. It would only be seconds before the attendant with them looked out too to see what the disturbance was.

"Run for the gate," I suggested, increasing my own pace.

Ross ran alongside me, asking no questions.

A window opened on the first floor, and somebody shouted down to us; I did not hear what they said. I was fumbling with the key I had taken off the board in the attendants' common room.

I flung the gate open, and we hurried though; I slammed it shut behind us and locked it, looking up in time to see Vanstone and Miller running towards us on the other side. I did not think they would have another key on them, as the others were in the superintendent's office.

"Stop!" shouted Miller.

"Sorry!" I shouted back, and we ran off, leaving them on the other side of the bars.

How much of a lead would we have? One minute, two minutes? I had not really thought beyond the bare necessity of getting the two of us out of there. Fortunately, mine was not the only brain at work on the task, and two streets away Ross slowed down.

"Don't run," he said. "Walk. And take my arm."

"What?"

"As though you were keeping me under control. That way we won't attract quite so much attention."

Of course, with me in my white attendant's tunic and him in his blue inmate's uniform, we did attract attention. But we did not look like an escape in progress.

"Is there a cab rank near here?" Ross asked.

"Not this side of Westow Street that I can think of," I said. "But there is a bus stop over there, and a Number Twenty coming down the street."

The conductor looked doubtful when I asked for two tickets.

"Don't worry about this man," I said. "I can manage him."

Ross kept his eyes downcast, every bit the depressed, lifeless shell.

"I don't know about that," said the conductor. "This is a public omnibus, not an ambulance."

"This man is a shell-shocked soldier who fought for his country," I said. "We can transfer one poor man on a bus when he's perfectly harmless, can't we?"

"He won't cause you any trouble," said a man sitting opposite. He was in civvies but had the ramrod carriage of an old ex-soldier. "Will you, matey?"

"Some people," remarked the woman next to me loudly, glaring fixedly at a point in space adjacent to the conductor. "You'd think it would kill them to show a little charity."

Only a little abashed, the conductor turned the little silver handle on his machine and cranked out two singles without any very good grace.

"What regiment?" asked the old soldier opposite.

"Royal Flying Corps," said Ross without looking up.

The man offered an open packet of cigarettes, and Ross took one gratefully. I politely refused.

"You boys did a grand job," said the man with the cigarettes. "Many and many a time, I saw your lot flying over the lines. You lost a lot of good men. We all did."

Luckily, he did not feel a need for any more conversation, he just patted Ross on the shoulder and went back to his newspaper.

"Where are we going?" I had become the follower, and he was the leader. He seemed taller now than he had inside, and certainly more commanding than the meek individual in his cell.

"We're not going anywhere without better clothes," he said, looking me up and down.

Through the window there were two police officers making

their way down the street, looking about purposefully, one of them fingering his truncheon. Was it paranoia to think that word about us would be out already? If so, we were a conspicuous pair.

Ross signalled to get off the bus at the next stop. He had seen the police, too. I tried to tell him that our best chance lay in finding a faster means of conveyance, but Ross had his own idea. He had seen a pawnbroker's shop from the bus, and we stopped in the doorway.

"You stay here. Get that white tunic off. Slouch here in your vest as though you were drunk."

I did as I was told, leaning against the wall in my undershirt. I had seen men hanging around, the worse for drink, in similar states of undress. It was a mild day, but it felt strange to be half-naked in the open air. Ross quickly started negotiations with the pawnbroker. He was obviously familiar enough with the workings of such places.

"How's this one for ye?" The pawnbroker had a noticeable Scottish accent.

"How much?" Ross was alert, commanding even.

"Five shillings, very good condition, as you see. If you want better, these are ten."

A woman carrying a bag of groceries and holding a small child by the hand passed by. She looked away when she saw me in the pawnbroker's doorway.

"This one is almost decent," said Ross. "But it's seen better days. Look, the pocket's torn."

"Ten shillings," said the Scotsman. "I told ye before, and the price is clearly marked. I don't have to haggle when I'm selling, so I won't."

Ross emerged soon thereafter with a parcel wrapped in brown paper. We retired to an alleyway, where he slipped off his blue inmate's shirt and donned my white tunic, then pulled the old Army greatcoat he had purchased over it.

"Pawnbrokers are always full of these," he remarked. The lining was riddled with moth-holes, but from the outside it looked respectable enough. And the character of the tunic underneath was concealed; it might have been any white shirt. He would not attract attention now, but Ross was still not satisfied with the effect.

"Tear this for me," he said, passing me his blue shirt. "See if you can get a good long strip about this wide."

I did as he asked, tearing it as easily as tissue paper. Ross took the best piece and tied it around his neck as a kind of rough cravat or bandana. He looked more raffish than shabby. Sort of Bohemian.

"Good," he said, admiring himself frankly in a window glass. "And here, why don't you take this?"

He took an empty bottle from a pile by the rubbish bins and pressed it into my hand. I could have objected that it was empty, but then again, drunks do hold on to empty bottles.

"Muss your hair up a bit and try to look more vacant," Ross suggested, smoothing his own hair. "Dab a bit of grime on your cheek. So long as we stay a few paces apart and don't look like we're together—oops!"

Ross pushed me back against the wall and flattened himself against it so we were hidden by drainpipes. I glimpsed a police constable walking past. If he had been paying attention, he might have spotted us, but he was probably looking for two men running away.

"How far is this going to get us?" I asked.

"Far enough," he said. "If we can make it to St John's Wood, there's a place we can go."

We followed his plan, keeping a good separation between us and boarding separate trams heading up to Elephant and Castle. If police were looking for two men together, they would never find us. Out of our hospital clothes, there was little to distinguish us from the crowd. People steered away from me in my character as a drunk, and I had disapproving looks from more than one matron, but there was no hand on my shoulder.

I met Ross again at the entrance to the Elephant-and-Castle underground station. Passengers streamed past in both directions, oblivious to us.

"You don't have to come with me," he said. "You've done enough already. I could never have got out without you."

"I don't have anywhere else to go," I said, though the truth was more complicated. It might have been more honest to say I had rescued him for my own purposes, and I meant to see those purposes fulfilled.

"In that case, I'll put you up."

I started relaxing on the underground, but began thinking about what I had done. It had been a desperate gamble, but there had been little alternative. Little as I knew about Dr Nye, everything seemed to point to him as the eye of the storm, the focal point of everything. Ryan's tiger. I asked Ross what he knew about Nye.

Ross shook his head doubtfully. "Never heard of him."

"He was the doctor who signed your papers when you were committed," I said.

"Strange," he said. "I feel as if I ought to remember him, but I can't."

I had never visited St John's Wood before; it's a fashionable neighbourhood, close to Regents Park, with streets packed with three-storey town-houses. I believe many of them are Georgian; it is certainly a contrast to the Victorian brick constructions that fill the streets of Norwood. Again, I was left waiting outside while Ross knocked on a door. A woman answered whom I could not see; a few words were exchanged, then he turned and waved to me, grinning. "Come on in!"

The entrance hall was a black-and-white pattern of chequered marble. The house had not seemed large because it was narrow, but it extended a great way back.

Ross later explained that the property belonged to a woman he called his aunt. Technically, she was his foster mother, but she had not taken to the role of mothering. She resided principally in the south of France, but maintained it as a what he called a *pied-à-terre* for when she came to London. She only used it occasionally when she needed to replenish her wardrobe or plunder Fortnum and Mason for delicacies.

Apparently, Ross was allowed to drop in and use the place any time he liked. There was only one member of the staff, a housekeeper whom Ross called Maggie and who seemed to view him with some affection. The young Ross had spent his school holidays there, and she insisted that his old bedroom was the same as ever and she would make it up for him at once.

That afternoon, I soaked in a long hot bath on claw feet. I would have liked a decent workout, but the house lacked the facilities. It had a library, a conservatory, a morning room, and, I gathered, a superior wine cellar, but nowhere for exercise. After my bath, I found that Ross had sent out to a shop, and there was a new set of apparel in a good approximation of my size. Maggie did not blink when he asked her to make up a room for me, too. I was almost embarrassed to touch the linen, which looked not merely clean but brand new.

Ross had busied himself reading newspapers and magazines, catching up on all that had happened in the world since he had been out of it.

At seven o'clock, Maggie struck a gong, and dinner was served to just the two of us on a table, lit by two candelabras, that could easily have sat fourteen. I had three different crystal glasses and a whole row of cutlery, laid out in descending order of size.

"Maggie wants to be formal because you're here," he said. "She'll get over it in a day or two." Ross filled my glass with sparkling wine and raised his own.

"Your excellent health," he said. "I don't know how to thank you."

It must have been real champagne, not that I can tell the difference. The setting was almost otherworldly; Beltov's death that morning seemed like a dream. Death and danger were not admitted to this lavish domestic scene, so utterly different to the white-tiled interiors of the asylum suffused with the odour of carbolic.

Maggie bustled in carrying a tray, stopping in the doorway to admire Ross. Cleaned up and in evening dress, he cut a smart figure. "It's so good to have you back," she said, smiling.

"Not as good as it is to come back to your cooking," he said.

"Oh, you," she said, placing steaming bowls of a clear soup before us. She served soft bread rolls with silver tongs.

I found I had a good appetite. Somewhere during the day, I seemed to have missed lunch.

"Don't worry," Ross told me after I mopped up the remainder of the soup with the final scrap of roll. "There's plenty more coming. Fish, and an omelette, and I think I smelled a venison pasty in preparation. And pudding—she makes a terrific pudding—and cheese and fruit."

That would explain all the cutlery. I found it hard to credit that one woman could have cooked so much at such short notice, but Maggie brought the food, course after course of it, beaming at the plates polished clean each time. Ross's foster mother had taken on other children at various times and paid them little attention; most of the care came from Maggie, and Ross seemed to have been her favourite.

I explained my role, which I perhaps overstated somewhat, as a sort of private investigator handling cases concerned with phenomena beyond the ordinary.

"Sounds very glamourous," said Ross. Perhaps I had made it sound that way, but there had been precious little glamour mopping floors and supervising basketwork for the last several weeks. "And this mysterious client of yours—they think I'm involved?"

"It was my deduction that you hold a piece of the mystery," I said. "My real business lies with Dr Nye, and you are my closest connection to him."

Maggie came in, took away our plates, and served us each a fried sole. Ross picked at his, and I did my clumsy best to extract the meat from the tiny, elastic bones. The sole was, of course, excellent.

"Well, you've told me a lot," he said. "I never dreamed that there was such a thing as a psychic detective, or whatever your correct rank is. Every day I discover something strange in the world. I owe you an explanation, too… but it can wait until the morning. I've had enough of madness for one day."

And, over several courses and as many glasses of wine, we chatted about sports, the geography of London, the war, his foster mother, and a hundred other things. In hindsight, he was trying to convince me of what a thoroughly ordinary and entirely sane character he was. It was frustrating not to be able to discuss the one issue that mattered most, but the wine and good food worked their magic. The next day, I would discover how we would tackle Dr Nye.

That night, I slept an exhausted sleep. It was not until the morning that I realised there had been no screaming in the night. Ross's night terrors did not follow him outside of the hospital.

Chapter Fourteen: Out and About

I spent most of the morning writing up my notes and correspondence. First I penned a brief note to my brother, advising him of my situation, so he could let Ma and Pa know that I was working on a case and they need not worry about me, whatever the rumours that were flying about might say. Then I wrote a slightly longer missive to Arthur Renville, presenting a perhaps unrealistically optimistic view of the chances of resolving the matter now that Ross was free. In truth, we could have taken shelter with Arthur, but I did not entirely trust his sympathy would lie with helping to free a mental patient.

I wrote also to Mr Hoade, the fount of all knowledge, to see what information he could glean on Dr Nye and other matters. I could try myself, but I was sure that Hoade could glean ten times as much information ten times as quickly. Naturally, I did not mention my circumstances, and I trusted that he was sufficiently removed from my normal social acquaintances not to have heard any rumours.

Finally, my most extensive letter which I put off til last was reserved for Sally, who was owed something of an explanation, and whom I had left in the lurch without any warning. I expressed the warmth of my regards and the hope that I would be able to return soon.

These literary exertions had given me an appetite, and I was on my way downstairs to see what the pantry might afford by way of mid-morning snacks when I heard voices from the drawing room. One of them was female, and it was not Maggie's. Two steps later, Ross called out to me, "Stubbs! Do join us, please."

He was seated on the sofa, with Miss Bentham at the other end. There was a shopping bag at her feet, and her little dog was standing guard over it. He wagged his tail as soon as he saw me, but Miss Bentham looked less charmed.

"Stubbs, I wanted you to meet my fiancée—"

"We've met," she said, cutting him off.

I was not sure whether to stay or go, but Ross indicated an armchair.

"And what the hell do you think you're doing?" she demanded.

For a moment, I thought she was offended by my taking a seat. It was nothing so trivial.

"This is all your fault, isn't it?" she told me. "Why couldn't you leave him there? Can't you see he needs help?"

"Darling—" said Ross.

"Don't 'darling' me," she said. "Who knows you're out?"

"Nobody knows," he said. "Except the hospital, obviously, and Maggie."

Her rage subsided slightly at that revelation. So far as the rest of the world was concerned, Ross was still safely incarcerated, and that was the way she wanted it.

"Did you bring my books?"

"Yes, I brought your bloody books," she said, bending over the shopping bag. There were three or four of them, hefty reference works with plain dust-jackets. He reached out as if to take them, but she held the books hostage on her lap.

"This is my final gift to you," she said. "Don't ask me for anything else."

"Thank you," he said. "I won't."

"What are you going to do now, exactly?"

"We don't know," he said. "But with the books, we might be able to find our way."

She addressed me. "Do you actually believe in this? Are you encouraging him?"

I felt as though I was caught up in a marital argument. It was a very disagreeable sensation. I had no experience of domestic disharmony; my father's response to trouble was always to heave a sigh and give in, attending to whatever minor task he had been neglecting with an air of martyrdom. But perhaps the fact was that my parents never disagreed about anything that mattered to them.

"Your fiancé's life was in danger where he was," I said. "I was compelled to take steps to remove him from that danger."

"Because of ancient Egyptian rituals?" she said.

I must have been gaping, because Ross spoke up. "Ellen is referring to my ideas about the Black Pharaohs," he said. Which did nothing to dispel my confusion.

"What 'danger' was he in?" she demanded.

"I can't go into details," I said, "but there were a number of deaths, and I have reason to believe murder was involved. And I suspect Dr Nye may be behind them. How did he come to be involved?"

"Only by pure chance," she said dismissively. "He happened to know someone who knew us."

"But he was keen to have your fiancé committed, even though, as far as I can tell, he wasn't a danger to himself or others."

That brought her up, but she was not stalled for long. "I accepted his professional opinion. As for not being a danger"—she turned to Ross—"you did try to kill him."

"Nonsense," he riposted. "Who told you that?"

She did not give the obvious reply but instead thought a moment, weighing possibilities and whether there might be more than one view. "I never liked him," she said at last. "He never seemed entirely trustworthy. He kept wanting to talk to me."

"Did he… bother you after he had me put away?" asked Ross.

"Of course not. You know I would never look twice at a man like that." She was almost indignant. "But he is highly respected in his profession. And for one, I listen to professional opinions."

"Those Egyptologists were talking rot," said Ross. "And I can prove it."

"Because you're the *only one* who understands," she said. "Because you have *cosmic insight*. Because you are the *one chosen to save the world*," she said with theatrical sarcasm.

"Now, that's not fair!" said Ross, with an outburst of feeling I had not seen before. "You can't ridicule me!"

"I'm not the one who had to be locked up," she said coldly. And then, to me: "You should have had him explain it all to you first. You might have had second thoughts."

"Wait a minute," said Ross. "You wait a minute, now. Have you seen the pyramids?"

She did not reply.

"Well, I have. They are a feat of engineering beyond anything we can even imagine. A wonder of the world, still standing after forty centuries. Can we agree on that?"

She waved a hand. "If you like."

"And you think all that skill, that scientific genius, that was as far as it went? You think they never grasped any metaphysics beyond the enumeration of childish, animal-headed gods?"

"You see?" she said to me.

"The evidence is there in black and white," he said.

"And, miraculously, you're the only one who can decode it," she said. "And all those Egyptian scholars who have been slaving away for years are numbskulls."

"No, it's just I'm the only one—" he protested.

"The only one who understands how an engine works?" she asked acidly. "None of this woolly-minded, namby-pamby, liberal-arts nonsense for you." I tried to remember what I knew of her education; I suspected his background was in the sciences and hers in the arts and it had become a bone of contention between them. "Or is it perhaps because you were there at the time, and you've been conveniently reincarnated?"

He flushed at that and was momentarily lost for words. Miss Bentham was a skilled debater. I would hesitate to argue with her as I would hesitate to step into the ring with Jack Dempsey.

"Miss Stopes had a vision once," said Ross to me. "Under a yew tree in her garden, God spoke to her. Miss Stopes wrote a letter to the bishops, telling them she was the prophet of God and they should ignore what St Paul said and listen to her on birth control. Is that sane behaviour?"

"There's no comparison," said Miss Bentham.

"Miss Stopes wants to save the world from *reckless breeding*—and so do you!" he said. "How does that make you any better than me?"

"I admit, I am even deluded enough to think I can make the world a better place for women," she said. "But I don't let my delusions destroy my life or make me incapable of acting like a normal human being."

"You think you're a normal human being?" he demanded.

She ignored him, turning to me instead. "You're his friend. Please think about his welfare," she told me. "If he would be safer in some other institution, we'll arrange it."

"I will bear that in mind," I said.

"I doubt it," she said. She sighed twice. "I don't know. I wish I could believe in your revelation—"

"It's not a revelation," Ross protested.

"Or whatever you call it." She looked down at the books on her lap. "But I can't entirely discount it, either. Dr Beltov had his doubts about Nye, didn't he? I was trying to remember what he said on the phone before I saw you." Miss Bentham took the books in her arms. She seemed to be wrestling with herself.

Ross said nothing, perhaps to avoid provoking her.

"I suppose I'll leave you to it," she said at last. It was not a happy decision, but it was a decision. She stood. Ross stood, too, and she thrust the armload of books at him. "Goodbye," she said before suddenly kissing him on the lips and pulling away before he could respond. "Do what you can," she said to me, and she was already walking out, her little dog trotting alongside with a backward look towards me.

"Goodbye, Ellen," Ross called after her. "And thank you."

The front door slammed shut a second later. She had gone off to save the world in her own way.

"Sorry about the scene," he said, looking at his feet. "I thought things might go better if there was a third party in the room. Ellen can be a bit of a handful at times."

"I'm sorry you two are arguing," I said.

"Oh, it's nothing," he said, but he sounded relieved it was over. "I'm for a whisky and soda. Will you join me?"

"I was contemplating the prospect of a cold beef sandwich," I said. "I don't mind assembling it myself if the makings are around."

"To each his own," he said. "I wouldn't mind a bite to eat myself, now you mention it. Maggie's out shopping, so we have the run of the place."

In the kitchen, I sliced bread and meat from the pantry, while Ross clattered about with cutlery and crockery.

"Of course, most of what Ellen said was true," said Ross. "It's the way she says things that makes them sound ridiculous. I don't go talking about her work like that."

I don't disbelieve in reincarnation, or spirits, or anything. I was willing to believe that a mind could flit from one body to another. And, on the basis of there being more things in heaven and earth than are dreamed of, I was prepared to believe a great deal more was possible. As Beltov had said, there were things beyond even our power to imagine them.

"Perhaps now would be a good time for you to tell me the whole story," I said.

Chapter Fifteen: Ross's Story

"This happened towards the end of the war. In '17, my squadron was stationed in Egypt. There was a hiatus after Romani, and command were trying to decide what to do with us, shove us into France or keep us in theatre.

"I longed to go home to defend London. We had read about the Zeppelin and Gotha raids. I was convinced it was my fate to crash my machine into a German airship and save London. I did not understand why it did not happen. We were left in limbo, near Cairo. I took myself off and found quarters out on the edge of the wilderness, miles from the aerodrome.

"There was a craze for cards then, mainly *vingt-et-un*. As men do in wartime, we played for high stakes. Money is a joke when you don't know if you'll be around next week, and they were gambling away a year's wages in an evening. If you were anywhere near the mess, someone would badger you to join in a game, and I had decided to quit. It wasn't that I lost money. I couldn't stop winning it. They said I had the luck of the devil. When anyone wins too often, a suspicion hovers over them. I've never cheated at cards in my life, and I didn't care to be thought of as a cheat. So, I found my own lodgings.

"I had a motorbike, a Brough Superior. When my duties were done, I could leave the camp behind me. It was a world away, in the quiet of the desert, but I could get back to camp in seven minutes. My unspoken status gave me privilege. Survival in the air is all luck. If you survive the first encounter, you will keep surviving. Eight out of ten never see the machine that shoots them down. After your first blooding, you are the old hand, and your enemies are the frightened pups. Becoming an ace is no harder than cutting cards and calling high or low, though the stakes are higher. Nobody grudged my eccentric lodgings.

"My billet was a tumbledown old mosque, or the ruin of one. The roof had gone, and I pitched my tent inside the prayer hall. On the outside, the walls looked like much of the rest of Cairo, but inside the lower courses were flat Roman bricks. I'm no archaeologist, but I could tell that those bricks were laid on older foundations.

"Before it was a mosque, the building was a temple. They worshipped some heathen deity there a thousand years before the Prophet's name had ever been heard of in these parts. I could lie on my back, smoking and watching the stars wheel overhead, listening to the insects in the night.

"It was an empty, godforsaken place, beside a wadi that was used as the town dump. That was no coincidence. The local worthies called the place cursed, and thought it was a fit place to empty their ash-cans.

"The days were brutal. Heat-shimmer danced all around the horizon. If it had not been for the aeroplanes, I should have thought myself the last man on earth.

"Rocks the size of skulls were scattered everywhere. Human skulls, cow skulls, dog skulls, white warnings of mortality. The only vegetation was a type of sparse yellow grass and scrubby acacia bushes with more thorns than leaves. In England, you don't realise that water is precious as diamonds. In the desert, you learn its true value and rejoice in the sheer blessing of every scrap of greenery. Every growing thing is a hymn to creation, and every flower is purest music. In England, you have a million plants and flowers, and you never notice them until it's winter, and they've gone.

"I liked it for the peace—rubbish dumps in the desert don't smell. The wadi was dry as a bone, and the rubbish desiccated rather than decaying. Household refuse mummified in the desert air, with only a few hardy rats to pick through it.

"After a time, I also found that there was a pair of sand-coloured cats with pale underbellies in residence. They prowled the rocks by the wadi, or lay in the shade, their tails flicking gently. I watched them, and they watched me.

"There were sparrows, no different to the ones in London, and sometimes hoopoes, small striped birds with comical crests. Mainly, there were vultures. They stretched out crucified wings and hung in the sky for hours, circling endlessly. The only time they were not on patrol was when a great squabbling crowd of them gathered around fresh pickings on the rubbish heap.

"One day, I found an emaciated old man sweeping out my quarters with a whisk broom. He said he was the attendant or caretaker or watchman for the mosque. I never learned his name. I called him Uncle, which is semi-polite address. He called me Emir, a high honorific. I first assumed it was because I was a British officer, but I later found he had no idea who the British were.

"I was learning Arabic, and I used him to practice. He was not talkative. He had lost the habit of human conversation. But he was patient. Much of his talk was about the desert, the winds, and the spirits that he saw. He lived more in the world of dreams than the world of men. There was a word, too, which he repeated several times which was not in any of my dictionaries: *Judwali,* and he struck his chest when he said it. But it was not his name.

"I gave him small coins. He must have had a shack somewhere nearby, and I suppose he spent the money on bread or whatever he lived on.

"One night, I was woken by a commotion outside. Expecting robbers, I went out with my revolver and a lantern. Better to face them in the open than let them get to throat-cutting distance.

"I found the old man leading a group of others in a dance, ululating and clapping their hands as they went, under the rising moon. My two cats watched from the gateposts. I observed this display from the shadows for some time. The old man saw me and gestured for me to join in, but I held back. There was something in his look I did not like. After a while, I returned to my bed.

"That night, I dreamed a strange dream. I was in Cairo, but it was the Cairo of the Pharaohs. Everything was the same, the pyramids and the brooding sphinx under the same yellow moon, but it was a different age. A great procession was making its way from boats on the Nile, with banners and musicians, and the main body was of hooded dancers performing curious ritual gestures. And at their head was the old man who lived by me in the rubbish dump, his head shaved, in the costume of a high priest. I danced with them and followed along, and the stars wheeled above us.

"It was a vivid dream, and I remember it all. I remember the crossed leather straps on my sandals. I remember the feel of the ground at every step.

"Dawn was a crimson stain on the sky. There was no sign of the old man, but I soon found the tracks in the sand from where they had been dancing all night. I followed them around and around. It seemed to me that there was something of the utmost importance. Something I had known in my dream, but which I had lost hold of between sleeping and waking. Not for my life, but for humanity. In that dream, I had a mission which I must fulfil.

"The tracks followed a spiral path that led across the wadi. On the other side, a gang of the vultures was tearing at something with their beaks and claws. The old man had dreamed his last dream.

"I was greatly troubled by this. Nobody had a ready explanation for it. I asked around the mosques, and in the marketplace. Nobody knew anything, except for one Imam who spat when I mentioned the word 'Judwali.'

"I kept asking stall holders, beggars, water sellers, porters, and that ever-present, ever-helpful class of 'guide' who appears whenever a white man is alone in a bazaar.

"Money finds a way. For a fee, one such guide took me to a storyteller, and I sat in front of him,

cross-legged on the ground next to our cups of tea. There was some dickering. The story I wanted was *haram*, forbidden, and he could not tell it. I put down more coins for him, and increased my guide's fee. The storyteller agreed to tell me, just once.

"And, when he had carefully placed the coins in a leather purse, the storyteller cleared his throat. There once was a wise sage brought before the great sultan Haroun Al-Raschid. The sultan demanded to know the essence of human nature. The sage could not explain in words, but danced in front of the Sultan. This was the dance of the Four Kings.

"The Sultan's followers thought their ruler was being ridiculed, and the sage was put to death. But the Sultan saw that the sage's footprints had left a pattern in the sand. He perceived that the secret was contained in these markings. He ordered scholars to make sense of them. The scholars spent many years on this. They went mad, one by one, but afterwards, they became wandering teachers. They founded a school known as Judwali, which means diagrammatists.

"The story said that the explanation was this: the pattern of the dance was a gyre—not a circle, but a spiral. It starts at a point and increases steadily in size until it reaches its maximum extent. Then, it diminishes again until it reaches a single point. Then, it becomes the start of another gyre. This pattern came not from men but was learned from the djinn of the desert.

"The gyre is a map of human existence, of all existence. Once you have discovered the movement of a human soul on its gyre and discovered its geometry, you can trace the gyre back or forward to any point in time. The storyteller said that the gyre was the pyramid, and the pyramid was the gyre, rising from a wide base to its point. It originated not with humans, but with the gods long before man walked the earth. This was long before the Prophet. The story was blasphemous, and I should be ashamed of myself for forcing him to recite it. He became abusive. I calmed him down with more coins. He went off to cleanse himself at the mosque, muttering pieties.

"Hardly anyone else would admit to having heard of the Judwali. A Coptic priest told me they were a tribe of wandering madmen, marked by the devil for his own, and that only Christ offered salvation. A Cabalist said they were cursed, that they had been trapped by their own magic; she offered induction into a secret society, for a price. I declined both.

"There were traces, though, just traces, which I kept following. One day I saw children playing in the dust. They had marked out a spiral path and moved pebbles along it. The game was called Mehem. It was a child's game. Everyone knew it, but they said it had no significance. But Mehem is the snake in the work known as *The Enigmatic Book of the Netherworld*—it's enigmatic because it is written in code. Mehem is a protector, similar to the alchemical Ouroboros, the snake which bites its tail, in the West... such were the scraps I gleaned that sustained me in the quest.

"I could not give up my mission. Money found the way. As I spent more, a network of informers and agents grew around me, spreading like the roots of a plant. They offered me interviews with madmen, trinkets inscribed with odd symbols, and mouldering books. The best of these was a work by Catholic scholars, a sustained attack on Rosicrucian book called *The Mirror of Angels*, itself long suppressed or destroyed. The good priests quoted or paraphrased sections of the banned work in their zeal to show its errors. They gave me the clues I needed: old Egyptian names, referring to papyri known only by reputation.

"It was an impossible quest. But I have always been lucky. My agents, fuelled by my winnings from the card table, scoured the markets and brought back the gleanings. Dry scrolls that cracked and split as they were unrolled, hieroglyphs undeciphered for millennia, and variation after variation of coiled snakes, snail shells, geometric patterns, gyres.

"I quickly grasped the elements. The hieroglyphs opened themselves to me, offered themselves, spilled meaning from the page. I knew them. I read them as easily as I read a newspaper.

"I had never considered reincarnation. But I knew this place. And I could translate texts that had baffled scholars for centuries. When I needed to refer to a passage in the *Book of the Dead,* it was as familiar as the Bible—no, as familiar as a flight manual. The passage of the soul through the afterlife is as simple as an engine schematic—the flow, the pistons and chambers, it was as though I was looking at engineering diagrams—so simple, so complex in elaboration.

"I was getting closer to the truth. Each time I tried to grasp it, it slipped through my fingers. Every time I thought 'yes, now I understand it,' the thought drained from me like water into the sand.

"By this time, the war was long over, and I was back in England. I found books—others had fragments of the *Mirror of Angels,* the *Book of Thoth* and the *Book of Moons,* and others, and tried to fill in the gaps in different ways. I brushed up against secret societies and queer religious sects. Odd, wild-eyed Egyptians adrift in London. Masters of sacred geometry fled from the Freemasons, desperate to babble their story to anyone who would listen and scratch out twisted gyres on café napkins. There is a whole hidden world if you look for it, and most of it half-mad, reading books that crumble into gibberish.

"Fortunately, I was with Ellen. Her project, Marie Stopes's project, was a welcome distraction for me. I loved her sense of purpose. Ellen's sense of mission was as strong as my own. You can disappear entirely into this sort of thing if you let yourself. Mysticism will float you out of your world. Ellen tethered me firmly in this one. There were always speeches to be typed and pamphlets to distribute. I needed the outside world to remain sane.

"In hindsight, perhaps that was why I stopped making progress. I clung on to sanity and the everyday world. If I had let it go, I could have understood more. Sanity held me back like a mooring rope. I hacked at it until I freed myself… and Ellen became alarmed, and I was committed to that place. Thanks to this Dr Nye, it seems.

"I sank into a black misery. I knew that I would never be able to get out, never be able to complete the gyre. Never fulfil my destiny.

"The doctors tried to persuade me that I was, or had been, mad. That my mission was a delusion, or an illusion. That all my gyres were confabulations, mistakes, misreadings. Sometimes I believed them. Sometimes, I did not know what to believe. It did not make any difference, though, in the end: my life was over. There was nothing for me except days of boredom and nights of terror.

"And… a temptation.

"You know the *Book of the Dead*? Or rather the *Book of Going Forth by Day*? It's a work of magic, a set of spells that are only useful when you're already in the other life. According to traditional Egyptian belief, once you die, you go through a series of trials, and you must get past all sorts of monsters. The book gives you the words and the tricks you need avoid them or subdue them. And to pass the final challenge, you must have your heart weighed against an ostrich feather.

"If your heart weighs more than an ostrich feather, the Necrosaceriliac, a monster called Ammit, eats it, and your soul is destroyed forever.

"That may seem harsh. But according to the arrangement in our own church everyone goes to hell, even the good ones, unless they know the right formula: 'Our Father, Who art in heaven,' and all that. And perhaps they are just two different versions of the same thing.

"The knowledge was originally restricted to the pharaohs alone. The pharaoh was supposed to be a god, an incarnation of Horus, replaced by another incarnation of Horus each time, though some, such as Imhotep, were identified with other gods. They were the agents on Earth of divine power... But at some point, the knowledge was shared. First the priests and then the aristocracy were let into the secret.

"Knowing it as I did—and I have the whole work off by heart—I knew how to survive the afterlife. I could get through all the tests, dodge Ammit, and get through to the other side. A door that leads to heaven, another to metempsychosis, the transmigration of souls. Reincarnation back on Earth.

"If I killed myself, I could get through and have another go. It seemed like such a sensible idea. That was when the night terrors started. Death, the afterlife, the underworld, Ammit... It ended differently each time, but I never made it through.

"I would have killed myself, though, or I thought I would. Other men have died in those cells, I know that.

"And then, this huge fellow turns up and says I'm being rescued. And suddenly, I had a second chance in this life."

Chapter Sixteen: Into the Gyre

Having been in the business of recovering debts, I had been to a good many banks. I have had occasion to accompany debtors when they cashed cheques, having learned long ago that this is the only way of ensuring payment.

I knew also that, while it might embarrass the party concerned, you need to accompany them closely, and not simply wait outside the bank for them to emerge with the readies. The temptation to slip out another way and make a fool of the debt collector is too strong for many to resist.

I was therefore reasonably familiar with the process of cashing a cheque, and I was equally aware that there might be some difficulty with Ross's. The clerk, wearing a wing collar that looked even more old-fashioned on a young man, went away and came back a minute later.

"I am aware of Mr Ross's situation," I said. "However, his creditors are less interested in his mental condition than his financial obligations."

"I'm afraid this account has been suspended," said the clerk.

"Of course," I said. "But the date on this cheque predates his regrettable lapse into being *non compos mentis*."

"That is so," he said. Of course, he knew as well as I did that the cheque might have been written yesterday.

"And, being as he was of sound mind when he wrote the cheque, I can reasonably expect it to be honoured." I said this in as mild and unthreatening a manner as I could. I had no wish to be heavy-handed and hoped to win out by force of reason.

In truth, I did not know the legal niceties of the situation any more than Ross did, and the easiest way to find out was to try the experiment. While it would have been foolish for him to expose himself in such a manner, someone turning up at a bank to cash one of his cheques would be unlikely to attract much interest or set off alarm bells.

"Can you wait here?"

"Of course. I can wait all day if there's specie at the end of it," I assured him.

Affecting casualness, I took the letter from my pocket. Hoade had been prompt in the extreme, though his replies were characteristically terse. He dispensed with the "Dear Mr Stubbs, regarding your enquiry of the 15th…" in favour of a series of brief notes. The biographical data on Dr Nye yielded some idea of his career; what stood out was the rapid rate of his rise and the speed at which he produced new research.

I learned also that the sphinx is a mythical creature that originated in Egypt. They had the body of a lion, as human head, and sometimes the wings of an eagle and the tail of a serpent. Recumbent sphinxes guarded temples, and upright sphinxes guarded the Pharaoh, always in pairs. They were depicted on two legs or four. Sphinx is a Greek term meaning "strangler"; in Egyptian, they are known as "living images," for reasons which were not explained. The sphinxes at Crystal Palace were exact copies of the Tanis sphinx in the Louvre, though the hieroglyphics were not on the original and were added by the artist. The goddess Hera sent the Greek sphinx, which was female, to plague Thebes, killing travellers who could not answer a riddle, invulnerable against all attempts to kill it until ill-fated Oedipus came along. The sphinx became an emblem of silent wisdom but was also feared, hence the Egyptian nickname "father of terror."

Hoade's notes were brief but gave me something to chew over in the twenty minutes it took for the clerk to carry out his enquiries. With an unchanged facial expression, he asked for my name and address, and whether I had any means of identifying myself. I doubted very much whether anything I could provide would pass muster, but on an impulse, I told him he could check with the solicitors Latham & Rowe. Even though I was no longer in their employ, my relations with the firm were cordial, and they would verify my identity.

The clerk went away again, and I could see him standing in a far corner, talking into a telephone and looking at me. For once, my distinctive appearance might actually count in my favour. There are not many people who can be positively and uniquely identified by a simple verbal description, but I felt I fell into that category.

Miss Bentham was the legal controller of Ross's assets. She had said she would not give him any more assistance. If she was on the end of one of those phone calls, would she actively hinder him? I thought not; I hoped not.

Ross's funds lay in a sort of limbo. That would have been behind the bank's calculations. Would withholding payment be more trouble in the long run, if Ross had outstanding debts and they stood between the creditor and the money? On the other hand, what was the likelihood of anyone raising a stink if they were to make a questionable payment?

Ross and I assumed that the bank would decide to pay up. The call to Latham and Rowe should be the final link in the chain, assuming that was who he was calling.

A distinctive appearance may also be a liability. The clerk might equally well be calling the police, who would no doubt have a description of me as the attendant who had helped Ross escape. I had also unthinkingly given my real name to the bank clerk, although if I had not done so, it would have been impossible to substantiate my identity.

My brain performed a number of these loops as I waited, and I struggled to stop myself from looking round for a squad of officers coming in through the door. Technically, I did not think that I was committing a fraud myself, but I was taking a chance. If I bolted for the door, I could be away before anyone had a chance of stopping me. Staying there was a gamble that I could not afford to lose.

However, a cool head won the day, and I stayed there, though I may not have appeared quite so relaxed. The clerk came back at last, seemingly satisfied with my bona fides.

"What denomination notes will you be requiring for payment, Mr Stubbs?"

"Ones and fives, please," I told him, leaving him to figure out a suitable ratio.

I then realised that I did not have a suitable receptacle for the bundle of notes. As casually as I could, I folded the wad and stuffed it into my jacket pocket, as though it was no great matter and that I was used to dealing with far more significant sums.

Back at the house, Ross was elated. Everything was possible with money.

"Splendid work!" he said, fanning out the pile of money. He immediately set out on a shopping spree, conducted remotely by telephone and by messenger boys. He sent out to tailors and bootmakers and others, and insisted on including me.

"No, really," I said, "I can send to my landlady's if I need any more clothes."

"Rubbish," he said. "You lost your job at the hospital for me. It's my treat."

"He's very generous," I said later to Maggie, as she was arranging a huge bouquet of flowers, his gift to her.

"He always was," she said. "A selfless little boy, always thinking of others. Not like some of the others Mrs Ross had—little scamps and villains, some of them!"

"And he flew in the war," I said. It was clumsy probing, but she was oblivious. "An actual air ace."

"He sent a picture postcard of the pyramids," she said, and I would bet you that postcard stood on her mantelpiece in a place of honour. "We were so frightened we'd never see him again. So many boys from his squadron never did come back." She moved some carnations.

"And that was how he met his fiancée," I said.

"Yes," she said and succeeded in conveying resigned disapproval in a single syllable. That seemed like a good point to end the inquisition.

I had half-wondered if Ross would change his plans once he was in possession of the money. A man who has been incarcerated for a while might want to enjoy his freedom.

"We process the gyre," he said. "I've done the calculations. We're going to do the whole damn thing, from beginning to end in one go."

Ross had explained the ritual spiral processions and shown me diagrams. The smallest could be completed indoors; others carried on for several miles. The largest of all, the Grand Procession, took several days and nights to complete. It was best carried out in a desert or other flat, featureless area, because there could be no deviation from the path without breaking the ritual.

I found it hard to imagine how it could be done in London, or anywhere apart from the Sahara, the steppes, the Arctic or some other wasteland. "That hardly sounds possible," I said.

"We have some advantages over the Pharaohs," he said. "They had slaves carrying palanquins, and horses and chariots and camels. But lying in my roofless mosque, looking up at the vultures circling the rubbish tip, I knew there was an easier way."

"Is it possible?" I asked. For the first time, I had a flicker of a doubt about Ross's sanity. Taken individually, his ideas about the power of spirals, the ancient cult of the diagrammatists, and even the link to reincarnation, made some sort of sense. But he was pushing it to absurdity. Using an aircraft was like performing a magic trick with a telephone.

"Nobody has ever flown a gyre in an aeroplane before," he said. "So, there's only one way to find out if it works."

The next afternoon found us at Croydon aerodrome. It looked like the newsreels. A big tower held several clock faces on it, all showing different times around the world. Planes were landing and taking off constantly; I imagined they were full of noted aviators and glamourous travellers, movie stars and opera singers, politicians and business tycoons. I did not see anyone famous, but Ross pointed out the hangar where Amy Johnson's plane was stored.

Ross had bought himself an aircraft, simple as that. It was a cash deal sealed with a handshake, as easy as purchasing a second-hand bicycle. The seller was a flyer whom Ross evidently knew by reputation and trusted.

I was walking round with him as he inspected his new purchase.

"Of course, it's mad," said Ross. "Because magic is madness. That's almost the definition of it. The ordinary mind, the sane mind, revolts at the thought of doing the impossible and cannot go further. But the magician—the madman—goes beyond that. Instead of being deflected, he matches his will against the world, and bends it. 'Magic is the Science and Art of causing Change to occur in conformity with Will.'"

"The madmen I have encountered do not bear that theory out," I said.

"I'm not saying that madness is magic, just that magic is madness," he said, loosening a nut with a spanner and peering into the space behind a hatch. "You have to disconnect the part of your brain that provides common sense and reach beyond."

"Deliberately drive yourself mad, in other words," I said.

"If you like," he said. "Let's get you some overalls. I don't think I can do this on my own."

My lack of knowledge was no defence. Ross said all he wanted was a pair of hands, and long arms and decent muscles were a bonus. In short order, I was drafted as a mechanic's assistant and was helping him dismantle some vital part of the engine.

Ross said it would not take more than a few minutes, but three hours later we were still at it, breaking only for tea and bacon rolls from the aerodrome canteen.

"There's a malign influence at work in the hospital," I said, holding a metal cover like a giant pot lid. "What my associate described as a tiger, and which may or may not have human form. It may or may not be Dr Nye himself."

"Those two fellows who came for Ryan sounded human," said Ross.

"Perhaps," I said. Privately, I entertained some doubt about how human they were under those long coats. To claim that someone is inhuman because of the way he seems to walk, seen from a distance at night, is a stretch. It was difficult to explain this to one who had not been there, though Ross was the most sympathetic of listeners. "And whatever it is, it can kill people inside locked cells or offices," I said. "Gillespy and Hooper and Beltov."

"They all died in different ways," said Ross. "And we don't know for sure whether they were all murdered. Also, why am I still alive? You seem to think this Dr Nye takes an especial interest in me."

I had to admit that I had a great many questions and no very substantial answers. Positing an enemy who could attack through solid walls, and whose killings could look like accidents, natural causes, or suicide meant that any death could be a murder. This perhaps is what they mean by the road to madness.

One immediate project was getting that reel of film back before Bellingham could start showing it to more people. That was a challenge in itself.

The chief mission, though, had to be confronting Nye. The *Phantom of the Cinema* was his doing: he had persuaded or encouraged Beltov to extract the mental images recorded by the Sarcophagus. Perhaps he even had an inkling, or more than an inkling, of what effect those images would have on the man who copied them. It looked like a deliberate attempt to multiply madness.

If I did that, though, Nye might simply laugh at me and say I was imagining things, before sacking me—or having me committed. Or, he might get his minions to follow and murder me, in a locked room if need be.

I would need some kind of weapon or tool to tackle Nye, and Ross was the only card I held. Nye had Ross committed and kept him in the asylum without killing him. That surely meant he had other plans. Ross was in some way special to him.

"What happens when you complete this grand gyre?" I asked.

"I don't know," said Ross, "but afterwards, I should have some clue about what I'm supposed to be doing. Some kind of… cosmic direction. I'll find out what I've been put on this earth for. Haven't you ever wondered what all this is for?"

I suppose we have all asked ourselves that in some form or other, but the question comes more naturally to some than others. My pa always said you had to do your bit, whether it was helping your family, your friends, or your country, and that pulling your weight was what mattered in life. Maybe it was not the sort of philosophy they teach at Oxford, but it had always stood me in good stead. People like Ross, though, they seemed to want something more.

"I suppose the Creator knows what he's doing," I said.

"Well, now's your chance to find out," he said. "You'll come with me, won't you?"

That stopped me in my tracks. I had not thought for a moment that there was a possibility. I had never been up in an aeroplane. I had seen them at Crystal Palace and elsewhere often enough, but rides were expensive, and I always had misgivings about my bulk in such a lightweight craft.

"It's a two-seater," he pointed out helpfully. "You might find it an interesting experience, especially as you've never been up before. And I need another pair of eyes."

"What for?" I asked, though I had some idea.

"Bandits," he said. "Or God knows what. But I can't help feeling that I'm not going to be allowed to get away with it this easily."

It struck me that if anything was going to happen, then it was not advisable to be in the plane, and he sensed my doubt.

"It would make a world of difference to have you along," he said. "You could keep an eye out and cover the rear hemisphere."

A biplane flew past a few hundred feet overhead, buzzing like an outraged bumblebee, leaving a faint trail of vapour behind. It seemed like a frail thing of paper and wooden struts, held together with wires. And we were facing unknown forces with unknown powers.

"Name your price, Harry. You can have anything you want—even unto half my kingdom." He looked away then looked back. "It would be an awful shame for me to get this far and not make it just because you weren't watching my back."

If Ross was to crash, I would be left stranded, without a clue on how to proceed, and the case would come to a halt.

If I could get over the embarrassment of having helped him to escape, I could start again with my life, which would mean asking Arthur Renville for assistance. Though, of course, if he died, my having helped him would be that much more awkward; his fiancée Miss Bentham would hold me responsible. More seriously, there was the possibility that the enemy who pursued him would be on my tail. Gillespy, who had been on the same mission, had ended up driven mad. I could only guess what had befallen Ryan.

"If you really think I can make a difference," I said, "you can count on me."

"I knew I could," he said. "Don't worry, I won't crash. I'm famous for my good luck, in the air and on the ground."

An hour later, Ross was satisfied that everything was set. He took a last look at his flight plan—a collection of diagrams, lists of speeds and bearings—rolled it up, and stuffed it into an inner pocket. I noticed then that a rolled-up piece of paper, like a scroll, was also a sort of spiral; and so was a film in a canister. Then, Ross grinned at me and scrambled up into the cockpit. "Go on, fire her up," he said.

I had expected we would take this by stages, assure ourselves that the plane was sound, and have a test flight, but Ross was nervous. He suspected, or his intuition warned him, that our time was limited, and Nye's agents, human or otherwise, would be closing in on us soon.

I took hold of the wooden propeller in both hands and gave it a good shove round. The engine caught immediately, and the unexpected noise of it was something shocking: it was like standing in the middle of a hundred motorcycles with broken silencers, all at full throttle.

Ross revved the engine a couple of times then gave me the thumbs-up sign. I removed the wheel chocks, dragged them a short distance away as I had been instructed, then climbed gingerly up to the rear cockpit.

Like everything else, it was designed for a smaller man, and I did not at all like the way the plane rocked as I clambered into it. We sat on the tarmac for some considerable time while the engines warmed up, and I had a chance to observe the comings and goings around the airport. A twin-engine passenger plane had newly arrived from Le Bourget, and a ladder was being wheeled out to meet it. As I watched, well-dressed men and two women descended, while porters were already swarming around at the back of the plane getting their luggage. The pilot and co-pilot were on the ground already, shaking hands with the departing passengers.

Then the plane lurched, and we were off, turning in a tight circle and taxiing for the runway. A man with two flags like a traffic policeman waved us on, and we motored down to the end of the runway and executed a turn. Then we were waiting again, I suppose while Ross made some final checks. I donned the leather flying helmet and goggles and buttoned up my new flying jacket. I kept getting wafts of exhaust fumes as the side-winds caught them.

It was the delays that made it all so nerve-shredding. Dusk was falling; Ross wanted a night flight under the stars. I badly wanted it over with.

The engine pitch went up, and the plane moved forward, faster and faster, the ground hurtling past more quickly than anything I had seen, so fast that it literally became a blur unless you turned your head to follow it. The roughness of the runway smoothed out, and I saw that there was nothing but grass beneath us—well beneath us. We flew over fences and hedges, Ross pulled the stick back, and we were on our way.

Ross turned his head to shout at me. It took a couple of attempts to understand him. "She's going well!" he shouted, and gave another thumbs-up in case I had still not heard.

The horizon fell away, an unforgettable sight, and I felt that we truly were ascending into the heavens. It was true exhileration, actual exaltation to a higher state.

The vibration was enough to rattle your teeth, and even in the back the noise practically blotted out everything else. My nose was full of the smell of aviation fuel, but the view was incomparable, even in the fading light. The ground beneath was dark, but there were lights everywhere, lights in houses, lights along the streets, and even the headlights of cars and vans going down Croydon Road.

I struggled to make out landmarks below. Everything looked so strange seen from above, and I had no luck, until I saw the towers of the Crystal Palace off to the north with the glow of the great glass building between them. Apart from that I could not orient myself.

The air blew past in a continuous hurricane. It was impossible to believe that the air was stationary and that it was us that were moving—it felt so much as if we were flying into the teeth of a storm.

A v-shaped formation of birds caught my eye—a skein of migrating geese. I marvelled that we could look down on them from above. In the distance were the moving lights of another aeroplane, and it was a strange experience to be on the same level.

The ground wheeled away as we turned, and then it actually tilted upwards so the horizon was at a thirty-degree angle. Again, it must have been an illusion: centrifugal force was holding me in place. I was tilted, and the earth remained on the level as it always had been.

A faint mist streamed past. There had not been much sign of cloud from the ground, but we had travelled some distance. The wind made the wire vibrate when we went into a turn.

After my initial apprehension, I was beginning to enjoy the experience of flight. It felt like freedom: escaping from the bonds of earth, breaking away from gravity into a new realm of endless possibilities where anything could happen, and the ordinary laws of earthbound life did not apply. Perhaps every flight feels like that, or perhaps it was this mission we were on. I tried to keep my emotions under control; we were here for a serious purpose. I was on sentry duty.

We went higher and higher, feeling lighter and lighter, until I could laugh for the sheer joy of it. The aircraft still felt as fragile as ever—every buffet of the wind made the wings ripple visibly, twisting like a cardboard toy—but it flew beautifully.

As we turned and the wire thrummed again, I kept looking about, wary of anything that might interfere with us but not knowing what to expect... A Fokker triplane with machine guns blazing, or storm clouds summoned out of blue skies by sorcery, or a flight of giant bats with fangs and claws—nothing could have surprised me.

We flew over a translucent sheet of cloud, and to my disappointment, the light-dotted landscape was erased, disappearing under a white film. Still, that narrowed my field of observation. I looked around and directly overhead, where the crown of the sky was unexpectedly dark. The horizon might be pale blue, but up there it was night with stars showing.

Ross steepened the turn, and I had a good view in the fading light of a cloud built like a towering fortress as we passed by. Either we had come farther than I had thought, which was highly possible at over a hundred miles an hour, or the cloud had suddenly grown up out of nowhere like Jack's beanstalk. I wished I knew more about clouds and what they meant. Tall clouds meant storms, I knew that.

Ross was pointing at the cloud and shouting, but I could not make out his words, and he gave up the attempt.

We turned again, and there were two more clouds, great slab-faced icebergs hanging in the sky. We flew in between them, and they seemed to be moving together to cut us off, but Ross pulled back the throttle and we sped through the narrowing gap before it closed.

My eye was drawn to an arrangement of red lights, like the lights that outline a steamer, but they were far above us, and I could not make out the colossal shape which they delineated. Ross pointed at them, too, without bothering to shout.

"There!" I shouted and pointed. Something flitted through the cloud above, beside, and slightly ahead of us. In the fading light, I could not be sure what it was.

Ross nodded, and I looked over my shoulder and tried to see it again, but Ross threw the plane into a sudden and violent manoeuvre. I gripped the sides of the cockpit as I was flung about. A dark-winged shape bigger than an eagle hurtled by, shockingly close and followed by a second. If pressed, I would say they were ungainly mechanical birds, but that was merely an impression. They were jerked out of my field of view as the plane banked and rolled. Ross turned his head, and he was laughing with maniacal glee at having outmaneuvered his opponents.

I twisted around, but they had vanished. From Ross's account of air battles, if they had dived and missed us, they would not catch us again unless he turned to seek combat. Given that we were unarmed, and the slightest contact would break a wire or rip a wing and send us plunging to the ground, I hoped he was heading away as fast as possible.

Whatever had attacked us had failed. I assumed they must have been sent by Nye in a last-ditch attempt to prevent us from getting further. And indeed, they had tried to intercept us at the very boundary of the normal world.

It was no ordinary flight, and as we raced towards a dark cloud, a tunnel, barely wide enough for the plane to pass through, opened in it like a mouth. The curving passage was so narrow that I could see the red-and-green glow from our lights reflected from its surfaces. The material looked too solid and well-defined to be cloud, but there was nothing else it could be.

Ross was vindicated. We had succeeded in processing the gyre just as he had hoped. Mysteries were opening to us, even if I could not understand them.

What happened after that became confused. My actual memory is curiously muted, as though I saw it at one remove. And I have dreamed about that flight so many times that I can no longer rightly distinguish the dreams from the memories. Both are equally strange and unbelievable.

To the best of my recollection, for as veiled and mixed in with the stuff of dreams as it became, we came out of that tunnel, perhaps after several similar passages, into an open space that was dimly lit by a greenish moon, which gave it the appearance of a wooded plain. I could attempt to describe the irregularities which appeared below, and you could try to determine for yourself whether they were natural cloud formations, fabrications of unreliable memory, or something else. Subsequent events make what I saw—or thought I saw—a moot point at best.

I was certain that tall obelisks projected from the cloud surface opposite, and that there were moving figures of men and animals, and lights like yellow torch flames moving with them.

As I looked around to take in the whole vista, I saw the men in white walking down the wing towards me.

Presence of mind had not wholly deserted me, and I shouted for Ross and pointed. He turned as they reached me, and I was hauled up bodily and whirled around.

I landed on my knees, striking my shoulder against something solid that could not have been there. Someone took hold of me—it was Vanstone!—and I shoved him away. There was confused shouting around me, and as Vanstone came at me again, I punched him solidly on the abdomen, then twice more until he fell back.

I reeled from a blow and saw Miller, who looked both elated and frightened. He had finally succeeded in hitting me.

"The needle!" someone shouted.

"Stubbs!" shouted someone else, right in my face. It was Miller, grinning cheerfully and shaking me. "Harry, wake up!"

I pushed him away, trying to make sense of my surroundings. The wind and the roar of the engine were muted and muffled, and another scene was superimposed on my vision. Clouds still rushed past, but at the same time, I was in a room with a solid floor and walls. The cockpit was fading; if I did not get back into the plane at once, it would dissolve altogether. I crawled forward and grabbed the handholds again, but before I could get myself in, strong hands were on me, and I was manhandled by men in white, who blurred and merged with the cloud then became solid and real.

I struck out and tried to free myself before the pain of a cold sting erupted in my arm. Still confused, I felt for it. The flying jacket melted away under my fingers.

Vanstone stood back, no longer a wraith but a substantial being. There was something long and silver in his hand—not a knife, but a hypodermic syringe. I was backed into a corner, and they were all looking at me.

"Don't you know us?" asked Donnelly, standing ready with a straitjacket.

I could see Miller and Vanstone quite clearly, along with another man behind them, who was not dressed in attendant's garb. "Quickly," he said. "Get him under control."

The scene blurred, and the walls behind me dissolved. Wind was rushing past, and I grabbed on to the plane, but I was trying to fight them off at the same time with one hand. Finally, the wind had gone, but shadows still flitted past and through me as I slipped away into unconsciousness. Then, the biplane was gone and the only wings I had were those of a dream.

Chapter Seventeen: Inside

Days in the cell were indistinguishable. The only variation was in the food they brought me, and in the fractional progress of the sunlight through the high window. Each day, the ray of light shifted around a little. Apart from these two things, it could have been the same day, over and over. I tried to keep track of time, but I quickly became confused. As a result of being drugged, my dreams intruded or overlapped with my waking life to start with, and I thought I had woken up more times than I had. After a while, the effect wore off, but the date no longer mattered.

My world entirely consisted of the cell. It was nine and half feet square, walled in cream tiles. The tiles themselves were not identical. I had not been there more than a few hours before I spotted where some of them had been replaced. Linoleum covered the floor, which was much worn around the centre by constant pacing and still with some spring to it out in the farther edges and underneath the bed.

The bed was a heavy iron construction of Victorian vintage, firmly bolted to the floor. For a mattress, it had three cushions, known as biscuits, of heavy canvas packed with coir. They were hard, but not as hard as the iron bedframe.

For sanitary purposes, a grate in one corner led into an open pipe. The smell came and went at different times of the day.

The windows were way up high—the cell's height was its largest dimension by far—and there was the iron door with its spyhole.

There must have been many more secure cells in this world, and no doubt an accomplished escape artist could have been out of there in a day. I might have even been able to think of a course of action myself, but my mind was not running in that direction. Stone walls do not a prison make, as the poet said. Imprisonment and liberty have more to do with mental condition, and my mental condition was poor. My world had been broken, and I could not mend it however long I sat and stared at the tiles.

I had gained a swift understanding of how the inmates felt and why they behaved as they did. They could not mark off days and wait for their sentence to be over. They could not hope to escape, because they had nowhere to escape to; their families had forsaken them. The only thing they had to look forward to was the next mealtime. If they clung on to wisps of their former life, pretending to drive a car, or drag a string instead of a dog's lead, it was because the rituals were comforting reminders of a better world, even if they were without substance. These and a hundred other things became plain to me on my first day of confinement, and I wondered how I could ever have failed to realise them before.

I could follow the course of events from inside my cell. I could hear the shouts and cries from the farther parts of the building as the place woke up each day. At mealtimes, the door in the segregation ward opened and closed, then the squeak-squeak-squeak of the trolley led to the next door, and the same sequence repeated until he got to me. Then, the key turned in the lock and, for a brief minute or two each day, I had company.

The attendants had been uncommunicative at best. Some of them were abusive. They wanted to avoid contamination by whatever madness had dragged me over from their side and into the cell. When it was Miller's turn, he was stony-faced and barely said a word to me. I had always known him as a cheery type, but as he slapped down the water cup I felt actual alarm. I was painfully aware how reliant I was on his goodwill. If he spat on me or kicked me, I could do nothing; no complaint would ever be heard.

Today though, it was Donnelly. Even though I had struck him, I hoped he might take a broader view of things.

"A fine afternoon to you, sir," he said. "Room service: your lunch is rissoles and rhubarb crumble with custard, still good and hot from the kitchen."

"Thank you," I said, keeping still, with my hands down so as not to seem threatening. I raised them slowly to take the tray. "Are you allowed to talk to me?"

"You know me, I'll talk to anyone." His cheer seemed forced.

"Getting me to shut up is the hard part. You're the last in the row, and they won't miss me for five minutes."

"What am I doing here?"

"What is any of us doing here?" The quip was not enough, though, and he added, "I'm not privy to the details, but surely it's connected with your helping Ross to escape, don't you think?"

I settled the tray on my lap and took a drink of water from the tin cup. Your mouth gets very dry when you cannot have water whenever you want it.

"That might be a criminal matter," I said, "but I'm not mad."

"Not for me to say," said Donnelly. "The doctors will explain it all to you in a day or two. Surely, they will."

I spoke carefully. I felt as tentative as a man trying to pick a lock with a twig. "Would you know if the superintendent is aware of my presence here?" With Beltov dead, the superintendent was the one person I felt I might be able to talk to. How many inmates, though, had asked me the same question?

"It wouldn't make any difference if he did or didn't," said Donnelly. "Wherever there's a case in question, he'd ask the doctors, as he's not a medical man himself. And Dr Nye is emphatic."

That was exactly the answer I would have given a few weeks ago—the same one I had given, in fact, almost word for word; I probably learned it from Donnelly. It was all too true. The superintendent had no special reason to take my word. No doubt the paperwork was all there, signed by a magistrate who was happy to accept the word of the esteemed Dr Nye.

A pang of sympathy seemed to strike Donnelly, the first inkling I had that he saw me as a pathetic figure rather than a menacing one.

"Sure, we know Ross is loaded and you were only going along with him for the money," he said. "I don't blame you a bit myself. Judging by that house, he's not short of a few coppers. But Dr Nye is... He doesn't like it. He thinks you've been infected, like all those others following FitzRoy. Once you set the record straight, you'll be out of here."

"What about Ross?"

Donnelly shrugged. "He's not far away from us now." I took that to mean he was also in the segregation wing. "He's quiet."

"Where did you find him?"

"Did that stuff spoil your memory?" he asked with genuine concern. Sometimes patients were confused and suffered amnesia after a dose of a sedative. "He was there in the same room with you. Playing aeroplanes."

"He was a pilot," I said.

"You do remember!" Donnelly's face lit up. "And I thought we might have addled your brains. Dr Nye measured out the dose, and I swear he put enough in there to knock out an elephant. Glad to hear there's no lasting effects. Anyroad, got to be going now." Satisfied that I was in something like my right mind, but evidently not keen to prolong the conversation, Donnelly backed out. The key turned in the lock, once, twice. The wheel of the trolley squeaked, and he was back on his rounds.

My stomach gurgled, reminding me how hungry I was, and I set to the rissoles with an appetite. My ma would have been ashamed to serve them, as there was so little meat among the stodgy potato. The runner beans with them were stringy, too, but everything is a feast to a famished man. I polished it all off in no time, and the rhubarb crumble did not take much longer.

Being on my own and unobserved, I licked the plate clean of the sweet custard and tart rhubarb juice. I was still hungry, but less so than I had been. Things looked slightly better on a stomach that was, if not full, not quite so empty. The situation was still desperate.

At least Donnelly had talked to me, but he had spoken to me as though I was an inmate, not a former colleague. The free-and-easy manner had been replaced with that guarded tone adopted when talking to a lunatic. And he had confirmed my suspicions.

There was a discrepancy between the version of events I had experienced with Ross and what everyone else saw. Common sense insisted that the flight had been a dream or a hallucination of some sort, but the facts and details kept presenting them to me. If I accepted what Donnelly said—and of course I had to—then they had found me indoors, "playing at aeroplanes."

By that account, the whole flight must have been a waking dream, like the storm at sea that had seen me blundering about and breaking roof slates from underneath. What about the man that Ross had bought the plane from—might he remember something?

We must have dreamed him as well. I wanted desperately to go to the aerodrome and see whether it matched my memory, even though I already knew that it was futile.

It seemed so real. That phrase kept floating back to me. *It seemed so real.* It was not like my earlier experience with the storm, where real life had overlapped with my dreaming and where I could separate the two. With the flight, I could not unpick what had happened and what had not.

The flight, however, was only part of a much larger problem relating to my mental condition. It had unfolded in the manner of a train wreck happening in stages. The locomotive runs into an obstacle on the tracks. At first, it seems to have escaped damage, but then the heavy freight cars behind start slamming into it, and the whole train crumples up like a concertina. The train was me. As long as I kept going forward, I had been fine, but then all my past and all those mad adventures began to catch up with me. At the time, I had been grateful to survive them, but their momentum and the freight-load of implications they carried was beginning to crush me, and I could not get out of the way.

The Shackleton affair, the Roslyn D'Onston case, and the Horniman investigation each trailed a long streamer of unanswered questions about what I thought was real and what I might have imagined. As long as there were others such as Yang or Skinner or Ross, who would more or less go along with the same narrative as myself, we could travel along together, shielded from the disbelieving world.

I had never before seriously doubted myself and my own sanity. Perhaps I lacked the intelligence or the imagination to consider the possibility. A mirror was being held up to me, and I was being forced to take a long, hard look at my actions. Evaluating your life from the vantage point of an asylum cell is not a pleasant experience. Even what is good in your life is soured from that view, because it all led to that cell in that place. Everything that seemed promising is revealed as false hope and self-deception. Everything bad looks like inevitable steps towards a bad end.

Nor does it get any better with time: as day adds to day, each one lays down a hard layer of regret, guilt, and confusion, building up like lacquer into a shell that becomes more impenetrable each day.

In that situation, you do not need anyone else to torment you: every man is his own torturer in that cell.

However, my morose inactivity was interrupted the very next day after Donnelly brought me lunch. Miller and Vanstone came to escort me to see a doctor.

I was braced for an encounter with Dr Nye himself, but instead was ushered into Dr Hamilton's office. The two attendants waited outside, ready to intervene, but the psychologist seemed quite relaxed, moving a few papers around his desk as I took a seat. It felt strange to be sitting down there, in one of the doctor's rooms, but then it felt more than a little peculiar to have left the cell at all.

"Well, well, well," he said, and you could hear the soft Edinburgh burr in his voice, before finally looking up at me. "Mr Stubbs. This is a most unusual situation. I hardly need to tell you that. What I would be most interested to hear would be your point of view. Would you like to elaborate upon the events that led up to your being here?" He was warm and sympathetic, an unlit pipe in his hand. The beard, perhaps, helped by masking the expression of his mouth and placing all the emphasis on those open blue eyes. "Tell me anything you like," he said. "I'm not asking you to incriminate yourself. I'd like to understand your thought processes a little better—maybe get you to understand them a little better, too."

Dr Beltov used to have a glass clock above his mantelpiece. Dr Hamilton had little figurines, elongated hunters and warriors and dancers, carved out of dark wood. They were African; Donnelly said that Hamilton had worked out in the Gambia for a spell. I tried to remember what Dr Beltov had said about Hamilton. I recalled that he was a Jungian, whatever that meant, and a follower of William James, and Beltov thought Hamilton was not sufficiently sceptical of telepathy and psychic phenomena. That was not enough, however, to tempt me into telling the full story.

I am no good at lying, but I had decided to follow the line that Donnelly had suggested. Ross had offered me a great deal of money if I helped him, I explained, and that was quite true. The offer had only come well after I had already rescued him, but I omitted that in my account.

I told him about the escape, Ross's experiences in Egypt, and his desire to complete his peculiar spiral pilgrimage. Dr Hamilton's brow furrowed while I was talking, and he made me go back and describe parts of it over and over again. He made no notes but sat with his hands clasped ostentatiously behind his head, the stem of the unlit pipe gripped between his teeth, in the manner of a listener rather than a doctor.

"And what did you think when he told you all this?"

"I like to keep an open mind," I said.

"Even so, reincarnation and ancient pharaohs and mysterious Egyptian sages." His tone was gently chiding, trying to get me to see how silly it all sounded. "It sounds more like something you'd see down at the cinema on a Saturday morning, doesn't it?"

That of course reminded me of something else. "Did you hear about that cinema reel?" I asked. "And Eric Woods, the projectionist."

"I'd be very interested to hear about it from you," he said, not put off by my change in direction.

I tried to give him as good an account as I could for a story told backwards, tracing the incident of the *Phantom of the Cinema* backwards from the picture house to the projectionist, then to Tom Reynolds, the photographer of the extraordinary and his source back here in the hospital. Finally, I offered my conclusions about the apparatus known as the sarcophagus.

"That has a bit of a flavour of Old Egypt about it too, doesn't it?" he said.

"Could it be true?" I asked. "Can you really extract images from someone's brain like that and project them on a screen?"

Hamilton chewed his pipe thoughtfully before replying.

"Have you come across any of Dr Nye's work on magnetic treatment?" he asked.

I shook my head.

"You were quite intimate with Dr Beltov, I believe. Did he ever discuss Dr Nye with you?"

Another shake.

"And you know, of course, that it was Dr Nye who committed Ross."

"I did know that," I admitted.

"And the Faradisation treatment, which Dr Easton says you found so objectionable—you knew that was Dr Nye's? Somehow, he seems a recurrent theme in your story."

He waited a moment, a trick that I was beginning to recognise. Leaving a silence is always a good way of prompting the other party to say more than they mean to. Silence can be better and more insistent than the most pointed question; it leaves the listener to answer the question in their mind.

"I don't know," I said, a little defensively. I had not mentioned Nye once, but somehow his absence left a lot of Nye-shaped holes in the story, which were as significant as if I had come in shouting that he was a fiend.

"Hmm-mm." Hamilton reached down and placed an open book in front of me, flicking away the tissue cover of a glossy illustration. "Take a look at this for me, will you? Tell me what you think that is?"

It was a symmetrical black-and-white shape, which at first looked like nothing but spilled ink. The caption said simply, "Plate Seven." It was one of those images made by folding the paper over; this one might have been the silhouette of a flattened moth, or at least a moth and a bee both squashed together, and that was what I said.

Hamilton made a non-committal noise and turned over another page, and again flicked the protective cover away. It was another winged silhouette, with a trunk and limbs that might have belonged to a squat human. The head was all wrong though, oddly shaped and with a mass of fronds or feelers radiating from it.

"What is this book?" I asked.

"The inkblots were originally developed by a Swiss gentleman named Rorschach," said Hamilton, taking the pipe from his mouth. "The set we have here are an evolution of his set." He hardly needed to say that Dr Nye was the mind behind them. "We use them to diagnose certain types of patients. Some of these resonate with the subconscious mind of patients with… particular pathologies. Now, what does this picture suggest to you?"

"I couldn't say. A sort of imaginary monster, I suppose," I said.

"Yes, it could be that," he said, in an encouraging tone.

Hamilton flicked over several more pages and unveiled Plate Thirteen. This time I recognised it at once. The image on the page was nothing; it might have been an old tree stump with a few twisting branches and projecting roots. But there was no mistaking its identity, and it brought back the memory of a terrifying encounter during the Shackleton affair with full force.

"A tree stump," I said, too quickly.

"Not a monster?" said Hamilton, tracing the outline of what could have been a leafy branch or a wing.

He shut the book and slid it to one side. I could hardly suppress a sigh of relief when he did. I was not sure what else there might be in those pages, but I was sure I did not wish to see any more than I already had.

"This has been most useful," he said, offering a reassuring smile. "It really has been very interesting hearing your side of things. I hope we'll get to have another chat soon."

"What is to become of me, Doctor?" I asked.

"Please don't worry," he said. "You're settling in very well. I expect you'll be able to leave segregation in a few days. Then, you'll be able to get out and join the other patients."

He smiled again without showing his teeth and held out his hand, inviting me to look forward to the prospect of becoming an ordinary inmate like any other. I did not have the heart to ask about magistrates or release or anything like that.

I should have guessed before I went in that the diagnosis of paranoid delusions had been affixed to me like a brand on a bull. Everything I said or did would be seen through the prism of that diagnosis. Mentioning Dr Nye or not mentioning him would both have had the same significance.

I racked my brains for anything I could say which would make it clear that I was not mad, that there really was a pattern behind it and that I, along with Gillespy, was working undercover for a mysterious secret society. Three random deaths with perfectly simple accepted explanations were really caused by some supernatural force. Somehow, the man in charge of the hospital, who appeared to be a highly respectable, eminent psychologist, was an evil genius masterminding it all for some unknowable purpose of his own.

"Thank you very much, Dr Hamilton," I said.

What could I say? My own tales were all too reminiscent of every other inmate's story. The interview with Dr Hamilton did nothing to settle my mind, and it set to growing the seeds of doubt that had already been planted. What if I really was mad?

Something of this had troubled me since the end of the

Roslyn D'Onston affair. The climax of that case had occurred in an underground cavern beneath one of the small factories on Brickmakers Road. Arthur Renville had later assured me that a couple of his lads had been over the area rather thoroughly and assured themselves that no such subterranean space existed. The entrance had been hidden to my eyes and only appeared by what might be called magic.

A simpler explanation would be that it was the fabrication of a dislocated mind. I had rescued young Lilly Wu, but I was not at all sure that her testimony would tally with mine, or that the memory of a terrified six-year-old could be relied upon.

My other experiences suffered from a similar lack of corroborating evidence. To the dispassionate observer, there would have been many explanations that made more sense than the actual existence of alien beings or uncanny forces at work. High among these would be the suggestion that the one reporting them is touched in the head. If the stories had come from anyone else, I too should have expected some convincing evidence.

I did have one piece of hard evidence: a small, star-shaped green stone, set in a ring. The ring usually hung on a chain around my neck. Given my circumstances, I assumed it resided in a cardboard box with my other belongings. Even if I had it, though, I could hardly wave it at Dr Hamilton, insisting that it proved there were alien civilisations and expecting him to agree.

I punched the floor with enough force to wake myself up and make myself think harder. There were powers at work—there could be no doubt about it. There were dead bodies from deaths caused by unnatural means, which others had seen. Why, a whole roomful of people had witnessed the events at the séance in the Theosophical Society. Estelle de Vere, who was dedicated to fighting those things, was no figment but a flesh-and-blood woman who rented a room and went about in a chauffeur-driven car.

And yet… and yet… the thought kept repeating itself in my mind, over and over: *it seemed so real.*

I could not deny the fact that I had been captured indoors, not in an aeroplane at five thousand feet. Plainly, I had not been where I imagined myself to be, if "imagined" was the right word.

I needed somebody to make sense of it for me, but the sense

was all too obvious. I was mad. I had a funny turn, or an episode, or whatever the medical term is. Under Ross's influence, I was temporarily insane. It was a *folie à deux*.

But if it had been my imagination, and if I could really stray so far from reality without knowing it, I wondered how much of the rest of my life was similarly made up out of the whole cloth.

Miss De Vere had once said something about magic and psychology, and how magic was simply working on the cosmic mind as a psychologist works on the human mind. Was that another way of saying that magic was insanity? Ross had said that magic and madness were one.

I punched the floor again—all the time realising that this act did not make me look any saner to the outside world, nor did it reassure me of my own mental condition—disliking the way the picture was coming into focus. How exactly ought a sane and balanced man behave in this situation?

I felt like a bull at bay, surrounded by dancing, taunting shapes that sting and stay forever just out of reach.

If only I could talk to Ross... but what if I could? I could not see that he would have any better explanation of what had happened other than magic or madness. Double or quits: having two of us believing it did not really make it any more plausible.

The attendants were never exactly cruel, but they were often hurried and indifferent, and the effects are the same.

Why I am here? Why has Nye left me alive?

There were things I was dreading. My parents' reaction, for one thing, and my brother's—not just the disappointment, but the stigma. Having a madman in the family would be a permanent embarrassment. They would stop mentioning Uncle Harry to my little nephews. Uncle Harry had gone away and was not coming back.

I was crushed to think what they would say in the pub, and at the boxing gym, or in my rooming house. "Did you hear about Harry? What happened, what did he do? Oh, oh, that is strange." It would be followed by a long, significant pause, and the speakers would wait to see if the other would say anything, in the wise, thoughtful way people always do. They'd say something such as, "He read a lot of those books, didn't he?" Or "He was involved in some funny business, wasn't he?"

People, myself included, want to make sense of things. We like to have a clear line of cause and effect laid out, so we can say, "Yes, that's what happened." We want that reassurance that overwork, nerves, or a touch of the sun can't happen to us.

There would come the questions about whether there was any of it in the family, and people would get even wiser, shake their heads, and say what a pity it all is. And they would look at my little nephew and watch him very closely for signs.

At least matters with Sally at last were settled. She was a single woman with a small child to look after, and the last thing she needed was a liaison with... I could not form the words, even in my mind. I hoped she did not hear it in a cruel way. I had not heard from anyone since I had been interned, and she was the person I dreaded hearing from most. Not hearing was a good sign. She must have found out where I was pretty quickly and come to a decision on her own accord.

As for Miss De Vere and her organisation, the way they had treated Hooper was enough of an indication. In their view, succumbing to insanity was tainted. Ryan had never even asked me whether Gillespy might be sane after all, or if he might have been faking it. At some point, they might want to snuff me out for the sake of tidiness, but no more.

Arthur was my one hope. Arthur was wise in the ways of the world, and he knew more about the sort of things I got up to than anyone, even if he was never entirely on the side of believing me. Arthur would not write off a good man, especially not someone whom he had known from boyhood. He would appreciate that there were things going on, wheels within wheels.

If only there was a way to get a message out to him and beg for his aid, Arthur could pull strings.

In the end, though, I did not need to send for him. Vanstone opened the door one day, told me I had a visitor, and indicated with a jerk of the head that I was to follow. I found Miller waiting outside with him; I was still not so sane that one attendant would be enough.

It must have been a Sunday, visiting day. Segregation inmates were not normally entitled to visits, so someone must have been bending the rules. My first thought was of Arthur, and he was there in the day room, sitting at one of the tables set out for visitors. He was dressed for a funeral and looked unusually sober. "Wotcher, Stubbsy," he said, greeting me with a handshake. "How are you keeping?"

I felt a tremor in my lip. Seeing an old friend in this blighted place was like rain on a parched field. I felt myself choking, and maybe I would have burst into tears if I had not been able to reply, with equal gruffness, "Can't complain. And yourself?"

"You know," he said, sitting down. "The usual." Arthur was a night owl, with business that was transacted in the hours of darkness. It seemed odd to see him in daytime and not firing off orders to the usual crowd of assistants and cronies that surrounded him. In that place and in that light, he looked not exactly worn out, but mortally tired.

"I've really dropped myself in it this time," I said. "You certainly are a sight for sore eyes. I was beginning to give up hope."

"Never give up hope, Stubbsy," he said in a kindly tone of the sort you would use for a sick relative, certainly not the hearty way you would speak to an old comrade.

"You were right to warn me about this place," I said. "I thought I was almost to cracking the case I was telling you about when... this happened."

"Well now, don't you worry too much about the case," he said. "We can sort all that out in due course. I hope they're feeding you properly?"

"Barely. It's like being on a diet. I'll be down to my fighting weight in no time." I patted my flat stomach. I dropped my voice, checking that Vanstone was not eavesdropping. "Like I told you earlier, there is something going on here."

"You're off the case now, Stubbsy," he told me, not lowering his voice in return. "You know what they say about when you find yourself at the bottom of a hole. You stop digging. Do you get my drift?"

It was never profitable to argue with Arthur Renville, and his mind was made up. I spread my hands flat on the table in front of me. "I see," I said.

"You get a lot of leeway with me, Stubbsy, you know that," he said. "I have a great deal of faith in you, and that's not something I would say about just anyone. And nobody understands better than I some of the things you've been through." He was speaking slowly and patiently, without a trace of the irritation that often overcame him. "But Stubbsy, I warned you. I specifically warned you, didn't I?"

"You did warn me," I said.

"What are we going to do with you?" he asked, and the note of sorrow in his voice cut deeper than his anger.

"Help me," I said.

"Even if I was to open that door with a golden key, what good would it do? You'd dive straight back into trouble, and you'd be back here within a week, wouldn't you?" I began to reply, but Arthur raised a hand to forestall me. "I've helped you time and again, and look where it's got me. No, I don't mean it like that, Stubbsy. Of course I'll help you, but you've got to understand that there's a lot on my plate. I can't drop it all every time one of my friends gets himself into trouble, especially if he starts making a habit of it. So, what you have to do is keep quiet here, keep your nose clean, put your feet up, and concentrate on getting better. Then, we'll see what we can do for you."

It was an offer of help of sorts, albeit a vague one with no particular timescale attached.

"Thank you," I said.

"There's a lot more going on in the world than your own little problem, believe you me," he said, sounding almost peevish. "But escapes from madhouses and dead doctors are downright irregular. I can't make head nor tail of it, and I don't think I want to."

"What are you going to tell people?" I asked, trying to keep my voice neutral.

"You're here, and you're in good health. You're the same old Stubbsy, not a raving madman."

He left it at that, but people could draw their own conclusions. They might decide I had suffered a bout of nerves, or a funny turn, or whatever people chose to call the temporary version of insanity which you get better from. What he was not saying was that I did not belong inside and needed to be released.

Arthur was offering me something very different from Dr Hamilton's position. If I showed no further symptoms, I would be considered sane, at least provisionally. I might even be released in due course, whatever that meant.

"Thank you, Arthur," I said. "That would mean a lot to me."

"I was worried sick," he said. "I thought I'd find you strapped into a straightjacket and seeing demons."

Arthur relaxed a little after that. He brought me up to date with goings-on in the local community, and with the dealings associated with his latest consignment for disposal, which had been a vast quantity of plush toys. The story of Arthur going around trying to get people to buy teddy bears had been about the lightest moment of the discussion.

He left me a paper bag of grapes. They were big and juicy, and I ate them greedily, popping them in my mouth and spitting the seeds out into my palm. I would have appreciated something more substantial, such as a pork pie or two, but nobody ever seemed to bring those. When I was an attendant, we had been warned that well-meaning family members might smuggle things in for the inmates. Even the most harmless object might be flattened out and sharpened to make a knife for an inmate to do mischief to himself or to some enemy.

Arthur had been about my last hope. If he had given up on me, which he more or less had, then I could not expect any help from the outside world. Arthur had warehoused me: like an inconvenient consignment which could not be sold, I had been securely stashed away out of sight, so he could get on with other things until the situation improved. If it ever did.

With no prospect of help, I was thrown back entirely on my inner resources.

Unfortunately, even your inner resources can turn against you.

If you get up, you get hit again. That was something you learned quickly in the boxing game. Sometimes, it's better to lie there and not try to fight against unequal odds. Knowing when you've lost is the only way to prevent being beaten and seriously injured.

When despair spoke to me, it used Ryan's voice. I had been pushing it away, day after day, but I could only sweep so much under the rug. The accumulated mass is enough to take on a life of its own. I would not accept despair. I would not admit it as a part of me, but it spoke from outside of me.

"It's all up, Stubbs," said Ryan.

Oddly enough, I knew better than to look around for where the voice was coming from. Some part of me knew that it was from no external source. I did not reply.

"Face it. Things are only going to get worse," he said. "You can stay here and wait for it to start playing with you. Because that's what it's going to do, isn't it? It's playing with you."

Cats play with mice sometimes; I don't know if tigers do the same.

"Nye will have some therapy arranged for you," he said. "Think you'll enjoy that? That's unless *La Belle Dame sans Merci* finds a way to finish you off first," he said. "You're only alive because she can't reach you. That's a pretty unsavoury way to go, too."

There was something especially demeaning about being assassinated by my own side because I was a liability. It spoke of weakness.

After a long pause, Ryan's voice spoke again, more quietly but with more of an edge. "And those are the more attractive options, if you think about it. What do you think you'll be like after a few years in here? You're already losing weight and condition. You'll get weaker and more addled every day. Better do something while you still can."

"Do something?" I spoke involuntarily. I had not meant to reply.

"It's over," he said, voice grating. "You've failed. Failed me, failed on your mission, failed your friends. What's Arthur Renville telling everyone who said you were a wild man who didn't deserve his support? You've failed your family. Failed your fiancée, too. You know, she really believed in you. Until then."

"I tried," I said, almost in a whisper.

"You failed yourself. You're not the big hero." Ryan sounded regretful and resigned. "Best thing you can do now is bring the curtain down. Do it on your own terms. That's the one thing you can do. Cheat the predator of its prey. Let TDS know you're still in control of your actions." They were all the thoughts I had been blocking out, not daring to think. Ryan spat them at me.

"Or, are you going to keep failing?" he asked. "You've only one thing left to do, Stubbs. Are you man enough to do it?"

I did not answer, and he did not stop.

Others who were there died, but only when they reached a final level of despair. Perhaps the game was that the victim had to be driven to death or suicide. In the Bible story, the devil was given the power to torment Job in every way, but not actually to kill him. He kept tempting Job to curse God and die, but Job held firm. I thought then what a fool Job was.

Suicide is the coward's way out, they say, though it must take a deal of courage to go through with it. Especially when you lack a convenient rope or razor. Ryan had suggestions, but nothing easy.

They say the darkest hour is before the dawn. For me, the daybreak came after a long and harrowing night of little sleep, when the cart with the squeaky wheel proclaimed the arrival of breakfast porridge and a cup of stewed tea. But the man with the tray was not one I expected to see.

It is always difficult when you encounter someone in an unfamiliar setting. The man sitting opposite on the bus might look terribly familiar but is impossible to place, until you realise that it's the baker, looking so different without his white hat and apron. No wonder, then, especially in my insomnia-benumbed state, that I gaped at the man with the pinched, ferrety face.

"Hello, Stubbs," he said. It clicked at last. He was a member of the loose-knit pack of criminals run by Elsie Granger out of the Knights Head pub in Norwood New Town. The last time I had seen him was after he and his cohorts had kidnapped Sally. It was strictly a business matter with no personal animosity, and Sally had even dropped around afterwards to chat with Elsie. I was hardly on good terms with the man, but even so, it was good to see a familiar face.

"Smith," I said. "What are you doing here?"

"Working," Smith said. "What's it bloody look like?"

He passed me a tray. Then, he surprised me by closing the door and offering me a cigarette before lighting one of his own. "Got the job because I was Ambulance Corps in the war," he said. Smith's legs, warped by rickets early in life, would have kept him out of the fighting units. "Spent six months with shell-shock cases, so this is all grist to the mill."

"How did you get a reference?" I could not hide my incredulity, but Smith was not insulted.

"That was your old lady's doing," he said, and it took me a moment to realise he meant Sally. "She knew a doctor from when she was on the streets—he does all the girls. She threatened to call down the law on him if he didn't give me a glowing reference. Blow me if he didn't do it."

It was moving too much too quickly. Sally had blackmailed a doctor into helping Smith get a job at the asylum. Why did a natural layabout like him want to work here, anyway? Could it be something to do with me? There was a painful flutter in my chest. Hope was stirring.

"Getting you out's a tall order, though," Smith went on. "They've put on new locks with double keys, and all sorts of checks and procedure so one attendant can't just waltz out anymore the way you did. That's your doing, that is. Your name is dirt with the other screws. You've given them a ton of extra work." He exhaled smoke. Smoking was prohibited in there, but that was the least of it.

"Thank you," was all I could think to say.

"Don't thank me, pal," he said. "Not yet, anyway."

"Is Elsie Granger in on this?" I asked.

"'Course she is," he said, as though to an idiot. "She and your old lady are thick as thieves right now. They needed someone on the inside, and muggins here gets the job. Hard bloody work it is, too."

"I know," I said.

"Suppose you do." He looked me up and down. "It's good you're still in one piece. Try to stay that way, or I'm wasting my bleeding time."

This expression of concern, rough and self-interested as it was, was strangely touching. Smith was no sort of friend, and had been largely indifferent to me. But somehow, the fact that I mattered to someone, that they were counting on me in some way, made all the difference. And Sally was behind it. I was part of a team again.

"What's happening out there?" I asked. "It's been getting noisier these last few days."

"Some of them kick up a racket after they've been treated," he said. "Just be grateful it ain't you."

"Dr Nye?" I asked.

"I keep out of his way," said Smith, flicking his cigarette butt into the grate. "Gotta go."

"Cheerio," I said. "Thanks for the porridge."

"You're welcome to it," he said, a little ungraciously.

Smith's visit left me elated and full of questions. Some of those were answered the following Sunday, when, by a minor miracle, I was let out and escorted for visiting again. Against all hope and expectation, Sally was waiting for me. I could not quite believe it. Against all expectation, and despite of all common sense, she was still with me.

She was dressed for an evening out, with her hair brushed and silver bangles on her wrist, looking rosy and healthy as a milkmaid. Her face lit up when she saw me. Arthur had visited me out of a sense of responsibility. Sally was here because she wanted to be.

"You didn't have to come," I said, overwhelmed by a jumble of emotions. There was shame and embarrassment for my situation, and more than a little relief for seeing her, and gratitude, and other feelings which I could not so easily put a name to.

"I wanted to see you for myself," she said. "Sorry I didn't write." She leaned closer, and I could smell her perfume. "Letters get read."

"Smith told me what you were doing," I said.

She looked at the other inmates, their visitors, and the attendants, who stood straight-backed against the walls like stone sentinels. "And how are you?" she asked quietly.

"To be perfectly honest, I don't know," I said. "You'd better ask the doctors."

Sally shook her head. "They don't know anything. You tell me what happened."

Reluctantly, and in a low voice, I tried to give an account of the escape, Ross's plan, our attempted flight, and its incomprehensible conclusion.

"That's how I remember it," I finished, a phrase I had cause to repeat several times during the narrative. And then, without even meaning to, I added: "It seemed so real at the time."

Her brow had creased when I described the strange flight and the way the attendants had appeared out of the air, walking along the wing, but she seemed to take it in her stride. I was worried that once she heard what I had to say, she would change her mind and decide that I was not worth helping. But that apparently never even crossed her mind.

"I don't suppose a lock pick would be any use," she said. We had talked about lock picking long ago. It was one of the topics covered in my correspondence course, and I had failed to master the skills on the basis of the scant instructions provided. "Whatever you need, though, I'll get it for you."

"I'm not sure what's what anymore," I said hesitantly. I had to be honest. "Sally, I'm not even sure I ought to be outside."

"Harry, look at me," she said. My gaze had drifted down to the table in front of me. Her eyes were bright and fierce. "You don't belong in here. There's something bad at work, I know that. I don't know what it is, but nobody can stop it but you."

When I did not reply immediately, she began counting off points on her fingers. "That strange film at the cinema and the projectionist going mad. The man here who died, Gillespy. Hooper, that other one who worked for Miss De Vere. Dr Beltov dead. All that story that Ross told you. I'm not a genius, but there are facts there. It's not only in your head—or if it is, it's in my head, too."

The web was far more fragile than she made it sound. I had been through it many times myself. "Sal," I said, and I reached out and took her small hands in mine. "These things can be looked at more than one way."

"And don't you go forgetting that gipsy fortune-teller, saying you'd meet a man with wings. This Ross, he's a man with wings. Isn't he?" I had completely forgotten this episode, but to her it was a clincher. "How much proof do you blooming well need?"

"I don't know –"

"Remember," she said, cutting me off, "that you're talking to a woman who got propositioned by a walking corpse, and ended up screaming her head off. Nobody ever believed what I saw, until I didn't know whether to believe it myself. They thought I was mad. But it was true – you proved that. The nuns would never have let me go if it wasn't for you. So you can leave this 'don't know' right out. You need to pull your socks up, Harry Stubbs, and start acting like a man."

That was telling me. I stared back. She was right.

"Yes or no?" she demanded.

"Sal, you're a wonder," I said.

"I am glad you finally decided to start listening to me," she said.

"That long face doesn't suit you. And with your shoulders slumped, it looks like there has been a landslide."

I squared my shoulders. She was right. My trainer would have been horrified to see me in that posture.

"You know," she said. "This is like one of those prison films, isn't it, where the moll visits her gangster in prison? Do you remember *Convict 13*? It's harder than they make out, though. You know they searched me on the way in? There's a woman warden for that, and she's a hard-faced baggage if ever there was one."

"Vanstone's wife," I said absently.

"Hard to get anything in, but Smith might be able to. Speaking of films," she said, "I got that reel. The *Phantom of the Cinema*. Before they could show it like you said."

"What? How did you do that?"

"The new projectionist, he's very young," she said, with what I could only call a coquettish smile, an expression I had not seen before. "I dressed up nice and gave him the eye. He let me into the projection box, and I nicked it when he was changing reels." She laughed at my shocked expression. "Don't worry, he didn't try anything. He's only a boy."

I could never have seen Sally as Mata Hari. She always presented herself as just another girl working at the pickle factory. She was more resourceful than she let on.

"The reel is in a safe place," she went on. "Getting you out, though… I don't put too much reliance on Smith." He was on the far side of the room, watching one of the inmates arguing with another man. "Elsie reckons he wants to impress her, but he's not Douglas Fairbanks hero material. He says he can't work out how to get all the doors open to get you out on his own."

"I don't know if I want to get out," I said. "No, I'm not starting that again. I mean, I think I need to be in here. I've got to tackle Dr Nye." I had some inkling now of what I was up against.

"How are you going to get to him?" she asked. "Maybe I should do it."

I had a vision of Sally marching in and demanding to be let in to Dr Nye's office, with a pistol concealed in her handbag. She would do it, too. I could not believe that it would serve any purpose. Nye could bend and twist reality to his ends. If she tried to shoot him, Sally would find herself looking at a photograph of Nye on the wall, with a cap gun in her hand, or some other twisted version of reality—along with Vanstone's wife with a straitjacket to haul her off to a women's institution—and she would be as baffled and mad as me at the shift in the world.

If I was not mad, then Nye could warp reality into any shape he pleased, making reality into madness and madness into reality. You cannot fight such power with ordinary weapons. The answer, if there was one, lay with Ross.

"I'll have to think about it," I said.

"You do that! About time, too. Oh, and I mustn't forget this."

She produced a long, flat object, wrapped in brown paper, from her handbag. It was the biggest bar of chocolate I had ever seen.

"To keep your strength up," she said. She smiled at me then, and in spite of it all, I could not help but smile back.

Chapter Eighteen: Fight Your Demons

Ross was only two doors down from me in the segregation block. There were no convenient pipes to tap on—not that I could remember Morse code, anyway—and I could not figure a way of using the drain that ran under all the cells. Smith accepted the task of messenger, but the answers he brought back were oblique in the extreme.

"He says you have to hold on," said Smith. "He says it'll all come right. You just have to 'fight your demons'." His tone belied the words he was conveying.

"Ask him—"

"I'm not asking him anything. I'll get another load of guff back." He mimed a talking mouth with his hand. "Ross is happy enough. Don't worry about him."

Smith did at least accept another commission: retrieving the storm glass from my box of possessions. I had little idea of what it might tell me, but I had all the time in the world to watch it. Wisps of green precipitate would form and dissolve at certain times. Each day they became more defined and lasted longer.

Smith also brought other things along with the dinner tray some days later.

"Message for you," he said.

"From Ross?"

"From 'is royal highness, FitzRoy. Sends his best wishes and that."

"What for?"

"As if I know anything about it," grumbled Smith. "He reckons you've been thrown in the dungeon unjustly. He doesn't like Nye."

"How do you mean?"

"Incidents," Smith said without elaborating. "You're lucky you're in here and don't have to join in the Kinotherapy sessions. All we do is stick them in a room and play a film, but they come out of it like bloody animals. Nye reckons it's helping."

It occurred to me then that Nye must be employing Eric Woods to make more films. Showing them to the patients pushed them to further extremes. The Sarcophagus would then record their brain waves, which would go into making the next film, and so on, in an ever-increasing spiral of insanity. It had to be stopped – but I was trapped here, and Smith was not about to take any chances by throwing a spanner into the works.

"Anyway," said Smith, "I also bear a love token from your lady friend."

I did not know what he meant until I lifted the plate and was surprised to find a pair of knuckledusters, extra-large size. My knuckledusters, reserved for those rare occasions when serious violence might be afoot. Sally must have gone to my rooming house and ferreted them out of the bottom drawer.

Of all the absurd things. A file, or bolt cutters, or some other sort of implement, that might have been of some use. But the idea that I could punch my way out was ridiculous. And there was an added risk: if they were discovered in my cell, further measures would be taken. Maybe I would be put under restraint and tied to the bed. Maybe they would discover Smith and fire him, or worse.

Ross wanted me to fight my demons. Sally wanted to help me fight someone. We must all have been as mad as each other.

I will always remember one occasion during the war, when I was with my battery, and we could hear the battlefront moving closer. The artillery tractors were standing ready, like great mechanical oxen. As soon as the order was given, we could hitch the guns up and haul the battery to a position farther back.

Our guns were silent; heavy artillery could do nothing when the armies were mixed up with one another. We sat around the big howitzers, their muzzles pointing at the sky, and the action moved so close that we could hear individual rifle shots popping from among the background noise.

"Sergeant," one youngster burst out, "they're getting closer."

"Very true," our battery sergeant said. He was regular army, and singularly unimpressed by us wartime recruits. He had fought in the Boer campaign, and was as tough as nails and respected for it.

"Sergeant, what do we do if the order to pull back doesn't come?"

It was possible that the line of communication would be broken, or even that German storm troopers, who were the new crack troops, had broken through and overrun our headquarters. It had happened before.

"In that case, lad," said the sergeant, "we will just have to stay here and fight. And die like men."

It seemed like a cruel answer for a frightened young man needing reassurance, and the gunner looked like he had been slapped in the face. After a minute, though, he straightened up and stopped shivering. His jaw was set. Vague and unknown dread had troubled him, but dying like a man was something else. It had a concreteness to it, and it gave him a goal to achieve.

The order did not come, but neither did the Germans; their assault was repelled. None of us manning the guns had to die like men that day, but we were ready.

The brass weapons before me looked bright and new. I picked one up and sniffed, detecting a hint of vinegar. Sally must have cleaned them in a pointless-but-thoughtful womanly gesture.

I fondled the knuckledusters then slipped them over my hands. They were solid and reassuring. They reminded me of other times, of other tight corners and impossible situations. *This is who I am, and this is what I do.* There was something else, too. It was like holding hands with Sally at one remove. She was there with me in spirit, and she wanted me to keep fighting. It always helps to have someone on your side.

"Nothing has changed, Stubbs," Ryan's voice told me. "Except you're slipping into delusion."

I was in no mood for his sniping. "Either say something helpful, like telling me the best place to punch a tiger, or else keep your trap shut. I've had enough of you." It was rude, but he had been harassing me for some time. And since he was a part of my internal self, I wasn't really insulting anyone else.

For all Ryan's urgings, I was certainly not going to kill myself. Not now. Maybe the others had not killed themselves, either, at the last, even though somebody wanted them to. Those deaths had been a little suspicious at the time, but there had been no physical way a third party could have been involved.

As a man who had been dragged from an aeroplane at five thousand feet straight into a drawing room at ground level, my faith in the solidity of things and the relative powers of mind and matter had been severely tested. If we accept that reality is more plastic than we thought… then what? You can tear up the manual, and nothing makes any sense at all. Perhaps there are limits to the powers of everything. Otherwise, why all this charade and sneaking about?

There must be some limitations, because… The thought almost eluded me, but I caught it mid-flight. *Because Nye needs to have a solid base to work from.* If everything about him was changeable and insubstantial, his own hands would turn to smoke, leaving him unable to hold anything, and he needed to have some things fixed in place. Without any rules at all, there is no game. And he was certainly a player of games.

As soon as Smith left, I checked the storm glass. The cloud had congealed into a half-recognisable shape which did not dissipate. Not quite a tiger, but similar in some ways, and clear enough to recognise. It was close. Tonight would be the night, and I finally had some idea what I was facing. There had been plenty of time to figure it out. I may have been a plodder, but plodding will get you anywhere if you are persistent enough at it. And I had to be ready to fight.

Boxing was the only thing I had ever been really good at; if I was going to fight my demons, that was how I would do it. I would change my cell into a stronghold, from a place of execution to my home turf.

A proper competition boxing ring is twenty feet square, though some are as small as sixteen feet. I had fought in confined spaces before, but I really preferred more room. Half the skill of fighting is movement, and if you're in a broom closet, you lose the advantage of that skill.

I paced up and down then dropped into a fighting stance. I shuffled and jumped about, getting the feel of the size and the angles of the space. I could dodge about quite well by pushing off the walls. There was no need to get trapped anywhere, except the bed was inconveniently placed.

A more formidable weapon would be handy, not that I really knew how to use any sort of weapon except the knuckleduster. Hercules used a club, and I reckoned a decent club might be more useful than a machine gun at that point.

The room was completely bare. The only furniture was the iron bed, which was bolted to the ground. If I could dismantle it, the legs would make pretty decent clubs. And iron would do well. According to folklore, iron has always been hated and feared by things from beyond, which I took to include demons. Nobody had ever succeeded in detaching a bed, as far as I knew, but maybe nobody of my size and strength had ever tried.

I explored the situation on my hands and knees. The bolts were firmly in place on three sides, but the fourth, which was at the bottom of the bed on the side away from the wall, had some play in it. No more than an eighth of an inch, but that was enough.

Heaving on it from the standing and kneeling positions did no good, so I lay on my back and braced my legs against the bed frame. I taxed the bolt with a series of sharp upward thrusts, pushing as hard as I could. Then I used the bed cover as padding, as the frame was digging into my thin shoes, and pushed even harder. The bed groaned but did not shift.

I could feel my face turning the colour of beetroot and veins standing out on my forehead. After a minute, I stopped, lay back, and relaxed. It was ridiculous; I was acting like a madman. Hundreds, maybe thousands, of men had been confined in that cell, and none of them had ever succeeded in breaking the bed. Misery and defeat threatened to engulf me.

"They may have tried," I said out loud. "The thing is, though, they weren't Harry Stubbs, were they?"

Where had that come from? Some deep recess of my subconscious mind, I suppose.

I am the celebrated Harry Stubbs, the Norwood Titan, heavyweight champion of South London. "The last man standing," as Ryan had called me, and he was right. I had fought beings that no other man ever faced, and I beat them, too. I was not going to give up over a bed.

But I needed some help. I needed to draw on my inner resources. I was not going to beat the bed by boxing it now. It was more like a wrestling match, one conducted across the span of years. It was me against the workman who fastened the bed down in place all those years ago.

How would a cleverer man than me tackle the problem? Hoade must have known all sorts of tricks involving leverage, metallurgy, and other technical approaches, and he could look something up in a jiffy. Arthur would do it by influence; he would make deals, form allies among the inmates, and find a way of getting the attendants on his side until he was running the place. Yang… what would he do?

I braced my feet against the bed again and pushed. But instead of straining, I listened, applying a steady force. I thought of the waves of the sea, breaking against a cliff. Water is weak and soft compared to stone, but waves will make a cliff crumble in time. I thought of tree roots snaking down into fissures in rock, then growing, slowly, year after year until the fissure widened and the rock split apart.

With a sound like an iron cork being torn from an iron bottle, the bolt wrenched loose, and the bed lurched upwards four inches. It was still held in place by the other three bolts, but that was not going to stop me. With the first bolt gone, I would be able to get a good leverage on the second. That turned the bed into a hinge, and by working it up and down I would be able to get enough play to pull the remaining bolts loose or break off the brackets that held them.

It was a fair amount of noise, but no attendants came. I had a feeling they were all otherwise occupied this evening.

One small victory for the Norwood Titan, I thought. *And thank you, Mr Yang.*

It's amazing how doing something—anything, in fact—can lift your mood when you are low. I was still a certified madman, locked in solitary confinement with death imminent. But now I was making progress, the outlook seemed to change. When you're stuck, you know you are going nowhere, however much time passes. Once you start moving, progress is just a matter of time and persistence.

My success was, I admit, a partial one. The bed could indeed be worked loose on all four legs, but it turned out to be more robust than I expected. The joints connecting the legs to the frame were as solid as rocks, without the hint of any looseness. Even when I stood the bed on end and hung on to a leg with both hands, lifted myself off the ground, and bounced up and down, I could do no more than bend it a little.

The bed was determined to stay in one piece, but at least it was no longer blocking one side of the room. I could move it around to my advantage, use it as a barrier. I could shape the battlefield, as our instructors said, though they were talking about barbed wire and minefields rather than a bed and three cushions.

Standing on its end, the bed reminded me of a gallows, and I hastily put the bed back on its four feet. I had a feeling that unlikely accidents might happen whenever it was a convenience to Dr Nye, and it would be unfortunate if I was lured into accidentally hanging myself.

If the cell door had opened outwards I might have tried using the bed as a battering ram. However, knowing the strength of the door frame, I doubted that any amount of battering was going to do any good. Besides, my destiny would catch up with me wherever I was. Better to get ready to meet it.

The mood had taken me. I carefully tore strips from the coarse linen sheet, which, doubled over, did duty as a pair of sheets, so I could wrap them around my hands as extra padding under the knuckledusters. I had one long strip left over, which, on a whim, I tied around my forehead as a bandana. It would keep the sweat out of my eyes and afford some slight protection against cuts and grazes.

The three biscuits, the hard cushions which made up the mattress, I piled in the corner, thinking of ways that they could be tactically employed.

I lay on the bed, looking at the ceiling and feeling both exhilarated by the exercise but also curiously peaceful.

I had an idea of what was coming, but I wanted it to come. The worst thing would be if nothing happened. That would mean I really was deluded.

Has there ever been another situation where a man actually wished for someone to come and try to kill him? Hard to imagine that there was, but I wanted them to come. It felt like hoping that a fight could be arranged—a match that gave me a shot at a title.

Previous occupants of the cell might have been drained, wasted, or despairing, as I had been a few days ago. But I had become another man. *Harry Stubbs, the celebrated pugilist, master of the art, invites and exhorts all comers to step up and try their luck. No offers to fight refused. Apply to cell six.* I imagined a packed crowd all around, with Sally in the front row, cheering me on, excited by the prospect of seeing their champion in action, already laying bets before the opposition had even been announced.

There was more noise than usual, enough to suggest that the place was in a state of disorder. They were shouting and yodelling, making animal noises or shrieking, the way they do at times of high excitement. The attendants should have been putting the lid on it and preventing things from getting out of hand, but they did not. Perhaps they could not.

Night fell, and my room was illuminated by the electric light outside the high windows.

I had no clock, but I could feel the minutes and the hours trickling past. I was not impatient. Maybe I even drowsed at times, but I was always within a hair's breadth of full awareness.

They were coming to kill me, as they came to kill the others. Unlike the others, I was going to give them a fight they would remember.

A door opened silently in the wall. A door where there was no door. Soft radiance from the other side silhouetted the two of them as they came through. Just as I had seen in the storm glass.

They were executioners. They had the build and the bearing—the calm, unhurried determination—of men who had come to kill. Their faces were absolute masks, like the faces of statues, and that made them more inhuman than if they had looked like monsters. They were perfectly identical. I suspected there was only one of them, though it happened to occupy two bodies.

They stood on two legs, so tall that we were eye to eye. I had wondered how big they might be. The Sphinx at Giza is sixty feet high, and he's lying down. The sphinxes at Crystal Palace are a good deal smaller, but still too massive to squeeze into my cell.

In mythology and art, the sphinx is a blend of man and lion, with a human head atop a leonine body, with the tail of a serpent. Seeing the real thing, you can tell there has been some poetic licence in the depiction. No lion on earth ever looked like that; they certainly had massive paws and clawed digits to match any lion, but it was not merely the tail that was snake-like. The body was more than a little reptilian, and shaped so that they could go on two legs or four with equal facility. Their wings, which they kept folded, were more like dragon wings than the eagle wings you see in classical art.

In another age, the sphinxes were the supernatural assassins of the Pharaohs and the High Priests. They were constructs, artificial things built or assembled to carry out their master's deadly will. They were living images of their master, fleshy automata produced by a lost art, their faces like a man's but somehow lifeless, or at least soulless.

Gillespy and Hooper and Beltov must have been astonished by the intruders appearing in their rooms. I was ready with my knuckledusters wrapped round my fists. This time I was the one with the advantage of surprise, striking the first before the second one was even fully in the room.

I doubted whether anyone had punched a sphinx in the last forty centuries, and I hoped the shock would be severe.

They might have been as insubstantial as mist or as hard as iron. I was hoping for something towards the softer end of the scale, and I was not disappointed. In any case, his head snapped back as he took the force of the punch, and he staggered back two steps into the wall. If you are not in a proper stance and your centre of gravity is too high, that's what happens.

It was not the hardest thing I ever punched, and perhaps no harder than punching a normal person, but it certainly felt different. Just as it wore a mask rather than a face, the resemblance was superficial something assembled or moulded into human shape.

"Get out of my room," I said, punching the second one in his midsection, guessing that maybe he would be vulnerable there. Lions and other cats are not meant to stand on their hind legs, as it exposes a broad stretch of belly. Their ribcage is higher than a human, and while a boxer is well muscled and so well protected about his middle, this thing did not seem to be either.

My punches landed well enough. Again, the texture was peculiar, as though it was stuffed with bowling balls rather than fleshy organs. I know nothing of the anatomy of lions, but I hoped I could give him a pain in his gut. A kidney punch is a deadly thing for a human. Maybe whatever they had inside could be broken too.

My onslaught did not delay them for long. As ever, when fighting one against two, I had to watch out for the first one, who shook his head and recovered then came for me. He had a longer reach than I expected—his arms or forelegs seemed to stretch like elastic. If my reflexes had not saved me by causing me to twitch my head to the side, the fight might have ended there. As it was, four giant claws sliced the air an inch from my nose. They seemed to leave trails in the air, as though they scored the fabric of the atmosphere.

My counterpunch was low, and he exhaled sharply, the first noise I heard one of them make. It wasn't so much a grunt as air knocked out of a bag. It gave me an indication that they breathed, and that the faces were not simply ornamentation like the face of a puppet. Before he could recover, I gave him an uppercut with my left.

The results were unsatisfactory. Hit a human like that, with the added impact force and hardness of a knuckleduster, and there should be blood all over the place, sometimes a spray of it on the walls. As I had half-suspected, their skin was as impervious as that of the Nemean lion. If they had battled warriors with swords and spears in antiquity, they must be armoured and impenetrable. Perhaps, like Hercules, I would be reduced to strangling them, a difficult enough task with one but barely conceivable when there were two of them to tackle.

At least with the knuckledusters, I could hold my own for as long as I boxed cleverly. Without them, I would not have had a chance. And, unlike the warriors of old, I was accustomed to fights where an opponent could not be felled at once, and where ducking and dodging and blocking were vital skills, which I used freely.

The first one swiped at me with that elasticated reach of his, as though his joints had some looseness in them. I blocked with my left against his wrist and threw out a quick jab—only just quickly enough, because his other paw moved with lightning speed. I felt my arm brushed. His claws were like razor blades, so sharp that there was no immediate pain, but I felt wetness trickling down my sleeve.

I ducked back, stepped sideways, and snatched up one of the

heavy cushions in my left hand. It was awkward, but it was the only shield I possessed. Maybe the creatures' claws would snag in the dense stuffing.

Two seconds later, the cushion had been eviscerated, and the heavy coconut matting tumbled out. I tossed the useless remnant at the nearest one, and he swatted it out of the air as if he was a kitten with a ball of paper.

What was happening could not be happening—and maybe it wasn't. It was far more plausible that I was lying on my bunk in a mad delirium, with Miller or one of the others despairing of my ever coming back to the real world. But it was the world I was faced with, and I would treat it in good faith, and fight this nightmare bout as though it was a normal match.

I fell back a step and a half, sensing the surrounding room. The fight was just beginning, and Harry Stubbs was landing some good blows and getting well ahead on points, but this thing was not going to be decided on points. It would be a knockout. Or death.

They moved forward to be side by side and fight two against one. It was foolish. Their fighting style meant they did not punch straight but swung round, so they needed clearance. I could punch them freely, bobbing from side to side while they jostled and swiped ineffectually, but I could not stay in one place long.

I grabbed the bed in one hand and dragged it, tearing up linoleum, so it was between me, and them. They would have to squeeze around or clamber over to get at me.

I dodged wrong, and a blow caught me on the side of the head. I rolled with it, but for a moment I thought I was done for, like a cartoon character who is sliced through but stays in one piece for a second before falling to the floor in pieces. The blow had not been well judged. Though it was as hefty as what many boxers could deliver, it did no great damage. It was not the neck-breaking blow of the tiger that Ryan had described, though wild animals probably have less skill at riding punches than I did.

They tried to reach me several times over the bed before finally realising it was no good and that I was dodging back every single time. They were fearsome enough, but my respect for them was diminishing. "Your reputation for wisdom has been greatly overstated," I panted.

I have never been one for trying to rile opponents in a fight, but I was seeking any advantage. If they could not or would not talk, then being mocked by a mortal might irk them even more. And an angry opponent is a careless opponent.

Acting in perfect synchrony, the two leapt onto the bed at the same moment. There was no room to back away, and I did not want to get into close quarters with them; a clinch with those claws would be like falling into a sausage grinder. There was one avenue open to me. Even as they moved, I was dropping flat and rolling under the bed. For an unrehearsed move, it was polished, and I rose before they turned. They had fast enough reflexes, but they were slow thinkers.

"You're supposed to ask me a riddle!" I taunted, and I turned the bed over on its side to make a higher obstacle, then delivered a cheeky left jab to the midriff of the nearer of the two before stepping back. Claws cut the air in front of me, but I had their reach and timing by then. There was little variety in their moves.

They seemed to pause and think. I was not going to give them time to do that, so I picked up the bed by the frame and swung it.

I had considered the bed as a possible weapon during my tactical planning cogitation, but it had seemed much too heavy to be practical. Now it seemed lighter, more like wood rather than iron. The legs were facing away from me, and I used them to jab at my attackers as a lion-tamer keeps his beasts at bay. It was more like Buster Keaton than boxing, but satisfying.

I half felt and half saw blows directed at the bed legs. That did not impress me, either—it was like a dog who tries to bite the stick rather than the man wielding it. Then, the shock of impact pushed me back and took a leg clean off. It clanged on the floor. If I had a second, I might be able to grab it and use it as a club.

I raised the bed chest-high, swung it this way and that, almost knocking one off balance. The other raised a hind leg, trying to claw at my shins. I dropped the bed on his foot, and as it fell, I stepped in to deliver a long right into the face of the other, planting my fist squarely on his nose. I did not have time to judge the effect of either, but hoisted the bed again.

One of them struck at my fingers; he missed me more by luck than any skill of mine. The blow left deep gouges in the iron frame.

Through the metal slats, I saw a raking blow raise a shower of sparks. It might have knocked me over had I been less well balanced.

Claws hooked through the slats as one of them took hold of the bed and tried to pull it away from me. I thrust the bed forward then turned it like a windmill, marvelling at how easy it had become. It had begun to feel not like a normal wooden bed, but one made of featherweight balsa. I hoped to get his arm twisted or, best of all, to break loose one of those curved claws. I had a hunch that if there was one thing that could harm them, it would be one of their own claws.

I spun the bed and thrust it forward, letting go suddenly. It went down with a great clang, with one of them under it.

"Riddle me that!" I yelled.

The second one advanced on me, his face blank and his eyes as expressionless as glass beads. There was no blood and no bruising, for all the battering he had taken. He rushed in for the grapple, opening his arms. It gave me a free shot at his chin, which I took with jaw-breaking force.

I realised my mistake as soon as the arms wrapped round me. If he had been more alert, he could have gutted me like a rabbit, but perhaps I had stunned him, because he delayed for some fraction of a second—long enough for me to grab his wrists and force them upwards.

The claws extended, silver-white knives longer than my fingers, and he tried to bring them to bear. That should have been hopeless, given the leverage that I had, but his strength was a phenomenon. It was all I could do to hold him at a distance.

From a few inches away, I felt metallic breath on my face. There was no trace of sweat on his skin, though I was bathed in it. A depression like a thumbprint in wax marred his forehead: he was getting a battering. It seemed their bones were not brittle like ours, and more like soft bronze. Maybe a hard-enough pounding would suffice. *If only I could get that bed leg.*

I kneed him with all my force where his groin should have been. The blow almost lifted him off his feet, and I surged forward, still holding his wrists in mine. He was fully off balance by then, and after two steps, his back struck the wall, and his head whipped back into the brickwork with a hefty thud. "Take that," I shouted.

By rights, his skull should have been crushed by the force of that blow, given our combined momentum. I had no time to assess the effect, though, as the second creature had crawled out from under the bed and regained his feet.

He swiped clumsily, and the blow went wide; he seemed too dazed to take proper offensive action, as though bashing the head of one of them had stunned them both. He had no defence, no guard to speak of, and I rained blows on him without mercy. It felt more like an exercise against a padded opponent than a real fight. Satisfying as it was, I might as well have been tickling him with a feather for all the lasting effect it was having.

Then I saw the impossible door. It was beside me, and still ajar. "When is a door not a door?" I taunted.

Faint light showed around the edges. By rights, that door should have opened into the next cell, but I was nearly certain that it led somewhere else entirely. And it was open. Sometimes, especially in a fight, you do not take too long thinking about things. You just act.

I was through the door and pulling it shut behind me before my two opponents could move to block me.

I did not know where I was. Given how little progress I had been making in the fight, it had to be an improvement. I had expected a holding pen where the beasts were kept before being unloosed. Maybe I had only escaped into another cell, but if it put a solid door between me and them, then I was in a far safer place.

To my delight, there was a sort of door bolt on the side I was on, a metal wheel like those used to make ships' hatches fasten closed. I spun it, and a bolt or bar or catch moved, and the door was solidly in place. They could hammer on it—not that they had proper fists to hammer with—but they could not get in.

It was not, however, the cell-within-a-cell that I expected.

It was more like a narrow corridor with white, lime-washed walls and floored with matting. The corridor ran perhaps thirty feet in both directions before turning, and what light there was came from narrow, rectangular windows set slightly above eye level. Ths was the only door.

There was a chemical smell like vinegar in the air.

After a minute, I cautiously put my ear to the wall to hear what was happening on the other side. There was nothing, only the rushing of blood in my head.

"Well, that's a strange thing," I said and burst out laughing. The whole thing was so utterly ridiculous, so entirely impossible, that it made no sense at all. I laughed hysterically for half a minute before I managed to bring myself back.

The corridor I was in could not be where it was. I knew the layout of the hospital perfectly well, and there was no room for a whole corridor to fit there. Only some mad freak of geometry could put the corridor there; but here I was.

The window showed an unfamiliar garden, bathed in moonlight. Strange topiary and peculiar metal statues were arranged around a sort of water feature. It was not an English garden, I could tell that much—it was more like one of those Chinese or Japanese gardens. Rounded shapes churned and flopped in the water feature.

One of the metal statues moved, and I ducked away instinctively. If I was seen, things could go very badly indeed. The inhabitants of the place were unlikely to be friendly.

I set off down the corridor, hoping for a way out. There were junctions and side turnings, but no doors. A steel plaque set into the wall looked as though it might be a map, but I could not make any sense of the hieroglyphic markings however long I stared. Maybe it was not a map at all.

The place simply could not be there, inside the asylum. Perhaps it was somewhere else. If doors could connect places a distance apart, maybe I could find one that would take me back somewhere else.

A few paces farther, an alcove housed a glass case on a stand. It contained what looked like scientific instruments, silver and glass things with quivering needles and dials, but the markings meant nothing to me. A glass cylinder was full of clear liquid which changed as I watched, forming murky scenes that dissolved into one another. For a moment, robed figures seemed to form, then dissipated. It was hypnotic, but I forced myself away.

A turn took me to a winding staircase, and I went up two flights. I stalked onwards with a growing sense of purpose. I had some idea where I must be going. My route was a spiral. An archway appeared ahead of me, like a light coming on. I suspected the arch would be gone in another second, but I was through it by then.

Perhaps I should have used my time better. I should have scouted the place out properly; I should have found a weapon. I could at least have broken the case and taken some of the instruments. It is easy to be wise after the event.

The two I had left behind me were still trapped in my cell, I hoped. They were only the minions of the one ahead of me. Dr Nye was a far more dangerous creature.

My job lay ahead of me, and Harry Stubbs was not one to avoid a fight.

Chapter Nineteen: Master of Chaos

The room was dark, with only a few circles of illumination. At the middle of it was Dr Nye.

When you're hunting a tiger, the last thing you see is the tiger, Ryan had told me. That phrase "the last thing you see" had a double meaning, I now realised. Dr Nye might literally be the last thing I ever saw.

"The end is nigh," Hooper said. But maybe it was really "The end is Nye." Hooper had been trying to warn me about Nye because he was in danger – but he was only in danger because he was trying to warn me about Nye. A vicious circle had taken him.

Dr Nye was a tall, slim man. His face was familiar, because it was exactly the face of the two things that had come into my cell. Except while their eyes were as dead as pebbles, his sparkled with a mischievous humour. He was younger than I had expected.

And I realised with a slight shock that I had seen him before. I had seen him visiting patients at the hospital. It was as though the memories had been blotted out, or rather misplaced, until this exact moment. He had been there in front of me the entire time. Laughing at me. The fact that I could see him now and remember him suggested that he no longer needed any sort of concealment.

The lighting momentarily confused me, and the room looked unfamiliar, until I saw we were in the superintendent's office.

Nye was sitting behind an enormous desk—the superintendent's desk—with an array of wooden boxes before him. Prismatic colours played on his face from the indicator lights. Thick wires sprouted and coiled around him to the mass of equipment that filled much of the room. It looked like a power station, with glass and metal columns and stacked copper plates all connected. The Faradisation apparatus had been expanded and extended almost out of recognition, like some sort of weed running wild and allowed to overrun the whole garden.

Facing him, strapped to a chair on the other side of the desk, was Ross. He was wearing a peculiar headdress which at first looked Egyptian until I saw that it was made of at least twenty thick electrical wires, each taped to his shaved scalp.

"We should work together," said Ross quietly. He sounded reasonable and not at all like a man who stood to be electrocuted at the flip of a switch. Maybe a low voltage would not kill him, but the apparatus was infinitely more powerful than the one we had used on poor Jenkins. Surely it would scramble his brains in an instant. "Do something constructive instead."

"I don't need help from a lunatic," said Nye. His voice was mellow and every bit as reasonable, and he stroked a switch before him teasingly.

"But still you hesitate," said Ross. "You are as unsure of me as I am of you."

"Don't you dare compare yourself to me," said Nye, peevish rather than angry. "You are a pathetic, insane prisoner. I am master of this place—and anywhere else I choose to go."

A contest was being played out between them, and it appeared to have been going on for some time. Ross looked to be in the inferior position, but he was the less agitated of the two. Nye had the irritable look of one who had cornered an opponent but couldn't finish him off.

"And yet, here you are," said Ross. "With me."

It had been my intention to talk to Ross and form a plan of campaign against Nye, but clearly it was too late for that. Nye could put a tremendous and presumably lethal voltage through the other man with a flick of his finger, which still caressed the device before him. The thick wires covered the floor like coiled serpents, blocking my way. I could never hope to cross to Nye quickly enough to stop him. I had fought past my—or Nye's—demons to get there, but I had no idea what I should do next.

"You should not have come," said Nye, turning and addressing me for the first time. It occurred to me then that my presence was not accidental, but that it was part the contest between them. I was as much a part of it as a card that had been played. If the sphinxes were Nye's pieces, then I was Ross's. "You have been certified insane, Stubbs. You are not mentally competent to make any sort of judgement. You have no lawful authority. Go back to your cell—before you have an accident with those electrical wires."

He spoke with such command that I almost found myself obeying him. But I stayed my impulse to move, and instead spoke up as firmly as I could manage. "I know who you really are," I said.

His gaze seemed to sharpen, but so did his amusement. "Oh? Speak, madman."

I spoke quickly, stringing together fact and inference and supposition. Everything I had gleaned must be used now or lost.

"You were taken from the gipsies as a baby and raised in a foster home. You were a spiteful and resentful child, and you learned early to lie and cheat. You were always jealous of another boy with the same foster mother. You were always lucky and took an interest in what is called black magic—tricks learned from gipsies, mainly—and how to twist people's minds. Maybe there was a real Dr Nye. Maybe he was your brain physician after they first realised what you were like and sent you for treatment."

"You took his place after you disposed of him. That must have been no great feat when you invoked or generated minions which can penetrate any closed space by using other dimensions." It was wild, half-made-up stuff, but it felt like a rough approximation of the truth.

"Really?" asked Nye, raising one eyebrow.

"The superintendent was seduced by your supposed triumphs, your standing. Beltov succumbed to you because he could not resist what looked like science. How was he to know that what he called 'statistical significance' was just your luck, or cheating? You're a fraud, you're not a doctor. And the name given you by your foster mother was Ross, not Nye." My aim was to convey this information to Ross. It was not entirely to be relied upon, but perhaps he could use it. I could not tell anything from his expression.

"Is that all you have?" asked Nye, mock-disappointed.

"It'll be enough to see you dethroned from your position," I said. I did not trouble to add "if anyone listens to me." Needing a stronger finish, I added, "And maybe you'll be the one that ends up in a cell downstairs, with a diagnosis of megalomania at the least."

"The gipsies are a tribe of outcast Egyptians," Nye said, invoking a piece of folklore of which I was aware but had not connected. "You omitted to mention that my gipsy blood is royal. It is the blood of the pharaohs. My soul, too, is the soul of a pharaoh."

As one who was supremely presumptuous himself, Dr Nye despised presumption in others. I was being put in my place for daring to suggest that I knew who he was.

"Perhaps I can guess which pharaoh," said Ross. "Not Amenhotep, or Akhenaten, or Khufu."

"No." Nye's voice was silky and superior.

"One of the Damnatio Memoriae," said Ross, "whose name was erased from every obelisk and stele, whose deeds are their only monument."

"Yes. I am Nyarlathotep," stated the other proudly. "Incarnate again as man after forty centuries. Pray that you never see any of my unhuman forms."

The name meant nothing to me. I guessed that it must be connected with the mummy whose spirit Mathers had tried to summon, the one that the Sphere group of the Golden Dawn had contacted and inadvertently guided back to our world. They had allowed it to be born here again, its hour come round at last.

Nye seemed to swell up at the sound of the name he had given himself. "I am not a man, but a god come again, come again to set intricate devices into motion and unwind this world."

"The anti-Messiah," said Ross, quiet as anything.

"You thought I was just a magician," said Nye, his eyes fixed on Ross. "One of those dabbling idiots, making cocktails of science and mysticism and getting drunk on the results. Petty little men who think that one glimpse of the ankles of Truth means they have seen all her glory. My roots are sunk millennia-deep; eternity and infinity are my playthings."

"What exactly do you want?" asked Ross, entirely untroubled. This was the calm courage that had made him an air ace, while my mind was turning somersaults.

"I am here to destroy madness," said Nye, his voice cool again. "I will stamp out every delusion and hallucination, chip away the accretion of defences which encase human minds, dissolve the comfortable illusions humanity clings to. I will dig down to the roots of the psyche, dig out the futility of life and the certainty of death. I will unbury what is hidden in dreams, bring back every dread thought pushed out of mind. I will draw out Leviathans from the pool of the subconscious with a hook and release them, lithe and glistening, into the waking world. I will reveal the truth everywhere by cinematograph and radio. I will not rest until all humanity stands bare, nakedly exposed to the cold wind of reality, unprotected by lies and fallacies, utterly and irrevocably *sane*—screaming endlessly into the night."

"Humanity is better left as it is," said Ross.

I felt as irrelevant to the larger struggle as an ant crawling across a boxing ring between two heavyweights. As that other Norwood Titan had observed, my arms are too short to box with a god.

Nye seemed to be building up his own confidence before launching the killer punch, uncertain as he was of his opponent. It was the moment he would commit himself to the blow. "I don't care if they like it," he said in the tone of one who enjoys crushing insects as a proof of the power that he wields. That was the only proof that mattered. He would not get pleasure from putting food out for ants or saving them from predators. But tormenting them would be a joy to him.

If Nye was a god, he was an egotistical and insecure one that needed to boast. "I am the incarnation of a greater power, the power that rules the universe. The one that wears mountains to dust, levels forests and burns out stars. The force of that tears down every man-built thing, the anarchy that eats away every civilisation. Eternal, unstoppable, crawling entropy."

Nye's voice was rising to a thunderous pitch. He was not shouting, but his voice was amplified as through a loudspeaker. "I am the Pharaoh Nyarlathotep. I AM CHAOS!"

I reeled. The whole building seemed to boom and resonate with the last three words. The air was unable to hold them but kept echoing them back and forth. Something ghastly had been unmasked, its very presence a threat to human life. I had the sense of standing close to a whirring piece of machinery, a whirlpool of sharpened steel blades that expanded to fill the room.

Sparks fountained around my feet. The electrical cables writhed like tentacles or fire hoses with high-pressure water blasting through them, leaping into the air. Balls of lightining shot out of copper columns as though they were so many Roman candles, and barbed electric whips lashed around, thrashing the walls and the ceiling.

The coil of cables leaped up from the floor and struck me.

Impossible as it was, and although there cannot have been any interval between Nye throwing the switch and what happened next, before the arcing cables struck me, I know I heard Ross's reply. He was as clear and quiet as the fighter pilot when the clouds part and he gets the Zeppelin squarely in his sights, and as level-headed as the tiger hunter when the beast breaks cover and leaps towards him, claws bared. "I am Providence."

The two men were incarnations of the same force, like those two haughty Cleopatras who refused to talk to each other. In this case, though, they were different aspects of that force, wearing the masks of angel and devil.

Ross could not match Nye's power; his own was merely an offshoot of the same elemental force, but it put a twist in that force and changed its direction entirely. Because chaos is chaotic, it cannot always destroy. Sometimes, despite of itself, it creates.

Providence is the twist of chaos that reverses its effects, the one random chance in a thousand that brings order rather than confusion. It is the serendipity that causes you to get on to the wrong train and find it is the right one after all. Providence is the cowpox that gives you immunity to deadly smallpox, malaria burning out syphilis.

The stirring up of primordial chemicals results not in ever-greater disorder, but in the molecules that form life. Providence is when the sports and freaks that affect reproduction instead turn out to be new species. Providence is when the lightning that smashes the cave dwellers' encampment gives them fire and everything that came after. Providence throws up the stepping stones of progress.

Providence is the madness that turns out to be genius. Providence means that even a shattered clock can be correct twice a day. Providence is when the secret door which admits assassins is the one through which the victim escaped.

Providence is the tiniest part of chaos, but it is the part by which we survive. It is the twist which makes the all-devouring serpent catch its own tail, swallowing itself before it can annihilate the world.

I did not appreciate any of this at the time: when I was struck, a reflex action sent my fists up to block the blow. I was hurled across the room as though by a giant hand. Thinking back, I assume the knuckledusters must have caused a short circuit that made the apparatus explode in such dramatic fashion. A one-in-a-million chance, but Ross was always lucky, and chance was serving his ends.

I rolled to my feet, and the fireworks were still in progress on Nye's side of the table. Ross's side darkened. There had been enough power there to kill Ross instantly a hundred times over. The electrical attachments fell away from his head as I watched, leaving small burned circles. Ross slumped forward, and a fine ash ran out of his open eye sockets. Ross's skin was perfectly intact, but everything inside his skull was a charred mass.

At the other end of the circuit, electricity coiled around Nye like swarming pythons. His arms were folded across his chest in a protective gesture. He appeared to be unharmed, but as I watched, a dozen more of the lashes found him, the tentacles an enraged monster made of living lightning. For another moment, an aura of electricity hovered around him without touching. Then, something gave way, and it collapsed, enveloping him and burning as it went.

Nye was not burned from the inside out, but from the outside in. The electric chair is a spark by comparison. Even lighting does not burn its victims completely, but as the fire went out it left Nye a blackened statue of himself.

The electric arcs vanished, leaving flame burning along the length of every cable. I was dimly aware of distant explosions downstairs: all the wiring in the building must have caught and the fuse boxes all blown out in that last orgiastic electric discharge.

Smoke billowed over and around me as the apparatus gave a few last electrical sputters.

The clamour from the rest of the building, screeching and screaming, started to press in on me.

I wanted to be sure Nye was dead. In their state, the two men looked even more like polar opposites, though they were really different versions of the same being, incarnated in two bodies at once. Positive and negative had met and cancelled each other out. Or had they?

I could believe Nye still was alive, for a time being; even if those burns only went down a quarter inch, the complete destruction of the skin is invariably fatal. Though it might take a while for him to die, someone—or something—like Nye might do further damage before he succumbed.

Then he moved, and I stifled a cry.

His chin had shifted, or had seemed to. Or was it just the carbonised flesh crumbling away? I moved forward gingerly.

There was a sound, a strange dry rustling, coming from him. Or, rather, from his body.

Part of his chest flaked away, and then a piece broke off from his shoulder. I could have persuaded myself that it was merely the final disintegration, except for that sound. Something was scraping and tapping.

A section of cheek the size of my palm fell away and clinked on the floor like a piece of thick black porcelain. It revealed a hollow cavity beneath. It was as though I was looking at one of those hollow chocolate animals.

Another section of abdomen was pushed out from the inside. The statue in the shape of Nye was an enormous black eggshell, and something was hatching from within.

Nye was dead, surely utterly dead. But even in death, he had somehow reincarnated himself, taking on another form, drawing on the electricity that destroyed him to incubate something and bring it to fruition in the blink of an eye.

A pale, worm-like limb emerged into the air. I caught only the shortest look at it, but it was too much.

Reading this, comfortable in your armchair, and with the cool consideration of relaxed surroundings, could again tell me a dozen things I ought to have done. I could have found a solid poker or other substantial blunt instrument and smashed the thing with all my strength. But few people, finding a scorpion scuttling across their desk, would be able to coolly crush it with a paperweight and ring for the maid to clear up the mess. No, faced with that situation, you might panic a little.

Filled with the most awful revulsion, I picked up Nye's chair, with his hollow remains in it, even as it cracked and split. Pale tendrils like the horns of snails started to protrude.

I was shouting, not words but that inarticulate roar they teach you to let out during a bayonet charge. It was a yell to overcome terror and convert it into sheer desperate action.

I took three running steps and flung the whole lot through the glass balcony doors with a tremendous crash. It sailed through the air, over the railings, to smash down in the shadows of the stone courtyard two storeys below.

With the electricity gone, it was dark except for the rays of the yellow-green moon. The charred outer body had been shattered to fragments on the flagstones. Nye's newest form unfolded and unbent itself, extending its many limbs. I could not see well enough to describe it. There probably is no name for it in any human language, and my powers of description are not adequate for the task.

I was paralysed by shock and confusion. Like a mouse hypnotised by a snake, or the soldier who stares stupidly at the smoking grenade that falls at his feet, or the boxer who cannot understand how his opponent has dodged a blow and fails to react for a fatal second. Whatever the thing was, my mental machinery was not able to compute a course of action but instead lay idle, waiting for a stimulus to which it could respond.

I was not the only one watching. A hundred other pairs of eyes, and a hundred other brains more attuned to understanding, had witnessed the fall. And while I gaped, stupefied, they rose and acted as one.

Windows burst into the courtyard on all sides, scattering glass stars everywhere. It was like seeing a dark wave strike a breakwater and shatter into spray, only this wave was human.

"...for Saint George, and for England!" boomed a voice. The figure below, leading the charge, must have been FitzRoy; like the others he was hooded, but a foil crown gleamed in the moonlight.

As though on cue, as though they had been waiting for this moment, the inmates poured into the yard from three directions, converging on a point directly below me, all of them. They were howling and screaming like banshees and silhouetted by the flames behind them, their limbs contorted by a wild fury. Instead of clothes, they had wrapped sheets around themselves, wearing them like hooded robes. I could see no faces.

I could not say really what I saw. They did not look like the stooped, weakened inmates that I knew. There was something more beastlike than human in their loping steps and hunched bodies. This was what a charge of Viking berserkers looked like, when unleashed ferocity turns men into animals. Nye had done it—with his meddling, he had pushed them through to another level of insanity—though he cannot have foreseen that it would be turned on him.

They hurtled forwards as though it were a race, with a golden prize for being the first to reach that thing. And perhaps there was a prize, one that all of these men had thirsted for so long: revenge on their tormentor.

The scene jumped abruptly, like a movie reel that skips some frames. The light in the courtyard changed, and the berserkers were gone. The pale thing stretched and struggled to get upright on flaccid limbs.

Then the howling mob smashed through the windows again as if replaying a different staging of the same event.

Another jump, and the courtyard was empty again. The shapes of the windows had changed, becoming more elongated and with Norman arches. The pale thing stretched and lurched, straightening out like a chrysalis starting to harden with exposure to the air. It needed just a few minutes more, but in seconds the horde burst through again, bearing down on it with maniacal fury.

Each time the Nye-thing tried to change track and shift to another world, the pursuers followed a second later, a pack of hounds baying for blood with as little care for the rules of the universe as he had. Their collective madness tore through the barriers between worlds that should have stopped them. If magic was madness, they had the gift; they bore down on him through a dozen transitions.

I imagined them skipping through other worlds and passing strange geometries, alien vegetation, and bizarre landscapes as they spiralled in, with each transition shorter than the last as they converged on the centre of the gyre and fell upon the soft, flopping thing there.

It fought them, but it was the fight of a newborn calf against a pack of wolves.

They say a shoal of piranha fish can strip a whole cow down to its bones in seconds. These were piranhas in human form, with teeth and jaws and tearing claws and a strength and savagery beyond anything human. Moonlight and firelight gleamed off their limbs, eyes, and wet hands. There were too many of them to all attack at once—they piled on like a rugby scrum. As they tore it and pulled it apart, more and more of them joined; there were several scrums instead of one, and it was not a fight but a cannibal feast, an unholy communion.

All trace of the thing disappeared as they ripped it into shreds and devoured it, scatter and squabble among themselves for the final few fragments.

Instead of spiralling outwards into the world, the gyre had reversed itself and spiralled back to its point of origin, becoming nothing again. The Ouroboros had devoured itself, leaving no trace in our world.

I staggered back and was enveloped by a choking cloud of smoke. Electrical insulation was still burning from a dozen fires. A funnel of light from an electric torch shone through the smoke.

"Stubbs!" It was Smith, stepping carefully over the debris of melted cables towards me. "Are you hurt?"

"Not particularly," I said, and it was true. I had plenty of bruises, and trickles of blood were running down me from the slashes down my side and elsewhere. I've come out of fights feeling worse.

Smith shone the beam around the room, lingering on Ross's body a moment. "We have to go," he said, leading me by the arm. "The Old Bill will be here in a minute."

Everyone we passed seemed too dazed to notice us. Inmates wandered around in states of undress and nakedness as though sleepwalking, or sat mumbling to themselves, or milled about staring. Donnelly was herding a group away from the building; he did not notice us. The mania had run its course, and they were exhausted, mentally and physically.

Looking back, the fire was still burning in the superintendent's office, and smoke poured from at least two other windows. It did not seem to be spreading through the structure. The fire service should be able to save the place if there was not too much delay. As if in answer to my thought, sirens started up in the distance.

Smith had provided himself with both the keys to the side gate in the confusion, and he opened it for me. "I've got to stay here and clean up," he said. "You scarper. You know the way to the Knight's Head from here?"

That was Elsie Granger's stronghold. The New Town is a walled enclave of six streets, and the gate that connects it with the high road is manned by a policeman at night.

"Go to the end of Rockmount Road and whistle twice," he said. "If they give you any trouble, tell 'em Smithy sent you."

"Thank you," I said.

"Now, clear off," he said, waving me away and locking the gate between us.

I wondered whether I should go and find Arthur instead. But after my last interview with him, Elsie Granger seemed the better bet.

The streets were deserted, and I slunk along in the shadows, all too aware of my outfit and how easily I might be picked up by police racing to the scene of the fire. But nobody except a few cats noticed me, and after a couple of wrong turns, I made it to Rockmount Road and whistled as instructed.

A moment later, a face appeared over the wall, and an electric torch shone in my eyes.

"It's Harry Stubbs," I said. "Smithy sent me."

A rope ladder was flung down, the wooden rungs clattering on the pavement. Without ceremony or very much welcome, I had made it to safety.

It was all anticlimactic, even when Elsie Granger stood me a couple of brandies. It seemed to me then that the difficulty was all still ahead of me. But events were to prove me wrong, as usual.

Epilogue

The extended spell of unnaturally warm, dry weather had ended abruptly. Autumn came to its senses as if making up for lost time with wet, windy days and lowering skies. The withered leaves were stripped from the trees and trodden black and slippery underfoot. Everyone was wearing overcoats and scarves, with umbrellas blown inside out. The news, too, had moved on, and all the talk of war with Germany had been overtaken with political scandal and economic analysis.

The fire at the asylum had attracted little attention; firemen had put it out in short order, and there was less damage than there might have been. There were few soft furnishings or other flammable content, and had been evacuated promptly. The only death had been Ross.

The investigation that followed naturally enough homed in on Dr Nye, and as soon as it did, his whole set of credentials collapsed like a house of cards. As I had guessed, he was a fraud. His imposture became transparent as soon as he died. His wild schemes for treatment, which had seemed so promising, were dismissed in a breath. Under the slightest examination, forgeries and lies turned up everywhere. Institutions where he claimed to have worked had never heard of him, papers which he published were nowhere to be found, colleagues were nonexistent, and experiments had never been carried out.

A bubble had burst, one which had only been sustained while Nye was alive by the force of his will. Not that anyone except me knew he was dead. He was assumed to be on the run after killing Ross; the patient's burned body still attached to the apparatus left little doubt as to the cause of death. There were warrants out for his arrest. The matter was kept quiet, with only a couple of stories in the more colourful newspapers, and they added so many fanciful details that nobody would believe it, anyway.

One immediate consequence of Nye's posthumous unmasking was that I found myself suddenly in the clear. The paperwork in my case was not in order. The magistrate's signature had been forged, and in any case Nye had no authority to certify me. If you care to see it, I have a certificate to say I am as sane as anyone. It is not a thing I treasure, but I keep it by me in case I am challenged by those who have not heard the full story.

My incarceration was an egregious act of malpractice. I suppose I could have gone to law. The superintendent wrote to me personally, enclosing a cheque in compensation. It was hush money by any other name, but I was happy enough to take it. I politely declined, however, his offer of my job back. I never wanted to see the place again. Curiously enough, Smith has continued to work there.

Although I have now had time to ruminate and digest my experiences, I am little the wiser.

The simplest explanation is that Ross and Nye were both mad, entangled in a *folie a deux* of mutual destruction that dated back to their childhood. I too was caught up in their madness. It is a neat explanation, which covers all of the publicly known facts of the matter. I do not relish the idea that I myself had "an episode," and that the balance of my mind was disturbed, even temporarily. To any fair-minded reader, though, this would be the most logical conclusion. The deaths in the asylum were accidents or suicides, involving no external actors.

Certainly, there was no physical trace in my cell of the two beings I left there to validate my story. Presumably they dissolved or vaporised the moment that Nye was destroyed… assuming they ever existed. According to Smith, the only riddle when my cell was opened was what had happened to the bed, how it came to be detached from the floor and short of a couple of legs.

Against the view that it was all delusion I would need to weigh the comments made by Ryan, and his apparent demise at the hands of Nye's agents. A sceptic might suggest that Ryan never existed, that I imagined him too. I have to concede that this too is possible. But then you have to ask whether I also imagined Miss De Vere, who provided my letter of reference and is clearly more substantial than any mere figment.

The other possibility though is equally disturbing. If I am not mad, then the world is. A person can be in two places at once, and bodies can pass through solid walls. Uncertainty pervades everything, and even history is not fixed. It is a world that mocks our attempts to make sense of it, where chaos rather than order reigns.

I struggle to accept that Nye was the incarnation of some cosmic principle, let alone a divinity, or that the god of elemental Chaos—supposing such a thing exists—should take such an interest in the human race. Again, it is easier to believe that his beliefs were a part of his megalomania. On the other hand, it is no stranger a story than scripture—and more especially if you take the Book of Job to be a historical account and not merely a fable.

I am edging my way towards a middle view. Nye and Ross did control powers beyond what is understood by current scientific thinking, but only imagined themselves to be gods. If unchecked, Nye might have succeeded in setting into motion an ever-expanding cycle of madness—or sanity, as he saw it—with consequences that can hardly be imagined.

This version of events is perhaps a self-serving one, as it represents me as being not only sane but actually heroic, albeit in a small way. Perhaps that is why this version of events makes most sense to me.

I was not the only one to be officially discharged. Not long afterwards I saw FitzRoy go by in a taxi, deep in conversation with another man who might have been his son. The face of a woman in a headscarf working behind the counter at a florist looked oddly familiar. It was fully five minutes later that I realised it was Grogan, living now as a woman.

There was one final act to carry out.

Sally insisted on coming with me to Ross's funeral. West Norwood cemetery is a grand Victorian necropolis with an avenue of great tombs. There are two angels everywhere, and even a few obelisks and pyramids. Perhaps it was grand enough even for a pharaoh. The day was foul, and it took an effort to keep my umbrella over the two of us.

There was a pretty decent crowd. I guessed most of them were his friends from his service days, but there were one or two queer characters who might have been friends from esoteric circles. The only people I recognised were Miss Bentham, of course, and Maggie. I shook hands with them both, but we hardly exchanged a word. Miss Bentham looked sad and solemn all in black; even her little Pekingese worse a black collar.

"You might not think it," I told Miss Bentham, "but he died a hero."

She smiled bravely and nodded, but said nothing. I think she believed me. I think she knew.

The coffin was closed. Ross's remains must have presented quite a puzzle for the undertakers; embalming him would have been impossible, but perhaps needless.

"Ashes to ashes, dust to dust," intoned the priest. Ross had certainly been reduced to dust and ashes. As for his immortal soul, and whether it had a separate existence from that being that called itself Nyarlathotep, that was impossible for me to say. Perhaps it was merely another spin around the whirligig for him, as Ross had appeared to believe. As always, when things receded in time, it became harder and harder to believe what I had seen. Both of them had been mad to greater or lesser degrees, and I no longer had so much faith in the reliability of my own senses.

Sally looked neat and dignified. She cried more than I expected, probably more from the memories of losing her own husband three years ago, as she had not even known Ross. But she recovered quickly when we were walking back, arm in arm. Instead of going to the nearest entrance, we walked around the long way, past the rows of stone urns and broken pillars and angels.

Sally blew her nose and then said, in a normal tone, "It's good to get it over with and give him a proper send-off," she said. "He saved your life, and I'll always be grateful for that. Poor man."

"He was a friend," I said. "And a hero."

"He wouldn't have succeeded without you," she said with a sideways look.

I shrugged. "I wouldn't have got through it without you," I said.

"You did the same for me," she said. "After I had my breakdown, I'd never have recovered if you hadn't brought Mr Yang to hypnotise me. Once he'd shown me how to push the memories away, I started living again." She shook her head, the black veil rustling. "I'd still be stuck with the nuns if it wasn't for you."

"So, we're even," I said.

I stopped there among the gravestones and turned to her. Sally's upturned face was curious, but not unhappy. Black was a good colour for her.

"You'll be burying me next," I said, "sooner or later. If I manage to stay out of prison or another mental asylum, that is. Being around me is dangerous. You took some risks helping me, and you've got your little boy to think about."

I was thinking of Miss De Vere. I had received her telegram the morning after the events in the asylum; she requested a full report as soon as possible. Communications had been re-established.

"I know," she said.

"I can't give you respectability, or money, or a stable home," I said. "Stick with me, and all you'll get is danger and mad adventures."

There was a long silence as she considered this.

"Well, Harry Stubbs," she said, and she was smiling. "If that's a proposal, then I accept."

I was speechless. Even after everything that had happened, she would not be put off. Sally believed in me more than I believed in myself. She had kept faith when nobody else had. And, despite of the prospect of more horrors ahead, she was determined to stand by my side.

It would take a heart of stone, which I do not possess, to resist such tender devotion.

Reaching awkwardly under my shirt, and I felt to where a ring with a star-shaped stone hung around my neck then snapped the fine chain. I did not exactly produce the ring with an immediate flourish, due to the awkwardness of coping with a multiplicity of layers of clothing, but Sally was patient.

I took her hand and slipped the ring onto the third finger. It fit perfectly.

Editor's Note

Stubbs's account appears to tally with historical records and other sources.

Vice-Admiral Robert FitzRoy was a pioneering meteorologist, who founded what is now known as the Met Office and invented the term "weather forecast." Many were sceptical of the possibility of weather prediction, and this contributed to his eventual suicide. As well as introducing the barometer, FitzRoy advocated the use of the storm glass, an instrument apparently derived from Italian alchemical work. Although still popular in some quarters, the storm glass is now considered useless by mainstream meteorologists. FitzRoy is better known as the captain of the *Beagle* during Darwin's voyage of discovery.

The sect of Judwalis, and the significance of gyres, are described W.B. Yeats's esoteric work, *A Vision: An Explanation of Life Founded upon the Writings of Giraldus and upon Certain Doctrines Attributed to Kusta Ben Luka*. Yeats did not distinguish greatly between objective fact and revelation, claiming that truth could not be discovered, only revealed, so the factual content of this work is dubious. The date of *A Vision*, 1925, coinciding with Stubbs's account is presumably coincidental.

The summoning of the Egyptian Astral by Annie Horniman's group, The Sphere, has been well documented. (See, for example, Christine Ferguson and ◎Andrew Radford's, *The Occult Imagination in Britain, 1875-1947*). The group was a splinter organisation of the Golden Dawn, of which Yeats was also a member. The summoning was achieved by Horniman's protégée, actress Florence Farr, with the fragment from a coffin-case in the British Museum. The coffin was originally believed to belong to an Egyptian noblewoman called Mutemmenu. Later museum dating and x-rays have shown that the mummy in the case was actually male and from a later era. Why a male body was padded to appear female and concealed in another's coffin remains unknown.

The supposed Pharaoh, Nyarlathotep—even the name is disputed—remains a shadowy figure. One theory suggests he was an apostate (similar to Akhenaten) who considered himself to be the incarnation of the serpent-god Apep, representing primordial chaos. Apep was depicted in Egyptian religious art as the opponent of the sun god Ra, but never worshipped. The most detailed account of Nyarlathotep is provided by H.P. Lovecraft's monograph of the same name. As with Yeats's book, this is a work of revelation rather than scholarship, and its accuracy must be considered highly doubtful.

WB

About the Author

David Hambling is a journalist and author who has lived in Norwood, South London since 2000. He writes about science and technology for New Scientist magazine, The Economist, WIRED, Popular Mechanics, and writes a science column for Fortean Times ("the magazine of unexplained phenomena"). In addition to non-fiction books, his "Shadows From Norwood" project seeks to bring HP Lovecraft's Cthulhu Mythos to South London, via the Harry Stubbs novels and a number of short stories.

Visit the Shadows from Norwood Facebook page :

https://www.facebook.com/ShadowsFromNorwood

...for links, photographs, interactive map and more about the Harry Stubbs Adventures series

Printed in Great Britain
by Amazon

55629177R00133